MW00935840

# IONA PORTAL

## BOOK ONE OF THE SYNAXIS CHRONICLES

**An Epic Science Fiction Thriller by**

**Robert David MacNeil**

## DEDICATION

This book is dedicated to Keith, whose words prompted the writing of this book.

To Susan, Pam, and Margie for reading and re-reading the manuscript, and making many helpful suggestions.

And most of all, to my amazing wife Linda, for her patience and continual encouragement, and for believing this book should be written.

Copyright © 2011 Robert David MacNeil
All rights reserved.
This book or parts thereof may not be reproduced in any form, stored in a retrieval system, or transmitted in any form by any means--electronic, mechanical, photocopy, recording, or otherwise--without prior written permission from the publisher, except as provided by United States of America copyright law.

Published by Robert David MacNeil
624 W. University Drive  PMB 137,
Denton, TX  76201

ISBN: 978-1467992541

Website:  http://ionaportal.com/
Email:  RobertDavidMacNeil@Gmail.com

# TABLE OF CONTENTS

## PART ONE:  ENCOUNTERS

## PART TWO:  PILGRIMAGE

## PART THREE:  SYNAXIS

## PART FOUR:  PORTAL

## EPILOGUE

"There is no question that there is an unseen world. The problem is,how far is it from Midtown and how late is it open?" – Woody Allen (*Without Feathers,* p. 11.)

"There are more things in heaven and earth, Horatio, than are dreamt of in your philosophy." – William Shakespeare (*"Hamlet"*, Act 1 scene 5)

* * *

The geographical descriptions in this book are accurate, including McCaig's Folly, which really is perched on the cliff above Oban.

Aidan's Pub is loosely patterned after Aulay's Bar, which is located on Airds Crescent in the city of Oban.

The Torosay Inn is based on the Criagnure Inn on the Isle of Mull. (The Craignure Inn was also featured in Robert Louis Stevenson's novel, *Kidnapped.* Stevenson called it the Torosay Inn, and I have followed his example.)

The only major departure from geographical accuracy is the description of Lady's Rock, which in modern times is topped with a light tower to protect shipping in the Sound of Mull.

All historical references in this book are accurate.

All present-day characters in this book are fictional, and are not intended to represent any persons, living or dead.

The SYNAXIS, of course, is real.

# MAIN CHARACTERS

**Lys Johnston** – Lys (rhymes with bliss) is a 26 year-old receptionist at a major Colorado law firm.  She doesn't know she has an ability that could save the human race from destruction.  All she knows is that mysterious strangers keep trying to kill her.

**Erin Vanderberg** – Erin is a 42 year old Dallas socialite.  She's the envy of Dallas society, until she discovers her husband's dark secret and barely escapes with her life.

**Patrick O'Neil** – An investment counselor with a corner office in one of the gleaming glass towers of Dallas.  When his world is torn apart, he's driven by a series of surreal dreams to abandon everything and travel to the remote Scottish island of Iona.

**Dr. Derek Holmes** – A clinical psychologist whose quiet life is shattered by a close encounter with mysterious humanoid aliens.  Holmes and his soul-mate, **Ginny Ann Piper**, are chosen by the *Irin* to assemble the first synaxis.

**Michael Fletcher** – Michael is an angelologist.  He's studied angels and demons all his life and written three books on the subject.  But he isn't prepared to meet one.

**Eliel** (An *Irin* warrior) – With wings concealed, Eliel appears to be an attractive 21 year-old woman, but she's visited our world for thousands of years and walked the streets of ancient Babylon and Rome.

**Kareina** (An *Archon* Commander) – Kareina is a killer.  She enters the earth-realm to remove those who pose a threat to Archon plans.

**Other Irin Warriors**:  Araton, Mendrion, Rand, and Khalil

**Other Archon Warriors**:  Pele, Botis, and Turell

# PART ONE:  ENCOUNTERS

# Chapter One:  Lysandra

The speeding BMW's green xenon headlights burned
fiercely in Lysandra Johnston's rearview mirror.  "They're
coming after us again…" she said, trying in vain to control
the tremor in her voice, "…*faster* this time!"

Clutching the wheel tightly, she slammed the
accelerator and let a wave of inertia drive her deep into the
seatback.  The soft, leather-trimmed upholstery enfolded her
torso, cocooning her in a protective embrace; but the
increased speed brought no illusion of safety--her Corolla
could not outrun the BMW.  Her pursuers' low-slung coupe
was effortlessly carving a path through the dark, twisting
curves, relentlessly devouring the pavement as it
approached.

With one eye on the mirror, Lys careened through a
double hairpin turn, dropping down a low hill to an
extended straightaway.  Tall Ponderosa Pines flashed past
as she accelerated hard, mashing the pedal to the floor.

Coming out of the straightaway, she squealed through
a tight S-curve, barely keeping four wheels on the road.
Her fading hope rekindled as the pursuing lights winked out
of sight behind a massive granite outcrop.  But that hope

was instantly crushed when the BMW re-appeared around the bend moments later, closer than before. The sudden burst of acceleration had temporarily increased her lead, but the men were now playing catch-up and overtaking her rapidly.

A flood of cold, unreasoning fear crept up her spine. "They're almost on top of us," she said, glancing nervously at her companion. "This has gone on *way* too long!"

Gritting her teeth in frustration, Lys looked for a place of refuge, searching the road ahead as it wound through a dense forest of Douglas fir... *a convenience store... a bar...some roadside café... any place with lights and people!* She saw nothing but cold, desolate pavement fading into darkness.

With no escape in sight, she fixed her gaze on her pursuers as they inexorably closed the gap.

The mysterious black BMW had come out of the gloom twenty minutes earlier and with no provocation engaged Lys in a harrowing game of cat-and-mouse-- hurtling past her on the lonely mountain roads, then slowing, almost to a stop, to force her to pass. She'd tried to tell herself the men were just toying with her, but the looks on their faces made her skin crawl.

Her stalkers were almost on her rear bumper and still accelerating; the throaty growl of the BMW's engine reverberated in her ears. She gripped the wheel firmly, bracing for an impact, but in the last instant the men swerved to the left and roared past.

As they sped by, Lys saw a now-familiar face pressed hard against the BMW's passenger-seat window. By the pale light of the near full moon, the man's face appeared wraithlike, almost skeletal, with coal-black hair falling in oily tangles down his back. His blood-dark eyes were locked on Lys, staring at her hungrily.

Lysandra Leigh Johnston was no stranger to the longing gaze of men. At twenty-six, with an easy smile, carefully-toned body, and light, ash-blonde hair tumbling loosely across her shoulders, Lys had often held the starring role in a man's romantic fantasy. But she sensed nothing amorous, or even sexual, in this man's leer. What she saw in his ashen face was a terrifying look of bone-chilling brutality.

She shuddered involuntarily at the sight of him--a tremor of revulsion snaking through her core. She struggled in vain to delete his lurid image from her memory. The cruelty in his eyes gave her little doubt of the sadistic fury playing out in his imagination. *He's abusing me…* Lys knew… *raping me in his mind.*

She let out a sigh of relief as the BMW sped down the road to finally disappear around the curve ahead. She eased up on the gas and felt her body relax. *Maybe it's over…* she looked hopefully into the darkness … *maybe they'll leave me alone now.* She wiped a bead of cold perspiration from her forehead.

Rounding the bend, her heart sank as a familiar set of brake lights flared brightly on the road ahead. *If I can just get by them one more time…* she thought... *in ten more minutes we'll be back home in Boulder.*

Her fingers shifted nervously on the wheel.

The BMW was still two hundred yards away, but the driver was pumping his brakes, rapidly decelerating.

Lys envisioned the cadaverous man in the passenger

seat waiting for her--obscene eyes following her approach. She lifted her foot from the accelerator. Her breath caught in her throat and an icy knot formed in her belly.

*Get a grip, Lys!* She scolded, struggling to shake off the disquiet.

She drew a deep breath, held it several seconds, then blew it out slowly, consciously attempting to rein-in her emotions. *We'll get through this...* she assured herself, inhaling deeply again ... *Just stay focused ... Take it one step at a time.*

As the receptionist for the biggest law firm in the Colorado Front Range, Lys was well-accustomed to handling stress. At the office she'd built a reputation on her ability to thrive under pressure--always maintaining control in any crisis. Right now, though, she was far from her comfort zone.

"I know it's a cliché, Kareina, but I've got a really *bad* feeling about this," she said, almost in a whisper, as the BMW loomed closer.

"Don't worry about it..." her companion smiled condescendingly, brushing a long strand of jet-black hair from her eyes. "They're just *guys*. They saw a pretty blonde driving and are having a little fun with you. You're much too suspicious."

Tall and gangly with a plain face and pallid, almost sickly complexion, Kareina Procel had dropped by Lys's desk three weeks earlier, looking like a lost puppy. As the two spent their afternoon break talking, Kareina said she'd just moved to Boulder from a small town in New Mexico, hadn't yet made any friends, and felt totally lost in the big city.

Compassionate by nature, Lys was an easy touch for Kareina's hard-luck story. She'd gone to lunch with Kareina several times and spent one Saturday afternoon showing her the sights of Boulder. Even before the BMW showed up, however, Lys regretted going to tonight's party with her. Something about Kareina just didn't seem right.

"*I'm* suspicious? *Yeah, right!*" Lys jabbed. "Coming from such a good judge of character… You thought *Carrington* was a great guy!"

"Well, how was I to know he only had one thing on his mind?"

"Listen Kareina, I'm the blonde. You're supposed to have a brain in your head. We never should have gone to that party in the first place."

The BMW was now stopped dead in the lane ahead. Lys slowed cautiously as she approached, then pulled out to pass, flooring the accelerator.

As the Corolla struggled to gain speed, she caught another glimpse of the BMW's driver. He looked young, maybe still in his teens. *Probably took his dad's car without permission.* But his expression showed no hint of playfulness. His face was as gaunt and pale as his companion's and was fixed on Lys with the cold determination of a hunter stalking prey.

Despite the blonde jokes, Lys was no fool. She knew this was not a situation to treat lightly.

A glance in the mirror showed the BMW accelerating again, its 400 horsepower turbocharged V-8 roaring loudly as it bore down on the defenseless Corolla.

This time the men made no attempt to pass. Instead, the BMW pulled within feet of her bumper and matched her speed.

Her speedometer was edging 60, but Lys knew she couldn't keep it up. She was approaching a set of treacherous hairpin turns where the road zigzagged down the mountain to Boulder.

Entering the first switchback, she slid her foot onto the brake, taking the turn much faster than she should have. Her tires squealed, but the BMW was still riding her tail.

Near the midpoint of the curve, Lys gasped aloud as a breathtaking panorama appeared beyond the guardrail. Like a billion sparkling gemstones flung across a field of black velvet, the lights of Boulder exploded into view. *Almost home! If I can just stay ahead of them through the switchbacks.*

Exiting the hairpin, Lys straddled the center line, trying to keep the BMW from passing. The men responded by blasting their horn and flashing their high beams repeatedly--nearly blinding her.

She punched her accelerator but the next switchback was already in sight. Warning signs flashed past. The posted speed limit for the curve was 35. She tried to take it at 50, tires screaming in protest. *Too fast!* Hammering the brake, she froze as the Corolla broke into a skid, almost slamming the guardrail before she regained control.

Lys could feel her heart pounding. Adrenaline was flooding her bloodstream. Her breathing deepened, her palms went cold, and her hands were beginning to tremble. She gripped the wheel with whitened knuckles, struggling to control her rising panic. As the road ahead straightened, she jammed the accelerator to the floor.

*This has been a night from hell from the start! It started with the god-awful party at Carrington's. Now this!* Lys was beginning to wonder if she'd survive the evening.

She shot a glance at Kareina, but her companion seemed oblivious to the danger. Kareina was watching her intently with an amused smile. She actually seemed to be enjoying Lys's distress. *No wonder she doesn't have friends...* Lys thought. *She's STRANGE!*

But Lys had no time to think about Kariena. The BMW had coasted through the last curve, but now charged ahead, engine thundering.

Approaching the next switchback, the BMW pulled up beside her. The mountain here loomed close on the left with a sheer drop-off to the right.

Another cluster of warning signs swept past. The maximum speed limit for the turn was 30 but the men were pacing her--she didn't dare let them pull in front. She started into the curve at 50, barely keeping control.

Lys chanced another look at the BMW. The man in the passenger seat was leering at her, not three feet away, and the look on his face made her blood run cold. Something dark, malevolent, and not quite human was staring back at her. Their eyes met for an instant, and his lips went taut, baring crooked teeth in a vicious grin... the gape of a wolf about to rip the flesh of its cornered prey.

And in a moment of chilling recognition, Lys finally saw what the men were after. With gut-wrenching certainty, her mind embraced the terrible truth she'd been struggling for the last thirty minutes to reject. For Lysandra Johnston now knew, beyond all doubt, that the men in the black BMW were planning to kill her.

Her gaze fixed resolutely on the rapidly-tightening curve ahead. *A thrill killing...* the thought came numbly to her mind ... *and I'm to be the thrill...* Resisting a wave of nausea, her mind raced, striving frantically to form a plan of escape. But it was not to be.

At the tightest part of the curve, as her tires shrieked, struggling to maintain their hold on the road; the men swerved abruptly to the right. With a resounding concussion and the sound of shattering glass, the BMW slammed the Corolla hard, lifting its front end from the pavement and driving it into the guardrail. There was an agonizing scream of ripping steel, a crash as the guardrail gave way, and a long moment of silence as the Corolla sailed through the air.

The welcoming lights of Boulder spread wide before her. Lys seemed to float for a moment in mid-air. Then, by the glare of her one remaining headlight, she saw the ground rising to meet her... Everything was happening in slow motion, but she was frozen to her seat and could not move.

Clenching the wheel in helpless terror, Lys glanced at Kareina one last time. But Kareina was gone.

# Chapter Two:  Kilauea

## HALEMA'UMA'U CRATER, MOUNT KILAUEA, HAWAII

Pele angled the tip of one dark, leathery wing and banked to the left.  Gaining altitude rapidly, she opened her mouth in an exultant roar as a blast of frigid, early-morning wind buffeted her face.  Eyes like glowing pools of lava scanned the horizon.  From this height she could see the whole island, from ancient *Kohala* on the north to wind-swept *Ka Lae* at the south.  She detected no sign of her enemies.  *Perfect!*

Long waves of ebony hair flowed behind her as she descended toward Kilauea.  Her prey was now fast approaching.  She watched as the silver Porsche 911 *Carrera* slowed to make its turn into Hawaii's Volcano National Park.

All had been prepared.  For two weeks, Pele had planted the sequence firmly in the victim's mind.  There would still be a need for subtle mental influence in the last moments, but that would be easily accomplished.  This victim *wanted* to be hers.

She bared her teeth in anticipation.  Pele was still revered as a goddess on Hawaii's Big Island, but it had been a long time since she'd savored the taste of human sacrifice.  Too long.

But her ancient enemies, the *Irin*, were in decline and would soon be vanquished. Even now, few remained who were strong enough to oppose her, and they were spread thin, distracted by pressing issues in distant places. The time was coming when she would again be free to do as she pleased on her own island. Then *all* of her ancient pleasures would be restored. Perhaps it had begun even now.

Pele had just begun her long glide toward the glowing pit of *Halema'uma'u* crater when she sensed something new. *No!* A presence had come … she felt it. It was a presence she'd not encountered for many years. Her oldest adversary had returned. She rumbled quietly under her breath, *Araton!* …then opened her mouth in a shriek of anger and frustration.

Erin let the door of the Porsche 911 *Carrera* swing softly shut behind her, waiting to hear the reassuring *thunk* of the engaging latch. She glanced quickly around in the pre-dawn mist to make sure no one was watching, then pulled her shawl tightly around her body against the early morning chill. Even in Hawaii it gets cold at 3700 feet.

Her eyes searched the darkness and found the path leading to the crater overlook, yet she hesitated, a look of confusion and uncertainty on her face. She glanced around again, eyes darting nervously like a frightened animal's. *Could she really go through with this?*

Most who knew Erin Vanderberg assumed she was in her mid-thirties, though in actuality, she was nearly a decade older. Taller than average, Erin stood five-eleven in bare feet, but she moved with the assurance and poise of a runway model. Her perfectly formed face was framed by rich cascades of silken, chestnut-brown hair.  Always impeccably dressed, she exuded an aura of beauty that women envied, and caused men to take a long and lingering second look.

That had been important to Erin once, but in recent years it meant nothing.  Erin was tired… tired with a weariness that went far beyond physical.

Gathering her resolve she tossed her purse and keys through the Porsche's open window onto the driver's seat.  *I won't need those anymore;* she thought to herself, then turned and strode briskly toward the trail.

It was a ten minute walk from the parking area to the *Halema'uma'u* crater rim.  The path was barely discernable in the early morning gloom, but Erin knew the way.  It had all been in the dream.

The dream had begun two weeks earlier, shortly after she arrived at the beach house, and had repeated every night since.  It seemed a pleasant dream, in a macabre sort of way, and it was always exactly the same.  By now Erin had every detail memorized.  She could re-play it in her mind at will.

The dream always began with her driving south along the windward coast of Hawaii's Big Island at four o'clock in the morning.  By 4:30 A.M. she'd slipped through the near-empty streets of Hilo and begun ascending the long highway through the cloud forest to Volcano National Park on Mount Kilauea.  Arriving at the park, Erin cruised through the entrance gate, unmanned at that hour, and turned left on the road to *Halema'uma'u* crater.

The area around *Halema'uma'u* had been closed to

visitors for several years, but in the dream the road barricades had been removed. Erin followed Crater Rim Road to the south and pulled into the deserted parking lot of the *Halema'uma`u* overlook at precisely five in the morning. The eastern sky was just beginning to glow with the faint light of a new day.

As the dream continued, she walked up the path to the crater's edge and easily vaulted the low fence designed to keep wayward tourists from approaching its crumbling rim.

*Halema'uma'u* looked like something from another world: an immense pit, 300 feet deep and 3000 feet across, set within the great caldera of the Kilauea volcano. Until the 1920s it had been a seething lake of fire, often boiling over its edges. But in 1924, following days of explosive eruptions, the surface fell to its present depth and hardened. Even now, however, lava often broke through, forming churning pools of molten rock on the crater floor.

Erin stood ten feet from the crater's edge and surveyed the chasm below. In her dream, *Halema'uma'u* was a pool of total blackness, an ocean of night. From its stygian depths, huge clouds of steam and sulphurous gas billowed skyward.

The ancient Romans believed the entrance to the underworld was located at *Avernus*, a volcano near Cumae. Erin had never visited that Italian volcano, but she wondered if it looked like this. It was easy to imagine *Halema'uma'u* as a bottomless pit stretching down into the interior of the earth--an open portal to the realm of the dead.

For her, that's what it would be... she would take a few quick steps and a long graceful dive into darkness.

She'd never see the jagged lava rocks rising to meet her. If she felt an impact at all, it would be a twinge of pain lasting only an instant.

As the dream progressed, Erin began to disrobe. That was an odd element of the dream, but it was the same every time. She would stand fully exposed at the crater's edge and casually remove every item of clothing; carefully folding her dress, shawl, and undergarments, and leaving them neatly stacked on her shoes at the craters edge.

*Tidy to the end,* she thought.

She'd read somewhere that those who commit suicide by swimming into the ocean often strip at the water's edge and swim naked to their death. She wondered if a similar etiquette applied to volcano divers. It made sense really, exiting life the way you entered, totally unencumbered.

Finally she stood upright, naked, facing the crater. She relaxed her body and took a deep breath, like an Olympic diver about to go off the high board. Then, as she stood before the waiting abyss, a wispy form materialized out of the surging clouds of steam. Vaguely humanoid, the apparition drew closer and solidified, until a beautiful Polynesian woman with an abundance of flowing black hair hovered in the air above the crater, not thirty feet away. Erin somehow knew the woman was *Pele*, the goddess of the volcano. Pele hung in mid-air, suspended over the darkness, watching Erin and smiling.

Pele was the oldest legend of the island. Even when white missionaries came and supplanted the gods and goddesses of ancient Hawaii with Christianity, belief in Pele had endured. Erin didn't believe in God or the afterlife, but she couldn't deny that Pele was a real presence on the

Island. According to legend, *Halema'uma'u* was Pele's home. Locals believed she lived in the frothing lava that still belched from the crater's floor. Every year, hundreds of sightings of Pele were reported all over the island, and the natives still brought her offerings... not the human sacrifices of ancient times, but rocks and fruit, and even bottles of rum were carefully wrapped in *ti* leaves and left for Pele to find.

For a moment, Erin stood motionless, face to face with Pele at the edge of the crater. Pele hovered a dozen yards away, bathed in the rising clouds of steam. Then Pele smiled at Erin again and beckoned, and in the dream Erin responded. She ran toward the vision of Pele.

It was a brief sprint, and with each step she felt her body become lighter, until at last, her feet barely touched the ground. As she gracefully leapt into the crater, it didn't feel like falling; it felt like flying. She closed her eyes and drifted through space in perfect peace. A warm breeze was gentle on her face. She opened her eyes again. She *was* flying, and Pele was beside her. She was as light as a bird, soaring out over the pool of night.

Gradually she began to descend. There was no fear, only a feeling of infinite freedom as she glided silently toward the ocean of darkness. She relaxed and let herself fall. It was the perfect escape. Escape from Rex ... from the crushing weight of unwanted responsibilities ... from clinging people who always demanded more.

With Pele still beside her, she sank into the darkness, feeling the stress and fears of life falling behind as she descended into the pit.

Erin always woke from the dream with an

overwhelming feeling of peace and contentment. It was a feeling she had not known for many years.

And now she was here, walking toward a volcano crater, following a dream-script that was embedded in her mind. It was a script that could only have one ending.

Erin walked in silence, purposefully. Scattered shards of *tephra*, tiny cinders of gas-frothed pumice, crunched underfoot.

*What would people say?* She thought to herself. She could picture the headlines… DALLAS SOCIALITE FOUND DEAD AT HAWAIIAN VOLCANO, APPARENT SUICIDE. *Would people even believe that? She was the envy of Dallas society. Everyone wanted to be Erin Vanderberg.*

*What would Rex think? Enraged probably.* Her husband would certainly feel no sorrow. Just anger that her choice of suicide could cause him to lose face.

Erin had considered leaving a suicide note. It seemed the right etiquette. But when she sat down to write one, she realized she had nothing to say, and no one she really cared to say it to. She just wanted everything to end.

Erin arrived at the crater's edge and quickly vaulted the low fence, then paused to survey the caldera before her.

To this point, everything had been exactly as she remembered in the dream. Even the barricades on the road to *Halema'uma'u* had been removed to allow her entry. *How had that happened?*

The eastern sky was glowing with the crimson light of approaching day. By its light she could just make out the great circle of the crater's rim. From somewhere far below an immense column of sulphurous steam and gas billowed skyward before the prevailing winds caught it and drove it to the southwest.

As she studied the scene before her, Erin was startled by the silence. In Hawaii there were always sounds… the chirp of insects, the call of birds. Hawaii was filled with life. But here there was absolute silence. There was no life in this place. She was suddenly aware of the sulphurous fumes filling the air, making it difficult to breathe.

Trying to stay focused, Erin again recalled the dream. The next step was disrobing. Erin considered it for a moment, but hesitated. It was *cold*. The dream had never been cold. Yet an icy wind was now buffeting her body. Occasional gusts tore at her clothing and caused her hair to whip around wildly. Even with her shawl drawn tightly around her, she was shivering and her teeth were beginning to chatter.

Something else was wrong. The pit before her was not the peaceful pool of empty darkness she remembered from the dream. Near the middle of the pit she could see a boiling cauldron of liquid rock illuminating the jagged boulders of the crater walls and causing the rising clouds of steam to glow with a hellish red. She looked around in confusion. This was not at all what she'd seen in the dream.

Erin drew back a step and glanced around, frightened, uncertain. This didn't look like a peaceful exit from life. It looked like the pit of hell.

In confusion, she studied the billowing clouds of steam rising before her, hoping for Pele's appearance. But Pele didn't come. The clouds of poisonous gas and steam continued to rise silently skyward. It was becoming harder to catch her breath.

Amidst rising panic, Erin pondered her options. Her two weeks on the Big Island had been a badly needed escape. The beach house was located on a cliff overlooking the black sand beaches of Honokaope Bay. Surrounded by three acres of meticulously landscaped grounds, it amply met Erin's need for seclusion and privacy.

Erin came to the beach house at least twice a year. It was a place to get away from incessant demands and endless responsibilities. And most of all, from Rex.

Sheltered on the lanai, she felt *life* slowly begin to return. She usually spent her first few days sitting on the lanai, not speaking, not thinking, barely moving. She'd fix her eyes numbly on the horizon and watch as the sun crept slowly across the sky to end the day in a blaze of glory as it sank into the western Pacific. Gradually the surging tide of stress within her began to subside. By the end of the first week she could actually sleep at night without drugs. Panic attacks came less frequently. She even drank less.

But then the time always came to return home, and each time it was harder. In two days Rex's plane would come for her. This time she knew she could not go back. Not to the life she had known.

But was *Halema'uma'u* the answer? Its reality was nothing like the dream. The dream had given her hope. But the yawning pit before her held no hope.

Erin again strengthened her resolve. So this was *not* the dream. It was not the peaceful exit to life she had hoped for. But it WAS still an exit. This place was cold and dead and filled with choking gas, but she could still jump. By the time her body struck the rocks below she would have gathered enough speed that she'd barely feel a thing. She could still do it. It would still be over. A fresh blast of bitterly cold wind hit her and she began to shiver again.

She looked around in desperation. *Oh God!* She thought. *This wasn't how I wanted it to end.*

But she saw no other way. Nothing would ever change. Rex's plane would land in Kona in two days, and that meant going home once more. She couldn't face the thought of it. Tears began to roll down her cheeks and her body was shaking uncontrollably.

She pulled the shawl more tightly around her and studied the short strip of earth between her feet and the crater rim, mentally counting the steps to the edge.

A brief sprint, no more than five steps. A quick run, and a leap, and it would all be over. She closed her eyes, took a deep breath, and prepared to make the final run of her life.

Suddenly a voice spoke… a man's voice. It was deep and resonant, and very close. The speaker was just behind her,

"I wouldn't do that, Miss Erin." The voice said, "*That* is not your destiny."

Startled by the voice, Erin's whole body shuddered. She spun around to see the speaker.

"Who are *YOU?*" She blurted, her voice tinged with both anger and confusion.

The stranger stood less than two feet away. He was tall. An African, apparently--his well-muscled body was cloaked in a colorful African robe that accentuated his rich, chocolate-brown skin. The man's head was closely shaved and his eyes were fixed on hers.

Erin froze in place.

He spoke again, his voice gentle, yet firm, "That is not your destiny, Miss."

Everything about the stranger exuded strength, yet his intimidating appearance was tempered by the kindness of his face.

As she stared at him, confusion quickly gave way to anger at the uninvited interruption.

"Who *are* you?" she demanded again, angrily.

"They call me Araton," he said calmly, and smiled.

Erin noted that he spoke with a strange accent, carefully enunciating each word. It sounded almost British, but definitely African.

"I've come to show you an alternative," he continued, glancing out across the caldera, "to this."

Erin followed his gaze across the crater. "There *is* no alternative." She said. "Nothing ever changes. Nothing *can* ever change. I can't take it anymore."

"Erin, you won't understand this, but I can see your destiny… I see what awaits you in the future. Or at least, what *could* await you. And if you choose the right path, I want to assure you that *everything* can change."

"What do you know about my destiny?" She shot back angrily, "You called me *Miss*. You don't even know I'm a married woman."

The stranger suddenly became very serious. "I called you 'Miss' because I *do* know you, Erin Vanderberg." He said, firmly. "We both know your marriage was a sham from the start. One of the reasons you're standing in front of this crater is that you know it's not real, but see no way out."

"Did Rex send you?" she demanded, spitting the name as though it was a dirty word.

The man laughed for the first time. A hearty laugh. "No, Erin. Believe me, Rex Vanderberg would have nothing to do with me."

"Then how do you know me?" she said sharply.

"I've watched you for some time now. I know many things about you."

"Like what?"

"For one thing, I know why you hate men. I know that every man you've ever known has only wanted to use you, abuse you, and control you.

"I know that you live in a golden prison. You have everything money can buy, and yet you have nothing. You've grown tired of inventing activities to fill up 24 hours every day.

"And you're weary of the causes to which you've committed yourself in a futile attempt to prove your own value. You're tired of bearing great responsibility for events you really care nothing about."

Erin's face hardened. He was reading her mail, but how could this stranger know her? She'd never seen him before.

Curiosity had now driven the thought of suicide from her mind. She turned to fully face the stranger for the first time. She tried to look him in the eye, but could not. There was something strange about him. She opened her mouth to speak, but could form no words. The stranger continued.

"Erin, the world is not as you've imagined it.

"It's like this volcano. You look into this crater and see a strange pool of liquid fire. You view it as an anomaly… something unusual and out of place in your beautiful world. You believe the real world is fresh and green, a place of oceans and forests and mountains.

"But the world you've experienced is just a small part of a larger reality. What you see in that pit is the true nature of this world. This planet is a spinning ball of molten lava. All you've known is a thin veneer of solid earth that floats precariously on that molten ocean.

"That's how you've lived your life. You've seen a tiny sliver of what is true, but there's a much larger reality beyond what you've known."

Erin stared at him in honest perplexity. "This isn't making any sense."

"Think of it like this," he said. "You've seen *The Matrix...*" The way he said it, it seemed more of an observation than a question.

"Of course."

"You're much like Neo. In *The Matrix,* Neo lived in his comfortable world and thought he understood it, but he never imagined the true nature of that world."

"And I suppose you're Morpheus?" Erin said with a hint of sarcasm. "You do look a little like him."

"Perhaps for you, I am Morpheus." He said. "I'm here to offer you the choice Morpheus gave Neo. Morpheus asked Neo to choose between two pills. The blue pill was a choice to continue to live in a false reality, oblivious to the truth. The red pill meant he wanted to know the truth, whatever it cost.

"My question for you, Miss Erin, is *which pill do you want?"*

Erin hesitated, uncertain where the conversation was leading.

He continued. "Choose the blue pill, and I'll turn and walk away. You can think of me as a kindly stranger who

27

saw you in distress and offered to help. I'll leave you free to jump… or not, as you wish.

"But choose the red pill, and I'll show you a world you've never imagined. The world as it really is. I can even show you the path to your destiny. But I must warn you it won't be an easy path… and you can't walk it alone."

"All right," Erin said, "Give me the red pill…

"But first," she demanded, her body shivering and teeth chattering from the bitter wind, "Tell me who you *are*."

"I'll tell you everything you want to know, but before we talk, let's get you some place warmer." He smiled, "I'd hate to see you die of pneumonia after all this.

"There's an old hotel called Volcano House," he continued, "perched on the upper rim of Kilauea just a few miles from here. Believe it or not, Mark Twain once stayed there. They serve great coffee, and there's an old stone fireplace just off the lobby. The hotel has kept a warm fire blazing continually in that fireplace for more than a hundred and thirty years. I happen to know there are two very comfortable old wooden rocking chairs standing in front of that fireplace right now, just waiting for us."

She looked at him, but her face hardened. She said again, "Who *are* you?"

Araton answered with a broad smile. "You wouldn't believe me if I told you."

"Try me." Erin insisted.

"Miss Erin…" he said, studying her carefully. The truth is, I'm not a native of your world. I'm not even a human being. You would call me an *alien* … but I assure you that I pose no threat. I've been sent here to help you."

Seeing her face flush red with anger, the man quickly added. "I told you that you wouldn't believe me… but perhaps a demonstration would be more convincing than an explanation. Let me show you what I really am..."

With no further explanation, the stranger walked past Erin to the crater's rim. Erin followed him with her gaze. At the edge of the abyss he paused for a moment, looked at Erin and smiled. Then, without a word, Araton stepped off the edge of the crater.

# Chapter Three:  Volcano House

Holding the coffee with both hands, Erin Vanderberg
leaned back in the huge wooden rocker Araton had pulled
close to the fireplace.  The room was old and slightly musty,
but very pleasant, and the warmth radiating from the
fireplace was already beginning to penetrate her bones.  She
glanced around, admiring the hotel's rustic décor.  It felt
more like a hunting lodge in Alaska than a Hawaiian resort.

Hot coffee in one hand, Araton pulled up the second
rocker and eased himself into it.  Erin stared at him, mouth
agape, still stunned by the recent revelations.

When Araton stepped off the crater's edge, of course,
he did not fall.  Instead, as Pele had done in her dream,
Araton floated in mid-air, high above the crater floor.
Gliding smoothly out about ten feet from the edge, he
swung around to face her, as a set of huge white wings
faded into view.

"My *God!*" she exclaimed.  "What…" she fumbled for
words, "…what *are* you?"

"I'm exactly what I claimed to be," he laughed.  "But
*you* wouldn't believe me."  Seeing her still shivering in the

cold he added, "And I promise I'll tell you the whole story as soon as we get to the hotel."

The ten-minute drive to Volcano House took place in complete silence. Erin drove, still glancing in unbelief at Araton every few moments.

Entering the hotel, they found a fire blazing in the old stone fireplace, just as Araton had promised. Araton seemed to know his way around the hotel, and soon had two cups of steaming coffee in hand and the massive chairs arranged before the fire.

Taking a sip of the coffee, Erin lifted her eyes from the roaring fire to find Pele staring at her. She started... almost spilling her coffee.

A large, cast-iron image of Pele was affixed to the fireplace in place of a mantle. Pele's visage was grotesque, with immense bare breasts and a glaring face. Pointing toward the image, Erin laughed, "Now, who thought *that* was a good idea?"

"Probably someone who never met Pele," Araton came back.

His statement raised a question she hadn't considered. "So Pele is... *real?*" Erin said.

"As real as I am," Araton assured her.

Erin studied the image for a few moments, then added, "Well, Pele was much more attractive in my dreams."

"Of course, what you saw in your dream was not the real Pele," Araton countered, "You saw only an image she projected into your mind.

"Even those who meet Pele in real life don't usually see her as she is. Pele uses mind control to affect how people perceive her. Up on these mountains, for example,

Pele usually appears as a beautiful young woman with long, flowing black hair. Down on the coast she's seen as an old woman in white hair. Neither is real, of course. The real Pele is barely humanoid."

Erin tilted her head questioningly. "Pele can really control how people *see* her?"

"Pele's race possesses formidable mental abilities." Araton explained. "If she were here now, you might sit and talk with her for hours, and never suspect you weren't speaking to a human being."

"What *is* Pele?"

"She's a member of an ancient race called the Archons. Her people have been visiting your world for many thousands of years. Many of them, like Pele, have chosen to live here. But their intentions are not beneficent."

"And now tell me exactly what *you* are." She looked at him intently.

"My people are called the *Irin.*" Araton responded. "We are, as you've seen, not exactly human, but we're similar to you in many respects.

"The Irin and Archons have both visited this world since ancient times, though only a few of your people have recognized our presence. However, our two races come here for vastly different reasons. The Archons' goal is to subjugate and destroy the human race and ultimately seize your world for their own. The Irin have been sent to prevent that."

With that introduction, Araton began his story. As Erin slowly sipped her coffee, Araton unfolded a picture of a world Erin had never imagined. A terrifying world. A battleground for alien races with the fate of the human race hanging in the balance.

At seven o'clock the hotel's restaurant opened, and Araton escorted her in. After filling their plates at the hotel's generous breakfast buffet, they chose a table by a large plate-glass window overlooking the Kilauea caldera. Erin's attention was captured by the huge clouds of steam silently ascending from *Halema'uma'u.* She shuddered at the thought that her body would lie broken at the bottom of that pit if not for Araton.

"Will Pele come after me again?"

"I doubt it," Araton responded. "Especially since you're leaving the Island. Pele is extremely territorial. She rarely leaves Hawaii. She sees this as *her* land, and in a way it is. At least she's helped form it. She's the one that keeps the volcano flowing, constantly expanding her territory. Once you're back on the mainland I doubt Pele will give you any trouble.

"But Pele is just one of the Archons. There are many others. And now that you're aware of their presence, they may target you more openly. But that *is* the path to your destiny."

"That's another question I wanted to ask. How do you know my destiny?"

"Let's just say my people relate to time differently than you do."

"You mean you time-travel?"

"Not exactly," Araton smiled, "but we can often see what lies ahead. Time has many corridors, many branching options. We have the ability to sense which corridor you're destined to walk, and what awaits you there.

"Right now, you have several corridors before you. Most of them are dark, but one is very bright. In fact, if you choose it, you may one day save millions of lives."

"What?" Erin said in unbelief.

Araton hesitated for a moment... "Erin, I'm saying that you are destined to be a person of great significance. You have things within you, abilities you're not yet aware of, that are vital to the future of your world. I see that clearly, and so do the Archons. There will come a time when you may save your entire race from destruction... but only if you make the right choices."

"What am I supposed to do?"

"Your next step is to go back home. You must return home and do exactly as you've always done. You must take up your responsibilities and fulfill your commitments." As he spoke he could see the light fading from Erin's face.

"I know that's not what you wanted to hear, but the days ahead won't be easy for any of us." He lowered his voice, looking more serious than she had seen.

"Great changes are coming for your world. Great destruction threatens, but my people will do all we can to help you prepare. You're one of a small group of humans who have the potential to save your world from disaster.

"We're preparing to gather the members of this group together and it's vital that you are part of it."

"When will all this start?" she asked.

"Within a month you should receive a phone call," Araton responded. "It will be an invitation to gather with the others we've contacted. From that point, things will move quickly.

"I must be honest with you, Erin," he continued. "Pele's choice of you was not accidental. The Archons know who you are. They know you have the potential to thwart their plans and they won't stop in their attempts to kill you.

"The Archons have already killed two of those we'd hoped to gather, and they *will* target others. They're very determined.

"The season ahead will be a precarious time for all of you," Araton said, looking intently at Erin. "You're in a battle for your life and a battle for your world, and I can't guarantee that you'll win. You may not survive, but I see no other path for you to walk. To arrive at your destiny, you *will* have to face death."

"I've faced death once already today." Erin smiled nervously, "Doesn't that count?"

"No, Erin, you haven't faced death." Araton countered, "You tried to escape life, but you have not yet faced death. That's a very different thing. But that time *is* coming."

# Chapter Four:  Mystery

## BRENTWOOD MEMORIAL HOSPITAL, BOULDER, COLORADO

The darkness lasted a long time.  Lysandra Johnston was dimly aware of unbearable pain.  Of movement.  Of people prodding and poking her body.  More pain.

She struggled back to consciousness.  There were vague shapes around her.  Voices.  One that seemed familiar somehow… but she couldn't place it.  Then a wave of darkness crashed over her.

Lys opened her eyes again and struggled to focus.  It was darker now.  Someone was leaning over her... a woman dressed in blue.

"So you're finally back in the land of the living?" the nurse asked casually.

Lys looked at the nurse.  "Where am I?  What happened?  I don't understand…"

It was an effort to speak.  She tried to turn her head, but it seemed frozen in place.  Bandages covered much of her face.

"Take it easy, honey," the nurse said softly.  "You've had a hard time, but I think the worst is past."

Lys faded in an out of consciousness several more

times. Doctors and nurses came and went, performing their nameless rituals.

A man came--a police lieutenant--asking questions about the accident. Lys mumbled something incoherent about a black BMW and men with cruel eyes. Then darkness overtook her again and she slept.

There were dreams. Strange dreams. Surreal nightmares that grew more and more bizarre. She was in the car. Kareina was with her, but she no longer looked like Kareina. Kareina's face had lengthened and distorted and gained reptilian scales. As Lys watched in horror, Kareina drew her lips back, revealing jagged fangs. She was leering at her with eyes like coals of fire.

The dream shifted and Kareina was gone. A man was in the car, a stranger. They were floating together in weightlessness. Time had stopped. The man reached out and seized her roughly, grasping her body in his strong hands. Helpless to resist, he pulled her close, and held her in a tight embrace. Then the world exploded.

Another dream. Lys was in a place she didn't recognize. The landscape was stark and rugged, and the sky swirled in a maelstrom of ash-dark clouds. There were birds in the clouds, thousands of them, great birds that fought and tore. One of the birds held a long gleaming sword in its hand. And one looked very much like Kareina.

And then it was morning. Lys was still in the hospital. She struggled to remember how she got there but her mind was filled with fog. Disconnected images jumbled together in her brain, tumbling over each other: The men in the BMW. The warning signs flashing past. The sound of ripping steel.

Finally Lys again heard a familiar voice. Climbing out of a deep well she struggled to open her eyes, and for the first time since the accident saw a familiar face.

"*Roger?*" She mumbled feebly through swollen lips. Then her face brightened in recognition as she flashed him a crooked smile, "Roger ... *DODGER!*"

Roger Johnston laughed out loud at his sister's greeting. Lys was still groggy from the pain medication and her speech was slurred. She sounded thoroughly *drunk*.

"That's *Doctor* Roger Dodger to you, young lady," he responded playfully.

Dr. Roger Johnston was a resident surgeon at Brentwood Memorial Hospital. Though he was seven years older than his half-sister, the two had been close since childhood. Lys hadn't called him *Roger Dodger* since they were kids.

"Roger..." she repeated, her voice clearer this time, "I'm *so* glad to see you."

He reached down and clasped her hand, "I'm happy to see you too, Sis, but next time you want to get together, just give me a call and we can do lunch. This is a hell of a way to get family time.

"But," he said warmly, "you don't know how glad I am to see you alive. For a while I thought we'd lost you. Mom and Dad have been worried sick. They're coming up to see you this weekend. They want to take you back to Dallas as soon as you're strong enough to leave the hospital."

Her mind was still foggy. It was hard to put words together. "Roger... the accident... those men in the BMW... Why did they want to kill me? I've never seen them before."

"I checked the police report, Sis. The black BMW was reported stolen in central Colorado. It was found abandoned, and heavily damaged, in Boulder. So it doesn't sound like they had it in for you personally. They were probably just strung out on drugs. You're lucky to be alive."

Lys again struggled to recall the accident. There was something important she needed to remember, but she felt confused, unsure which memories were real. Finally she looked up at Roger and asked, "What happened to Kareina?"

"Who's Kareina?"

"She was the woman in the car with me. We were coming back from a party when the BMW showed up."

Roger looked puzzled. "Lys, the police report said you were alone. No one else was found at the scene, and there's no chance anyone could have walked away."

"No, Roger... Kareina was with me," Lys objected, trying to sort out her memories. "She was the one who invited me to that god-awful party in the first place. I never would have been on that road if not for her."

"What can you tell me about her?"

"Not much, really. I've only known her for a few weeks. Her last name is Procel. She's about twenty-three, thin, with long black hair. She said she works down the hall at another office. I'm not even sure which one. She said she's new in town and I looked like a friendly face. She always dropped by on her break to talk."

"Lys, you're still pretty shaken up." Roger sighed. "I'll check with your office about Kareina, but believe me, you don't need to worry about her. There's no way anyone was with you in the car."

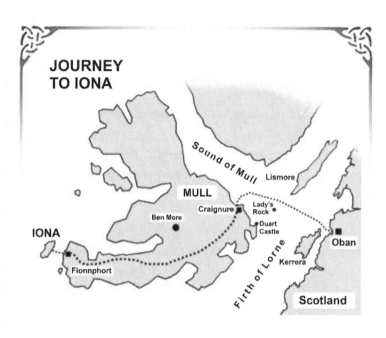

JOURNEY TO IONA

The Isle of Mull

# PART TWO: PILGRIMAGE

# Chapter Five: Patrick

## THE PORT OF OBAN, WESTERN COAST OF SCOTLAND

The deck plates shuddered with a deep rumble as the 4800 ton *Isle of Mull* eased from her moorings and began churning across the placid waters of Oban harbor. The *Isle of Mull* was a handsome vessel, over 90 meters in length, one of the largest in the Calmac fleet. Her gleaming white superstructure was accentuated by a distinctive red and black funnel towering above her decks, but her most notable feature was the company name proudly emblazoned across her black hull in huge white letters: *Caledonian MacBrayne.*

The MacBrayne fleet is the lifeblood of the Western Isles. There's a saying in the west of Scotland, "The earth belongs to the Lord, and all it contains, except the Western Isles, for they belong to the MacBraynes." That statement is not far from truth. The tiny, windswept isles of the Inner and Outer Hebrides have but one real lifeline to the rest of the world: the intrepid fleet of ferries operated by Caledonian MacBrayne, Inc.

Patrick O'Neill stood wearily in line at the ship's bar. It had been a long journey but he was nearing its end. Two years ago Patrick was a twenty-nine year-old investment counselor with a corner office in one of the gleaming glass towers of Dallas. He thought he had it all--until his marriage disintegrated in a messy divorce in which his wife got the house, the kids, and everything else important to him. After six more months of pointless activity, he walked away from his job, cashed in what remained of his invest-ments, and bought a ticket to Ireland.

Through the year-long trauma of the divorce, Patrick had been tantalized by a recurring dream. In the dream he sat on a green hill with the sea in the distance. Huge slabs of rock protruded from the ground around him. The countryside was rugged with few trees, mostly moss and grass. What he remembered most was the green. It was a shade of green he'd never seen in Texas. He assumed it was his ancestral homeland, Ireland.

There'd been a *presence* with him on that hill. He had no name for it, but it was very real. Every night as he approached the top of the hill, the presence enveloped him. It penetrated his pores and filled him with an overwhelming sense of peace and well-being. Nothing else seemed to matter as long as he was in that presence. He always awoke from the dream feeling strengthened and refreshed.

The dream-hill became his sanctuary, a refuge of healing amidst the turmoil of his shattered life. Month after month it was the same. At the end of long days filled with frustration, anger, and loss, Patrick would yearn for sleep and hope the dream would return. And it always did.

After the divorce was finalized the dream stopped coming, yet the Hill still called to him. When he set out for Ireland he told his friends he was searching for his roots. But he was really looking for the Hill.

Ireland had been as green as the pictures in the travel books, but he never found the Hill. His itinerary had retraced the life of Patrick, patron saint of Ireland. He wasn't sure why Patrick was important to him. He'd grown up Catholic but rarely attended Mass. In college he dabbled briefly in Buddhism, had a two-year fascination with "New Age," and ended up a mildly convinced agnostic.

Yet he somehow felt a connection to his namesake, Patrick. Guidebook in hand, he walked the Hill of Slemish where Patrick tended sheep as a teenager. He visited the Hill of Slane, where Patrick defied the High King of Tara. He finished his tour on Cathedral Hill in Downpatrick standing over Patrick's grave. He had no words to describe it, but being in Ireland was somehow a healing experience. Yet he knew his quest was not over.

There was still one place calling to him: a tiny, storm-swept isle off the western coast of Scotland. Though seemingly nothing more than a treeless sliver of rock and earth, historians consider the island to be one of the most significant places on earth. It's been given many names over the millennia, but in recent centuries, it's simply been called *Iona*.

Yet Iona is not easily reached. Patrick's cramped coach flight from Dublin to Glasgow had been followed by an hours-long rail journey to the city of Oban on the Scottish coast--a trip made infinitely longer by the screaming child in the seat behind him. After an overnight stay in Oban (which included visits to several of the local pubs), he awoke just in time to catch the MacBrayne ferry to Mull.

Yet his journey was still not over. Disembarking at

Craignure on Mull's eastern shore, Patrick would next board a tourist bus for a long trek westward--traveling a winding one-lane road the length of the island--to the village of Fionnphort on Mull's western tip. At Fionnphort he'd catch yet another ferry for the crossing to Iona.

The summer he graduated from college, Patrick signed-up for an adventure tour and spent ten days backpacking the Gobi Desert in Mongolia. At the time, Patrick thought Mongolia was the remotest place on earth. It now struck him that Mongolia had been much more easily accessed than this little Scottish Isle.

Patrick slapped a five-pound note on the bar and ordered a pint of Velvet, the thick, foamy Scottish ale he'd discovered the night before in a crowded Oban pub. Pint in hand, he retreated to the rear observation deck to watch the port of Oban and the western shore of Scotland fade into the distance.

Driven by its eight-cylinder, 3100 horsepower Mirlees Blackstone diesel, the *Isle of Mull* was already making fifteen knots across the smooth water of the sound. The ship was designed to carry a full complement of 80 cars and 972 passengers but the summer crowds were still weeks away. Lightly loaded today, she carried barely half her maximum capacity.

Patrick took a seat next to an older man who looked like a college professor enjoying an early summer vacation.

The morning was bright and clear, and unusually warm for this early in the year. Patrick leaned back in the deck chair, stretched out his legs, and enjoyed the sensation of the warm breeze gently ruffling his hair. He closed his eyes for a moment, took a deep breath and let it out slowly. *This sure beats flying in a jumbo jet.*

Taking a sip of the ice-cold Velvet, Patrick savored its rich smoothness while surveying a scene of almost surreal beauty. Receding behind him was the port of Oban, "gateway to the Western Isles." Tucked at the foot of massive wooded hills, the port was laid out in a natural amphitheatre with the harbor as the stage. At the end of the 19th century, Oban flourished as a Victorian seaside resort and many of the buildings still had that feel. Gingerbread villas clung to the hillside while majestic old hotels lined the Esplanade. Along George Street, busy shops and restaurants provided a quaint backdrop for the fishing boats crowded against the quay. Further to the south stood the historic Caledonian Hotel with its ornate façade of towers and gables rising above the harbor.

As Patrick studied the scene his attention was captured by an unusual structure on the hill above the town. Looming high above the picturesque Victorian village was a structure that looked for all the world like the coliseum of Rome.

Patrick's mouth opened, and without thinking, he said aloud, "What the hell is *that!*"

"Ah," the man next to him responded, "sounds like you've noticed McCaig's Tower."

Patrick glanced at the man. He appeared to be in his early-fifties with an untrimmed beard, horn-rimmed glasses, and a floppy white hat pulled down over a tangle of graying hair. Yet he carried a quiet air of confidence and intelligence.

"What *is* that thing?" Patrick asked. "It looks like the Roman coliseum."

"That's exactly what it's supposed to look like." The stranger laughed. "It was built by a wealthy banker named John Stuart McCaig back in 1897. Folks around here call it McCaig's Folly. Old man McCaig wanted to build a replica of the Roman coliseum here in the Scottish highlands and fill it with statues of himself and his family. It was supposedly a philanthropic project to provide work for the unemployed stonemasons of Scotland. McCaig only got the outer wall completed before his death, when his sister went to court to stop the project. It's a public park now. Really quite lovely."

Patrick offered his hand. "Patrick O'Neill... Dallas, Texas. You sound like an American, but you seem to know the countryside here pretty well."

The man shook his hand and laughed again, "Call me Michael. Michael Fletcher. I'm actually Canadian, though I've spent some time in the states. But I've spent many *more* years studying this part of the world. Sort of an amateur historian. Tell me, what brings an Irish cowboy to the Western Isles?"

"That's a long story," Patrick replied, sipping his pint. "I grew up in the states, but had an Irish grandmother who loved to tell me stories of the old country; so I've set out to explore my roots. I've spent the last four weeks in Ireland and have one more place to visit."

"And that would be... *Iona?*"

"How did you know?"

"You've the look of a pilgrim about you," Michael observed, "and pilgrims come from all over the world to Iona."

"I don't know about the pilgrim part... " Patrick responded, laughing. "I grew up Catholic but ditched religion in college. I'm an agnostic now, which doesn't make me very good 'pilgrim' material.

"My interest in Iona is sheer curiosity. My grandmother's stories of the old country included one puzzling detail. She said our ancestors left Ireland and for almost two hundred years lived on the Island of *Hy*--what's now called Iona. She described *Hy* as a mystical place. 'An isle of lights and faeries' she used to call it. She said our ancestors built a school there, attended by kings and princes from all over the world... and faeries would come down and teach them." Patrick laughed and shook his head, glancing at Michael to gauge his reaction. "I guess that's one part of our family history I may never understand, but I had to come here and see the place for myself."

"That sounds like Iona, all right," Michael said with a straight face and stared out across the water as though focusing on something Patrick couldn't see.

Michael excused himself and returned a few minutes later with his own pint.

The *Isle of Mull* had passed out of the Bay of Oban into the broad estuary known as the Firth of Lorne. To the right they were passing the Island of Lismore, marked by the picturesque Lismore Lighthouse at its southern tip.

Visible ahead, off the port bow, was their destination, the ship's namesake, the Island of Mull. The hulking form of an old castle was perched on the cliffs above the shore.

"Michael, do you know what that castle is?"

"That's called *Duart* castle," Michael answered, pausing to take a sip of his ale. "It's the ancestral home of the Clan Maclean... dates back to the thirteenth century.

*Duart* means 'Black Point' in Gaelic, and that is where it sits--on the point--standing guard over the Sound of Mull. Quite a history this place has."

Michael stood and scanned the water on the port side of the ship, finally pointing to a jagged rock just breaking the surface of the water. "Do you see that rock over there? It's called *Lady's Rock.* It's only visible at low tide.

"They say that in 1523, Lachlan Cattenach, the ruler in residence over at Duart, tied up his wife Margaret and marooned her on that rock, hoping she'd be drowned by the incoming tide.

"When the rock reappeared above the waves the following morning, Lachlan sadly reported her death to her brother, the Earl of Argyll."

Michael eased back into his seat, "Unfortunately for Lachlan, that wasn't the end of the story. A few weeks later the Earl invited Lachlan to dinner at his castle, supposedly to console him on the death of his wife. As he entered the hall, Lachlan was shocked to discover Margaret sitting next to her brother at the head table.

"Turns out she'd been rescued by a passing herring fisherman. Nothing was said at the banquet, but it's reported that Margaret's cousins met Lachlan outside the hall after dinner and administered some rather severe Scottish justice."

With a twinkle in his eye, Michael added, "My understanding is that it was all handled very quickly… *without lawyers!*"

Patrick took a long last sip of his pint, and looked at Michael. "Michael, what do you know about Iona?"

"Sounds like you already know a good bit about

Iona," Michael answered. "It's a tiny island of course, just three miles long and a mile wide, and about as remote a place as you can imagine." Michael took a quick gulp of his ale, then continued, "The usual history goes something like this... An Irishman named Columba and twelve followers came to Iona in 563. By the way, Columba was a member of the *Ui Neill* clan--what's called the O'Neill's today--so he really was your relative.

"Columba and his followers built a community on Iona. The history books call it a monastery, but it wasn't the kind of monastery most people think of. It wasn't even Catholic, at that time. It was more like a town... a cluster of thatched huts, surrounded by a stone and earthen embankment. Their 'monks' were allowed to marry and have children. They tended fields, raised livestock, practiced crafts, and worshipped God.

"As remote as it is, it's amazing the influence Iona had. At one time, the place was known all over Europe. Kings of many lands sent their sons to study on Iona.

"It's always been an unusual place. Many strange things happened there. Visitors sometimes comment that the barrier between the material and spiritual realms is very 'thin' on Iona."

"What kind of things happened there?" Patrick asked.

"A man named Ademnan--one of Columba's successors as the head of Iona--wrote a description of Columba's experiences on the island. Interestingly, he described pretty much the same things your grandmother told you about... strange glowing lights, angels, demons, and supernatural manifestations.

"According to Ademnan, Columba and his followers

went out from Iona with supernatural powers. They performed miracles, healed the sick, drove out demons, and converted all of Scotland from paganism to Christianity in a single generation.

"So Iona developed a reputation as a holy place." Michael continued, "During the medieval period, kings from Scotland, Ireland, Norway, and even France chose to be buried on Iona because they believed it was close to heaven."

Patrick stared at Michael. "How do you know all this?"

"It goes with the territory, you might say." Michael paused and returned Patrick's stare. Then he leaned closer to Patrick and confided, "You see, I've a unique field of study. I'm what they call an *angelologist*. I study *angels*."

Patrick barely suppressed a laugh. "*Angelologist*? I didn't know there was such a thing."

"Most people don't," Michael said. "But I've spent most of my life studying the creatures you call angels... and of course, their dark counterparts, the demons. I've written three books on the subject! Angels don't fit easily into our modern worldview. But when you begin studying them, it's quite addictive."

"So... you really *believe* in angels?" asked Patrick.

"Oh, absolutely. We've been visited by these creatures throughout our history."

Seeing the skepticism on Patrick's face, Michael added, "Did you know that every society in human history has recorded contacts with angels?"

"They're part of every religion. You were raised Catholic... Your Catholic Bible is filled with angels from cover to cover… and demons. In the first book of the Bible, angels visit Abraham. Do you know what he does? He fixes dinner for them! Abraham and the angels sit down and eat together as though it was the most natural thing in the world."

"But angels aren't just Christian," Michael continued. "The pagan Greeks and Romans painted pictures of angels that look exactly like your Christian ones. In every generation there are those who've claimed contact with these beings."

Patrick looked at Michael with suspicion, "Are you a priest, or something?"

"Heavens, no!" Michael laughed heartily. "I'm not even religious. When I talk about angels, I'm not talking about weird ethereal spirits. I'm talking about beings that are as real and physical as you and I. But they have some unique abilities. They appear to be *trans-dimensional.*"

"Trans-dimensional?" Patrick questioned.

"Yes." Michael explained, "You see, you and I are limited to a universe of three dimensions… length, width, and height." Michael gestured broadly to illustrate the dimensions, taking care not to spill his ale. "We can't imagine moving in a direction that doesn't fit one of those categories.

"However, science now recognizes there are dimensions beyond the ones we know. The latest theories point to the existence of at least *eleven* dimensions."

Patrick arched his eyebrows. "*Eleven* dimensions?"

"That's not some crackpot idea, Patrick," Michael laughed again. "It's mainstream quantum physics! And by the way, eleven is the *conservative* estimate. Some hold there are as many as twenty-six dimensions. Some believe there's an infinite number. That's why many cutting-edge physicists don't even talk about a "*uni*verse" anymore. They call it a *multi*verse."

"You've lost me again." Patrick laughed. "Now explain *multiverse*."

"Well..." Michael said, pausing to take another sip of his ale. "Back in 1954, a Princeton University doctoral candidate named Hugh Everett III came up with a radical new idea: the existence of parallel universes. It seemed the only explanation for the data his experiments had produced.

"Many physicists accepted his theory, and many have since tried to develop it further, but it was always considered unprovable. Then in 2007 it was announced that a team led by Dr. David Deutsch of Oxford University had actually succeeded in proving the existence of these parallel worlds.

"So we now know that our universe is not alone," Michael said with rising enthusiasm. "The universe we've known is part of a whole series of *universes* occupying the same physical space. Each universe exists in a different dimension, totally self-contained. You might picture them stacked up, 'superpositioned' upon each other, like layers on a cake. That's the *multiverse*."

"So, you're saying if we could shift into a different dimension," Patrick asked, "we would find ourselves in a totally different *universe*?"

"That's what the physicists tell us. In *our* universe we're sitting on the deck of this ferry headed toward the coast of Mull. But if we could shift into a different dimension, we could find ourselves in a totally different *version* of this world. It might be quite similar to the world we know, but there could also be some surprises. A parallel universe might operate with a whole different set of physical laws. It could even have its own inhabitants.

"And that brings us back to *angels*," Michael continued. "I'm convinced the beings we've called angels are the inhabitants of one of those parallel worlds. They live in their own world--their own *universe*--but they have an ability we lack. They can move from one dimension to another. They shift in and out of our world as easily as we move from shadow into sunlight."

"That makes my head hurt." Patrick laughed again.

"Think of it like this..." Michael said, pointing out across the water, "Suppose you're in a small boat out there on the Sound of Mull. Beneath you, just a few feet away, are many kinds of fish. You and the fish are in virtually the same location, yet you are totally unaware of each other's existence. You live in different worlds, different dimensions. You occupy the "air" dimension. The fish live in the "water" dimension.

"But you have an ability the fish don't have," Michael added. "You can travel between worlds. If you put on a scuba tank you can leave your own dimension and enter the realm of the fish. For a brief time you can swim among the fish as though you're one of them.

"That's how angels and demons interact with humans. They're as real and solid as we are, but they have the ability to move in and out of our world. They can enter our realm and walk among us. Then, just as suddenly, they slip out of our dimension and disappear. To primitive man that made angels seem like supernatural beings."

Patrick shook his head and smiled in disbelief, but Michael drained the last of his pint and continued, "Here's what's really interesting, Patrick.  The fact that twenty-first-century thinking has little room for angels hasn't hindered the angels in the least.  In fact, reports of angels and demons have skyrocketed in recent years.

"Something unusual is happening in the angelic realm right now… some kind of battle is brewing, and I've a sense that Iona will be right in the middle of it."

# Chapter Six: Across Mull

Dark clouds were moving in from the west as Patrick and Michael exited the MacBrayne ferry at Craignure on Mull's eastern shore.

Craignure was a tiny village whose main industry appeared to be servicing the ferry passengers waiting for connections to other parts of the island. Michael and Patrick grabbed a quick lunch at the inn across from the ferry terminal, then found the waiting area for the tourist coach that would carry them westward to the town of Fionnphort.

By the time the bus for Fionnphort arrived, big drops of rain were spattering the ground around them. They were soon inundated by a cold, steady downpour. Boarding the bus, Patrick and Michael took a seat together with Patrick by the window. The bus was packed, with nearly every seat occupied.

Almost immediately, the driver began a cheerful monologue that seemed somehow out of place on a day that had suddenly turned so gloomy. "Good afternoon," he said in his delightful Scottish brogue. "Welcome to Bowman's coach service. We'll be motoring today through Glenmore, along the shores of Loch Scridain, to finally arrive at Fionnphort on the western tip of the island."

The driver continued with a rapid patter describing the scenic details of Mull, apparently using a memorized script. "On the right, weather permitting, you might catch a glimpse of *Ben More*, which in *Gaelic* means 'Tall Hill.' At 3169 feet high it's the tallest mountain on the island, but it was once much taller. Ben More was the last active volcano in northern Europe. Geologists tell us Ben was 10,000 feet tall before it blew."

As the driver droned on, Patrick leaned back in his seat and tried to relax. The driver's voice was soon lost in the sounds of wind-driven rain. The bus traveled a winding, one-lane road across the island, stopping at times to let sheep cross, and pulling over frequently to allow cars traveling the opposite direction to pass. When most of his passengers appeared to be dozing, the driver abandoned his efforts as tour guide, leaving them to travel the rest of the route in relative peace.

Patrick gazed out at a lonely landscape of desolate moorland and steep, heather-clad hills. Ancient brooding castles flashed past the coach window. Deep lochs, impassible bogs, and deserted glens appeared and were quickly lost in the driving rain. Patrick had never imagined a place so desolate, yet so beautiful.

It was raining harder now. Dozens of waterfalls cascaded down every hill, turning small streams into rushing torrents.

Watching the fog-shrouded hillsides gliding past the window, Patrick felt he was being transported to a different world. Time itself seemed to have ceased. The whole island was brooding with a gloomy, other-worldly charm.

He leaned his seat further back and listened to the rain thundering on the roof of the bus. Perhaps it was the surreal setting, but Patrick suddenly had a great fascination to learn more about Michael.

Noticing that Michael was still awake, Patrick began, "Michael, how did you decide to become an angelologist?"

"Well…" Michael responded, smiling slightly, "you might say I was *chosen*.

"It began with an experience I had as a child. I still remember every detail. I was nine years old and was in bed on a rainy night about to go to sleep. As I lay there, listening to the rain outside my room, I heard a strange noise and opened my eyes. Standing at the foot of my bed was a figure, glowing in bright light. His hair was as white as snow, but he didn't look like an old man. He was dressed in a white robe, too bright to make out any details.

"At first I was terrified. I tried to lie still, but my whole body was shaking. Then a sense of incredible peace settled over me. I felt completely secure. My mind couldn't process what was happening, but I knew I wasn't in danger.

"Finally, the man saw I was watching him. In a smooth motion he unfurled huge white wings that hadn't been visible a moment before. He extended his wings horizontally, rose quickly from the floor, and disappeared up through the ceiling of my room.

"I closed my eyes, rolled over and tried not to breathe. Finally I fell asleep.

"For years I searched for an explanation of what I saw. I knew I wasn't dreaming, and I wasn't hallucinating either.

"I attempted to put the experience behind me, but then, in college, I made the mistake of majoring in history. The more I studied the ancient world, the more I found that many, many others have had experiences like mine.

"Did you know that students of pre-historic cultures have found pictures of winged humanoids scrawled on the walls of caves in every part of the earth? Creatures like these are described in the writings of Plutarch and carved in the monuments of Egypt, Babylon and Persia. All of these ancient peoples, in all parts of the world, had seen the same thing.

"They've been known by many names. The Hebrews called them the *benai Elohim*, or the 'sons of God.' The Jews also called them *watchers*. The Christians called them the *angelloi*, or *angels*. Pagan Greeks called them *horae*. The Vikings knew them as *valkyries*, and in Persia they were *fereshta*. To Hindus, they're *devas*, the "shining ones." In primitive Shamanism they're simply called the *bird people*, or the *bird tribe.*

"Reports of these creatures have continued throughout history. George Washington spoke of his guardian angel and credited his success at Valley Forge to 'a visit from a heavenly being.'"

"One of the most famous accounts in modern times is the legend of the Angels of Mons. The Battle of Mons took place in Belgium in August of 1914 during World War One. Within weeks of the battle, the story was already legendary.

"Soldiers returning from the battle reported seeing an army of angels led by a towering, winged figure that spurred on the English forces during their assault on the German trenches. These beings were observed by many soldiers and supposedly corroborated by German prisoners.

"Of course, angel sightings can't be proven," Michael admitted. "Some are certainly hoaxes. But the persistence of these accounts throughout history, along with the amazing similarity of the reports, tells me we're dealing with something very real."

Patrick was genuinely fascinated now. "Tell me more about angels."

"To begin with," Michael said, "most of them look just like us. They usually appear to be normal human beings. Sometimes they have wings--but often no wings are seen. And they come in all varieties; male and female, young and old, all different races.

"A common misconception about angels and demons," Michael continued, "is the idea that they don't have physical bodies. Some people picture angels as wispy spirits, 'beings of light' and nonsense like that.

"The records show just the opposite. When these creatures enter our dimension, they're as real and solid as you and I. They eat and drink. They use weapons, cook food, and play musical instruments. And they're highly intelligent.

"Most traditions teach that angels and demons frequently walk among us unnoticed. Your Catholic Bible warns you to always treat strangers kindly, because you never know when a stranger might be an angel.

"There are even accounts of angels--presumably of the 'fallen' variety--having *sex* with humans. The Hebrew Bible tells of a time when males of the *benai Elohim* bred with human women and produced a fearsome race of hybrids called the *Nephilim*. What's interesting is that the Greeks record the same story in pagan terms. For the Greeks, it was the Greek *gods* having sex with human women, producing a race of *demigods*."

"That definitely sounds like they have physical

bodies." Patrick agreed. "So where did we get the idea that angels are just spirits?"

"That comes from their ability to move in and out of our dimension," Michael replied. "Angels have the unsettling ability to fade in and out. They can also shift slightly out of our plane and pass through walls.

"Sometimes they don't appear visibly at all," he added. "Many traditions describe a shadow realm on the edge of our dimension where trans-dimensional beings can interact with us without becoming visible... So you can be visited by an angel without ever *seeing* one."

"How would you know an angel is visiting if you can't see it?"

"One way is through dreams," Michael explained. "Angels appear to have telepathic ability. They can communicate directly into our minds, and that most frequently happens in our dreams. So if you have an unusually vivid dream, particularly if it's a *recurring* dream, it could be a message from an angel."

Hearing Michael's comment, a chill shot down Patrick's spine, but he wasn't yet ready to tell Michael about the Hill.

Attempting to shift the conversation, Patrick ventured, "And you also believe in *demons?*"

"Absolutely!" Michael said. "That's one of the most important things you can know about these creatures. Some have the misguided idea that all angels are friendly, but the eyewitness accounts tell a different story.

"The truth is that some angels are benevolent and try to protect us, but there are also dark or 'fallen' angels that intend great harm for mankind. These dark angels are often called *devils* or *demons*."

Sensing Patrick's skepticism, Michael added, "I've interviewed many people who've had encounters with demons, Patrick, and believe me, they're quite real. Some of the accounts I've heard would make your skin crawl."

"What are demons like?" Patrick asked.

"They're cold malignant creatures... totally without compassion," Michael said. "They come into our world to kill and destroy, and they're sadists at heart. They love to inflict pain. They sometimes seem to make a game of it-- tormenting their victims for months or even years, prolonging pain to the point of madness. The victim's death can be almost anticlimactic."

"What kinds of things do they do?"

"Demons appear to choose their victims randomly-- any age, any sex, any walk of life--and they've a variety of tactics... Sometimes they target the victim's body. The unsuspecting victim is suddenly bombarded by a bizarre series of painful and debilitating symptoms. There's never a medical explanation and never a cure. Doctors sometimes label these people as hypochondriacs, but the agony they experience is quite real.

"At other times, demons attack by amplifying or distorting our natural desires. The victim is seduced into destructive behavior or overwhelmed by uncontrollable urges for violence.

"On occasion, dark angels even work by affecting our circumstances. We've all known cases where it's happened. A normal, well-adjusted individual suddenly finds everything in his life falling apart. He loses his job and every employer slams the door in his face. As he struggles to pay the bills, he finds himself inundated by an avalanche of bad luck. His kids get sick. Appliances break, computers crash, his car is totaled in a freak collision. He plunges into deep depression. His marriage falls apart. Helpless to resist, he endures one disaster after another, becoming more and more despondent."

"And you would attribute something like that to a *demon?*" Patrick asked.

"You can always tell when a demon is at work," Michael said, "because a demon always overplays his hand. When someone is targeted by a demon, their loss goes far beyond a normal run of bad luck."

"That sounds like a recipe for paranoia to me," Patrick chided. "If you talk like that, you'll end up with people running around crying, 'Help, the demons are after me.' …blaming all their problems on demons."

"Patrick, it's not paranoia if something really *is* after you. And this is *real*. The demons don't always show themselves openly, but in many cases the victims are haunted by a shadowy presence. The same dark figures show up, over and over again, at odd times and places.

"And since their lifespan is incredibly long, it's not unusual for a dark angel to torture his victim for years, or even decades, before destroying him.

"Demons have even been known to attach themselves to a family line and torment its members for generations. In some families, oppressive poverty, incurable disease, and just plain 'bad luck' are passed from generation to generation and no amount of effort can break them free. I've interviewed families where no one has survived past the age of forty in six generations. And always the demon is present. Sometimes you see the same dark figure in the background of family photographs, generation after generation."

Patrick was feeling overwhelmed. He'd never met anyone like Michael and wasn't quite sure what to make of him. The rational part of his brain wanted to reject everything Michael said. Yet Michael spoke so confidently, there was something in Patrick that wanted very much to believe him.

He glanced out the window. The bus had pulled off to the side of the road to allow a car traveling in the opposite direction to pass. The rain was letting up a little, but ghostly tendrils of mist still haunted the desolate moor.

As the bus pulled onto the road again, Patrick turned back to Michael, "You mentioned on the ferry that something unusual is happening in the angelic realm. What do you see?"

"I see two trends," Michael answered. "In the last few years I've documented a remarkable *increase* in the activity of angels. I've investigated more than five hundred reports of angel encounters in the last decade, and close to a third of them have been in the last twelve months.

"What I've noticed is that angels are openly revealing themselves, speaking to people and intervening in human events to a degree never before seen."

"That's fascinating," Patrick said.

"It is," Michael agreed, "but the other trend is quite alarming. While reports of angels are dramatically increasing, the reports of demons are increasing even faster. In fact, they've gone off the scale. Demonic encounters now outnumber the angelic ones by more than four to one."

"What does that mean?" Patrick asked, genuinely intrigued.

"It means," Michael said, suddenly dead serious, "that in recent years, the balance of power between angels and demons appears to have shifted.

"Angels have always protected the human race. Because of the presence of angels, demons have been afraid to show themselves openly. They've been forced to operate covertly, working behind the scenes in the shadow realm. But all that's now changed. The powers of darkness are moving among us with a new boldness. They seem to have lost their fear of angels."

"So what does *that* mean?" Patrick prodded, truly curious.

"It means," Michael said, leaning closer, "that in the age-old battle between good and evil, the forces of evil are now *winning*. And their goal, I believe, is to destroy us all!"

The rain had finally stopped, though the sky remained dark and overcast. As they followed the road on a long curve to the left, all conversation on the bus suddenly ended. For coming into view was the windswept strip of water called the Sound of Iona. And there, across the water, less than two miles away, was their destination. The home of Patrick O'Neill's ancestors. The burial place of kings. The legendary dwelling of angels and faeries. The Island of Iona.

# Chapter Seven:  Sylvia's Story

## THE NEIGHBORHOOD OF TREMONT POINT, NEW YORK CITY

Sylvia Romano no longer questioned the existence of demons.  She knew one.  And if there is a hell on earth, Sylvia had found it.

Sylvia sat hunched on the edge of a filthy mattress in the middle of a dark, litter-strewn floor.  She was naked, and the tangle of unwashed walnut-brown hair tumbling down her back did little to conceal the protruding ribs of her gaunt body.  Her pale, emaciated limbs--marred by overlapping bruises and streaked with grime--gave her the ghostly appearance of a death-camp survivor.

Tears still trickled down Sylvia's cheeks, but her concentration was fixed on the familiar ritual before her. Opening the crumpled, brown paper bag she kept beside the mattress, her trembling fingers carefully removed its contents, placing each item on the floor between her feet. Beside the packet of white powder bequeathed by her latest visitor, she placed a blood-smeared syringe and needle, a spoon with a bent handle, a cigarette lighter, a half-empty plastic bottle of water, a wad of cotton, and a length of electrical cord.

As she set the items neatly in place, the voice in her

mind began to speak again. The voice had been speaking to her off and on for several days, growing more and more insistent… warning her, telling her to get away. She knew it had something to do with the dream.

The last few nights Sylvia had had the same dream. A nightmare. In the dream something terrible was happening to her. She was being ripped apart. There was blood and smoke and fire and death. People were crying in pain. All around her little children lay on the ground screaming… and dying. The dream made no sense to her, but she knew what it meant. She knew if she didn't escape, she was going to die.

She emptied the packet of white powder into the spoon. With the syringe she drew water from the plastic bottle, and carefully squirted it into the spoon around the heroin.

The voice in her head was speaking more urgently now: *Get up, Sylvia. Run. You must get away… now!*

But an escape attempt would take so much effort. Her body hurt all over. The pain was constant now. And they would beat her again. And besides, it just didn't matter. Hardly anything mattered anymore.

Sylvia had just been raped, and even that didn't matter. Over the past six months she'd grown used to that. The only thing that mattered was that she'd been paid.

That was an unwritten rule in the house. They called Sylvia the *freak*… the freak in the back room. She was there for anyone to use, at any time. But when they used her, she had to be paid. And they paid her in the only currency that mattered … heroin. She needed heroin at least four times a day.

She flicked the lighter a few times and held the flame under the spoon, steadying her trembling hand against her knee.

Waiting for the mixture to boil, Sylvia looked down at her body. She hardly recognized herself. She'd always been proud of her body. She had liked the way people looked at her. Her senior year in high school some friends talked her into entering a beauty pageant, and she'd won second place. But she never really wanted to be a beauty queen. Her dream was to be a teacher. She loved kids.

And she'd been smart. She graduated from high school near the top of her class and was accepted at NYU. Her first two years in college she studied hard and earned a 3.5 average… but her third year she met Botis.

She was at a party at a friend's apartment when Botis tapped her on the shoulder. That night she smoked her first joint with him. "Come on, Syl," he smiled, "You'll like it!"

After that she saw Botis more and more frequently. They would sit and talk for hours, and he always brought drugs, all kinds of drugs. She hadn't known there were so many. Over the next few months a whole new world opened up to her. And she thought she was in love.

Botis was unlike anyone she'd ever met. He seemed young, almost a teenager, but he assured her that he was much older than he looked. He was dark and mysterious, and always wore black. And he was brilliant… he seemed to know *everything*. His knowledge of history, art, and religion would put any of her professors at NYU to shame. Many evenings they'd sit together on the floor of her apartment sharing a joint, and she'd listen in fascination while he expounded some complex point of esoteric philosophy.

Then, just before they slept, he'd hold her close and they'd make warm romantic love.

One night he told her that Botis was the name of a powerful demon from medieval lore… To the ancient writers, the demon Botis was a prince in hell with many legions of demons under him. At the time that seemed very exotic. Syl reached out her hand and lovingly tousled his raven-black hair.

As the months passed, Botis became her life. Her old friends gradually stopped coming around, and she spent more and more of her time stoned. She skipped class and her grades plummeted, but she no longer cared. Knowing she was failing anyhow, she dropped out of school.

The day she quit NYU, Botis introduced her to heroin. And after that, the heroin was all that mattered.

A year later, when she'd lost her job and was evicted from her apartment, her mom pleaded with her to come back home and get her life together, but instead she went with Botis.

That night he took her to the house. She was frightened at first. She had never been to a place like the house. But Botis assured her that the best drugs were always plentiful there.

He led her up darkened stairs to a back room, and they did drugs together… but then, without warning, he began to beat her. It was a side of Botis she had never seen. He screamed obscenities, shoved her into a corner, and pounded her body with his fists. Terrified and confused she sank to the floor and tried to shield her face, but he kicked her repeatedly, then--with seemingly superhuman strength-- he picked her up and threw her across the room. Finally, he raped her brutally and left her in agony, barely conscious.

When she finally awoke the next morning, she was alone on the mattress and the door to the room was locked. Her purse and cell phone were gone. Sylvia was trapped.

That afternoon Botis came again. Again he beat her and raped her and left her locked in the dingy room. For a full week the pattern repeated, with never an explanation. Occasionally he brought her food, and always heroin, then left her alone--imprisoned in darkness.

In anguished tears, she pleaded with him to tell her what she'd done... why he was doing this to her... but he just smiled and beat her more.

Then others in the house began to come. They came at any hour, individually and in groups. Some raped her savagely and left her bleeding. Others came gently in the night, whispering words of love while they were on her. Some felt sorry for her and promised to take her away, but never did. A few were so stoned they barely knew she was there. Gradually, as the agonizing months dragged by, she'd grown numb to them all.

The only one she dreaded anymore was Botis. She knew now what he was.

One night, two weeks into her imprisonment, Syl had been hunched over on her mattress sobbing. Hearing a noise outside the room, she looked up and saw Botis appear--walking right through the closed door--leering at her with his demonic grin. At first she thought she was hallucinating. But then she knew. Botis truly was a demon.

The day after that encounter someone left her door unlocked and Sylvia made her first escape attempt. She almost succeeded, but they caught her a few steps from the front door, and beat her severely. In the following weeks she tried several more times with the same result.

After a while, even escaping didn't matter. The last few weeks they hadn't even bothered locking her door. Syl was just the freak in back room. And she was numb… she didn't care about anything, as long as she got her next fix.

Botis still came every day. He rarely spoke, and didn't even seem to enjoy the sex. He just wanted to hurt her. And each time he came, her depression and hopelessness deepened.

Her mixture was boiling now. The heroin had dissolved. She sat the spoon down on the floor in front of her. Rolling a small wad of cotton into a ball, she placed it in the spoon, then pushed the tip of the syringe into the center of the cotton and pulled back the plunger until all the heroin was sucked in. She tapped the syringe with her finger, checking it for air bubbles.

Then she picked up the electrical cord and tied it around her arm as a crude tourniquet. With her forefinger she palpated her skin, searching for a vein. She inserted the needle, drew back on the plunger and looked to see if blood was entering the syringe. It was not. Syl shifted the needle under the skin probing for a vein. Four times she pulled back the plunger but without success.

The voice was louder now… she could hear it plainly. It was pleading with her, screaming at her, telling her to stop. To run. To try *one last time* to escape.

Finally she found a good vein… She carefully pressed the contents of the syringe into the vein, and in a few moments felt the warmth spreading through her body. And then nothing else mattered. The voice stopped screaming. She lay back on the mattress in momentary bliss. For the moment she didn't hurt anymore. That was what mattered. Sylvia closed her eyes and sank into a dreamless sleep.

\*\*\*

There was a flicker of light, then the rasp of leathery wings sounded from the dark alleyway. Three gaunt figures emerged from the alley and walked purposefully down the row of crumbling, three-story tenements.

In the lead was a woman who called herself Kareina. A tall, thin, plain-faced woman with a pallid complexion and long black hair, Kareina looked to be in her early twenties, but was, in fact, much older. Her subordinates, Botis and Turell, followed a few steps behind her.

The street around them was a picture of devastation. Broken glass crunched under their feet and the stench of garbage rotting in the gutter assaulted their nostrils.

Tremont Point had been an exclusive suburb of New York City in the late 1800's. After the First World War, however, when its aging mansions were supplanted by cheaply constructed apartment blocks, the neighborhood became a melting pot for the city's immigrant masses.

As the community aged, living conditions deteriorated. By the late 1970's, a dramatic rise in violent crime and random shootings forced the city to cut off essential services. When police patrols, fire services, and even garbage removal finally ceased, there was a mass exodus from Tremont Point.

Those bold enough to drive through Tremont Point today pass block after block of burned out or abandoned tenements. While other neighborhoods in the Big Apple have experienced a measure of renewal in recent years, Tremont Point remains one of the most dangerous in the city, a haven for gangs and drug dealers.

Near the middle of the block, the trio turned and climbed garbage-strewn concrete steps to the door of an abandoned tenement. Not a single pane of glass remained unbroken on its dingy façade, and the front door had long ago been ripped from its hinges. As they crossed the threshold into the dim interior, a rat ran across the hallway in front of them.

The stench of urine and feces permeated the hall. Fearful eyes peered through the narrow cracks of chained doors as the three intruders walked past. Through an open doorway they glimpsed a cluster of emaciated people lying motionless on soiled mattresses scattered around the floor.

Ascending a narrow, creaking stairway, they made their way to the third floor and walked a darkened corridor to the back of the building. They paused before the closed door of the last apartment. On the door, someone had clumsily scrawled two words in dark red paint, *"THE FREAK."*

The three did not knock. They simply walked through the closed door.

The only light in the room came from a small window opening. The glass was broken out, leaving an open hole overlooking the trash-filled alley far below and the shell of the burnt-out tenement next door.

The room reeked of vomit and the floor was strewn with piles of garbage and scattered remnants of soiled clothing. In one corner sat a grimy, lidless ice chest where roaches skittered around scraps of moldy food.

In the center of the room Sylvia Romano was sprawled, naked, across a filthy mattress. At the sound of intruders, Syl stirred slightly. Empty eyes peered through a tangle of matted hair, struggling to focus on the figures standing over her. Finding it too much of an effort, she sank back into unconsciousness.

Botis gave her a leering grin and took a step in her direction. A hard slap in the face from Kareina stopped him in mid-stride. "That's NOT what you're here for this time."

Like her companions, Kareina was a killer, and one of the best. She was sent to do only one thing... to destroy human life, and she had a long history of success. But Kareina had grown weary of just killing. Like a cat with a mouse, she liked to play games with her prey. When the assignment allowed, she would get to know her victims, befriend them, earn their trust... and then look into their eyes in their final moments to see their helpless terror.

But she couldn't do that on this assignment. This assignment required a human instrument. She needed a body she could possess. And Botis had offered Sylvia.

Kareina eyed Syl for several minutes.

It was obvious that Sylvia had once been attractive, but long months of neglect and abuse had taken their toll. She was emaciated, almost anorexic, with track marks up and down both arms. From the bruises on her limbs and face, it was clear that she'd been severely beaten many times... and recently.

Kareina twirled a wisp of her long black hair around a slender finger and smiled. She found it amusing that her easiest recruits were always found among self-righteous religious fanatics... or among the burned-out husks of humanity in a crack house.

Approaching Sylvia, Kareina leaned down and gently touched her forehead. If a casual observer had been present, they would have been shocked at what happened next. For Kareina suddenly faded from sight and disappeared, slipping effortlessly into the concealment of the shadow realm.

A moment later, the body on the mattress contorted in a violent spasm. Sylvia's head rolled back and thrashed from side to side. Her eyes rolled up, exposing only the whites. Another spasm, and then her body sat up.

Botis had almost done his job too well, Kareina thought with disgust. There was barely any humanity left in this body. She preferred at least a moderate amount of resistance when she took possession, but this ruined creature offered none. It was hardly worth the effort to destroy her. *Still, she'll be a useful tool for our purposes.*

Under Kareina's control, Syl stood shakily to her feet. The drugs coursing through her veins made her body sluggish and unresponsive. Sylvia's lips opened, and in the gravelly voice of one possessed, she barked, "Quick, help me dress."

From the parcel he'd been carrying Turell unwrapped a loose-fitting garment.

"No, first the bomb," Kareina directed.

Botis and Turell hastily fastened a harness around Sylvia's torso, then lifted the explosive device into place. Sylvia's frail body could barely support the weight of the 30 pound suicide belt, but Kareina would provide all the strength she needed. Kareina quickly pulled on the rest of the clothing.

Her eyes fixed on Botis and Turell. "Quickly, now… we must be in Manhattan by four o'clock."

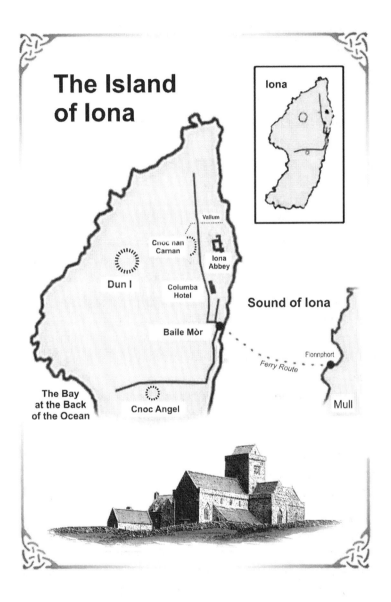

The Island of Iona

Iona

Vallum

Cnoc nan Carnan

Iona Abbey

Dun I

Columba Hotel

Sound of Iona

Baile Mòr

Fionnphort

Ferry Route

The Bay at the Back of the Ocean

Cnoc Angel

Mull

# Chapter Eight:  The Island of Iona

## THE ISLE OF IONA, ARGYLL, SCOTLAND

For Patrick's first morning on Iona the sun rose bright in a cloudless sky.  From the window of his room in the Saint Columba hotel, Patrick could see sheep grazing contentedly in the nearby fields.  Beyond them, the early morning sun glistened across the calm waters of the Sound of Iona and starkly illuminated the distant, red granite mountains of Mull.

Michael was already eating breakfast when Patrick entered the hotel restaurant.  He motioned for Patrick to join him.

"Good morning, Patrick," Michael said cheerfully as Patrick took his seat.  "How did you sleep?"

"Wonderfully," Patrick responded.  "I don't think I've slept that well in years.  There's something very peaceful about this place."

Glancing around the restaurant, he added, "How's the breakfast?"

"Outstanding, as usual," said Michael. "I've stayed at the Saint Columba several times, and the food is always superb.  They have their own organic garden behind the hotel, and much of the food is grown right here.

"By the way, might I suggest the blood pudding?" Michael pointed to a black sausage-like disk on his plate. "Most Americans are afraid to try it, but once you get used to it, it's really quite tasty."

"I think I'll have to pass on that," Patrick laughed, as he glanced at the menu, "but the food does look good." Patrick ordered a full breakfast, beginning with strong black coffee, which was promptly brought to the table.

Taking a sip of his coffee, Patrick again looked up at Michael. "So, what will you be doing here on Iona?"

"I want to start by interviewing some of the locals," Michael replied. "There are *always* new angel stories on Iona. Just about every inhabitant is ready to bend your ear with story after story of strange events.

"But mostly, I come here to write. I'm working on my fourth book, and somehow Iona just seems like the right place to write about angels."

As they ate, Michael quizzed Patrick about his recent travels in Ireland. Michael seemed particularly interested in Patrick's visit to the city of Bangor--situated in a section of County Down known as the Valley of the Angels. According to legend, Saint Patrick had once encountered a large gathering of angels in the place. Michael hadn't yet visited Bangor, and immediately began to pepper Patrick with questions.

Unfortunately for Michael, Patrick's most vivid memory of his stay in the Valley of the Angels was of a pub called the "Salty Dog," a few blocks north of his hotel on Quay Street. He couldn't recall seeing a single angel.

When they finished eating, Patrick stood and stretched, still stiff from his long journey.

"Before I get to work," Michael said, pausing to drain the last of his coffee, "How about a quick tour of Iona?"

"I'd like that." Patrick replied. "You know, if you ever give up writing, you'd make a great tour guide. Your knowledge of this part of the world is incredible."

"Having a photographic memory does help."

"I have a photographic memory too ..." Patrick quipped as they walked from the restaurant, "I just keep forgetting to buy film."

Patrick purchased a map of the island from the little display beside the front desk, and they were off to explore Iona.

"Let's begin in the south," Michael suggested as they exited the hotel. They turned to the left and followed a winding road that led past the crumbling ruins of a medieval nunnery, through the tiny village of *Baile Mòr*, and along the waterfront. Odd formations of twisted rock lined the shore.

"Patrick, on the map, Iona looks like a little sliver of land that crumbled off the end of Mull. But actually, Iona is enormously older. In fact, the rocks on Iona are some the oldest on Earth... four billion years old. Iona literally dates from the beginning of the earth itself. These rocks formed when the molten mass of the globe first formed a solid crust."

The road along the shore took a sharp turn to the right, heading inland across the center of the island. Walking between lush green fields on a spring morning, with sheep calmly grazing on either side of the road, was one of the most peaceful experiences Patrick could remember. The view was breathtaking in every direction. Clusters of multicolored wildflowers were splattered across the landscape, while steep, heather-clad hills rose to the north and south.

Seeing the look of wonder on Patrick's face, Michael said, "Do you begin to feel the uniqueness of this place? There's really nothing else like it. Sooner or later it affects everyone who comes here.

"The Scottish mystic Fiona Macleod wrote that Iona is 'the one bit of Eden that had not been destroyed.'

"Historians call Iona, 'The Light of the Western World.' You're no doubt familiar with Thomas Cahill's popular book, *How the Irish Saved Civilization.* Well, the Irish *really did* save western civilization, and they did it--for the most part--from Iona. For centuries--during the darkest of the dark ages--Irish monks from Iona went throughout Europe, teaching, and founding schools.

"And then there are the angels. Many writers describe Iona as a 'thin place' where the material and spiritual planes meet. Angelic beings seem to pass in and out of our dimension very easily here. But at least one writer attached a strong warning to that description. He said that great care must be taken to prevent Iona from becoming a 'demoniacal centre.'"

As they neared the center of the island, Michael gestured toward a nondescript mound of grass-covered earth rising to the left. "That mound is one of the most significant sites on the island. It's sometimes called *Sithean Mor*, 'the faerie mound.' Through the Middle Ages it was known by its Latin name, *Colliculus Angelorum*, or its Gaelic equivalent, *Cnoc Angel.* In English that means 'The Hill of the Angels.'

"Your cousin Columba used to come to this hill to pray. It's recorded that he climbed to the top of that mound, lifted up his hands in prayer, and that 'citizens of the heavenly country' flew down to meet with him.

"Columba had a special relationship with the angels. Ademnan relates that angels often visited Columba as he prayed. It was rumored that they revealed to him secrets hidden since the beginning of the world.

"They say the night St. Columba died, all of Iona was filled with the brightness of angels as thousands of them descended on the island. One contemporary writer said an immense pillar of fire appeared at midnight at the eastern tip of the island, illuminating the earth like the summer sun at noon."

An old woman, who had been approaching on the road, saw them looking at *Cnoc Angel*, and stopped to listen in. When Michael paused, she stepped closer, tapped his arm with a bony finger, and in a thick Scottish brogue, whispered, "They still come here, you know. Last month, I saw three of them, *right here*."

Then, pulling her shawl tighter around her head against the morning chill, she added, "And last week, down in the village, Agnes McClean and I was walkin' outside at dusk and saw two of them angel beings flying over us, headed toward the East. They flew directly over our heads… and they had a otherworldly glow."

Michael pulled out his dog-eared journal and made some quick notes, then got her name and asked if he could speak with her again.

"Looks like you've got your work cut out for you," Patrick smiled. He didn't want to admit it, but being on

Iona, he was actually starting to believe the angels might show up.

They continued across the island. Topping a rise, Patrick could hardly believe his eyes... the road ahead ran down through the middle of a golf course! "So this is where my ancestors *played golf?*"

"Well, actually, your ancestors grew wheat here, but this *is* Scotland, you know." Michael smiled. "Of course, everything on Iona is a little unique... notice the cows grazing over there near the fifth hole.

"But, now look straight ahead..."

Beyond the golf course Patrick saw something else that looked out of place on a wind-swept Scottish Isle. The path they were walking ended at a broad, crescent-shaped white-sand beach that looked like something out of a Caribbean travel brochure. All it needed was a few palm trees.

"That's called *The Bay at the Back of the Ocean*." Michael explained.

"Michael, I must say, Iona is an amazing place."

"Patrick O'Neill, you haven't even *begun* to see the wonders of this place. But, that's enough of the tourist sites. The southern part of the isle has some interesting spots, but it's pretty rugged, so I'll let you explore that yourself. But wear boots when you go... the bogs will pull the shoes right off your feet.

"For now, let's head back to the northern end of the island. I want to show you one more place."

They retraced their path past the Hill of the Angels and along the winding road until they passed the hotel.

A short walk north of the hotel, on the right side of the

road, stood a lovingly restored medieval monastery, the majestic Iona Abbey.

"Believe it or not, this was a crumbling ruin for hundreds of years," Michael commented. "The 8th Duke of Argyll began preservation work in 1874."

"So this was Columba's monastery?"

"Hardly." Michael laughed.

"As old as all of this looks, everything you see here was built at least 500 years *after* your ancestors retreated to Ireland. By the time this was built, the Catholic Church had taken over Iona, and the power of the ancient Celts was lost.

"The Iona Columba knew was entirely different than what you see here. The original 'monastery,' if you want to call it that, was a collection of small beehive-shaped huts. They called those huts 'cells.' Each monk had his own cell, or in the case of married couples… each couple had their own. Together, they formed a small community. For protection, they built a ten-foot tall earth and stone embankment called a *vallum* around the cells. Within the *vallum* they also built a mill, a barn, a church, and several other buildings. Of those buildings, of course, nothing remains.

"All that remains of the original Iona monastery is a trace of the *vallum* that surrounded the encampment. Let me show you the wall your ancestors built…"

Walking north past the medieval monastery, Patrick saw, running east-west across the middle of a field, the crumbling remains of a rock and earthen wall. "That wall was the northern edge of the original monastery. Your ancestors built that wall in an age when Roman legions still battled barbarian hordes all across northern Europe.

"Now, Patrick, there's one more place I want to show you. It's not mentioned in the tour books, but it's really my favorite place on the island. It's a little hill called *Cnoc nan Carnan*. That's Gaelic for 'Hill of the Cairns.' Most tourists never even notice it, but I believe it's where your cousin Columba lived.

"Historical records agree that Columba's cell stood at the top of a rise overlooking the rest of the monastery. That puzzled me, since the monastery now is pretty much on level ground. Then I realized that the original monastery was much larger than the medieval one. If you notice the remains of the old wall, it continues past the road, and up over that rise of land on the west. So part of Columba's monastery was actually up on that rise."

They crossed the road and passed through a gate. Just to the left, rising above the coastal plain, was a small green hill. At the top of the hill, Patrick could see huge rock slabs jutting from the ground, forming a sheltered area between.

Michael pointed to the top of the hill. "That's where Columba's cell must have stood, nestled in the protection of those rocks. How many times did Columba converse with angels in that very place? Let's go take a look."

Patrick and Michael walked up the hill. The grass underfoot was covered in wildflowers. To the east was the medieval monastery, and beyond that, the Sound of Iona and the distant mountains of Mull. To the west he could see the rugged, green landscape of Iona, and in the far distance, the endless sea.

As they reached the top of the hill, Patrick walked between the huge rock slabs, his feet sinking into the soft heather. It was like walking on holy ground.

There was no mistaking this place.  He was returning to a place he had visited many times before.  It was the place of peace and refuge he'd left America to find.  Patrick had found The Hill.

As Patrick glanced around in amazement, surveying the beauty and serenity of the place, he had no way of knowing that in less than three months time, the fate of the world would be decided on this very spot.

# Chapter Nine:  Aftermath

## BRENTWOOD MEMORIAL HOSPITAL, BOULDER, COLORADO

The next morning, Brentwood Memorial Hospital, along with almost every place else in America, was buzzing with the news of the latest suicide bombing in New York City.  In recent months there had been a series of New York bombings, but this was by far the worst.  It took place in Grand Central Station at four in the afternoon.  There were twenty-seven dead, most of them children returning from a school field trip.   Many more were injured and maimed for life.  The explosives had been heavily laced with nails and broken glass to produce maximum damage.

The news reports, as usual, replayed the security tapes over and over, with endless commentary and conjecture.  No one had yet taken credit for the atrocity.

Lys Johnston had been watching the reports all day, and was literally shaking when Roger came in that afternoon.

"What's wrong, Lys?"  Roger asked with genuine concern.  "You look like you've seen a ghost."

"I don't know..."  Lys answered haltingly.  She was still in pain and heavily sedated.  "Maybe I am seeing a ghost.  I'm seeing *something* and I'm not sure what it is.

"The networks have been replaying the footage of the suicide bomber all day. In the video, you see the bomber enter the station and walk to the center of the floor. From the first time I saw it I knew something wasn't right. She looked like she was already *dead*. It was like watching a zombie."

"She gets to the center of the station and stands there, watching a crowd of school children come toward her. She waits until they're all around her. Then, just before she detonates the bomb, she looks up at the camera… and smiles.

"The look she got…" Lys said, struggling against the pain, "It's the same look the men gave me just before they tried to kill me. And every time I watch it, I see the same thing. Something's there, and it's not that poor woman. Something is *in* her. It's looking at me through her eyes… and it isn't human." Lys's body shuddered and she shook her head, as if trying to shake the image from her mind.

"Roger, I know this sounds crazy, but that suicide bomber… I'm sure she's somehow tied in with the men who tried to kill me."

Roger reached out and rested his hand lightly on her shoulder, "Sis, you're still shaken-up from the accident. Don't let your mind get carried away. That woman was just mentally unbalanced."

"No, Roger. I know what 'unbalanced' looks like. This was different. It's like the woman wasn't even there. Something was *in* her, using her body. And whatever you call it…" Lys fumbled for the right word, and finally found it. "It was…*evil*."

The news channel was beginning another security

camera replay. Roger reached out and switched off the TV. "Lys, you've had a horrible experience, but I know you'll come through it. When they catch those men, you'll see they were just strung out on drugs. And that woman was just a brainwashed fanatic. Don't let your mind make this into anything more."

Roger hesitated. "Lys, I have to tell you something, and you need to listen. Your office called me earlier this afternoon. They checked on that woman, Kareina, you asked me about."

Lys looked up, "Did they find her? Is she okay?"

"Someone from your office went door-to-door, checking every office on your floor, then every office in the building. But no one in your building has ever heard of a Kareina. Two floors down they found a *Katrina* working as an accountant, but she's a 54 year-old blonde and weighs 250 pounds. In other words, sis… no matches."

"But that's impossible," Lys objected. "I *know* her. She came by my desk almost every day. I remember talking with her in the car just before the accident. I didn't make her up."

Roger reached down and held her hand. "You've been through a terrible ordeal… something most people wouldn't have survived. It's natural for you to be confused."

"What are you saying?"

"I'm saying that your mind is playing tricks on you. You've had a serious trauma and it's left you mixed-up, but you need to face the facts. There was no Kareina in the car. There was no Kareina in your building. Lys, this 'Kareina' person doesn't exist."

\*\*\*

## PLANO, TEXAS (A SUBURB OF DALLAS)

*I'm going mad,* Erin thought. *Absolutely stark-raving mad.*

Erin Vanderberg sat numbly on her patio pouring her fourth glass of wine of the afternoon. She tilted the bottle to the vertical and held it a moment to drain the last drops. Then she raised the glass and admired its rich red contents. It was her favorite wine, a little-known *Sangiovese* from a remote village in Italy. She had it shipped in by the case.

Taking a long, slow sip, she leaned back on the chaise again to watch a beautiful pump-driven waterfall cascade down a carefully-landscaped artificial cliff and into her swimming pool.

*Why am I doing this?* She thought. *Why do I keep going?*

Three weeks earlier she had returned from Hawaii, nursing a glimmer of hope. Since then, however, her doubts about the events at Kilauea had begun to grow. She pondered the scene with Araton on the edge of the crater, replaying it endlessly in her mind. It seemed remote, like something she'd watched a long time ago in a bad movie.

She and Araton had spent most of that day at Volcano House talking. It had given her a fleeting sense of purpose and a hope that things could change, but she'd heard nothing from Araton since returning to Dallas. Had it even been *real*?

Maybe she'd imagined the whole thing. Perhaps that whole day was just an unusually vivid dream that somehow lodged in her memory.

After a while she began to chide herself for even *thinking* it could have been real. *Erin Vanderberg rescued from the clutches of an ancient Hawaiian volcano goddess by a winged alien who warned of coming global catastrophe. Yeah, right!*

In the weeks since returning to Dallas, absolutely nothing had changed. The only good thing was that Rex, as usual, seemed preoccupied with activities at the ranch. She'd only seen him once since her return.

But she'd quickly jumped back into a swirling tide of endless responsibilities. *The curse of doing things well,* she thought. *Do one thing well, and you'll be given more. Much more.* She was torn by constant pressure from a dozen directions.

*The mayor has opposed the new plan for the arboretum. No problem. Erin Vanderberg just got back from Hawaii. She'll take the mayor's new wife to lunch and get things back on track.*

*And by the way, Erin... we're so looking forward to your presentation at the Dallas Arts Council luncheon. The governor will be there. This is very important.*

*And, Erin, the entertainment for the Charity Ball just canceled. The tickets have already been printed. Details have fallen through the cracks and no one is sure what to do. We need your help, Erin. You're the only one that can pull this together.*

*Erin can fix it. Erin Vanderberg can do anything.* They all depended on her.

After all these years, Erin knew she was still trying to prove herself. To prove she was not Rex. And to do that, she had to be perfect. She had to know the right people and have the right answers. And above all, she had to be strong. Always. She could never let anyone know what Erin Vanderberg was really like.

The momentary refreshment of her time in Hawaii was now a distant memory. Despite the Xanex, her panic attacks had resumed, and against her doctor's warning, she drank a full bottle of wine every night just to get to sleep.

Then last night she'd lost it. It began with a middle-of-the-night panic attack. She awoke at 2:00 AM feeling frightened and alone. Her legs and shoulders were twitching. She felt lightheaded. There was a smothering sensation… the sense that there was no oxygen in the air she was breathing. Next came the pressing tightness in her chest. She tried to scream, but could not. Her heart was a sledge hammer pounding in her rib cage. *Was she having a heart attack?*

In her mind Erin knew there was no danger… just the classic symptoms of an anxiety attack. They would pass in a few minutes, leaving her shaky and drenched with sweat. She'd experienced these attacks on and off for years. It didn't matter that the symptoms weren't real. They always *felt* real.

When the symptoms finally subsided, she'd flipped on the TV and for the first time saw the reports of the New York bombing. That's when she fell apart.

She didn't know why the news hit her so hard. Terrorist attacks seemed to happen all the time now. She felt little connection to New York City, and certainly knew none of the people involved. Even the *Nine-Eleven* attacks had not affected her like this. The moment she saw the report she began to weep uncontrollably.

She never got back to sleep. She had her secretary cancel everything and spent the morning numbly watching and re-watching the reports.

*What's happening to me?*

She'd nearly finished the wine when she sensed a presence close by. She looked up to see Araton standing beside her.

*"Araton!"* she gasped as she lurched clumsily to her feet, then stared at him with her mouth agape. His appearance was every bit as unsettling as their first meeting had been, but in a different way.

On the one hand, Erin had a strong urge to throw herself into his arms, embracing Araton like a long-lost love, finally reunited. With another part of her mind, however, she wanted to collapse in tears and pour out her frustration. Reigning in her emotions, she managed a middle course.

"Araton," she repeated, struggling to remain standing, "I'd almost convinced myself that you weren't real… that it had all been a dream."

"I assure you, I'm very real." He smiled. Then, noting the combined effects of a sleepless night and a full bottle of wine, he added, "… but I think you'd better sit back down."

He helped her into the chaise, then sat down cross-legged on the patio beside her. "Tell me what's happening."

"I'm not sure *what's* happening." She answered. "This morning when I heard about the bombing, I just fell apart. I don't even know why.

"What I'm feeling… it's not the kind of grief you feel about terrible events in far-away places. It's not even the sympathy you feel for people you know. Araton, this feels *personal*. It feels like I'm mourning a personal loss."

Araton looked at her quietly for a moment, then said, "When I heard about the bombing I knew I needed to come. I expected you'd have this response when you saw her."

"You assumed I'd fall apart when I saw the video of the suicide bomber?" Erin said, puzzled. *"Why?"*

"The woman in the video was Sylvia Romano."

Seeing the questioning look on Erin's face, he added, "No, you've never met her, but your destinies were closely intertwined."

"Sylvia was supposed to be part of the group we're forming. If her path had not been interrupted, the two of you would have worked together closely. In fact, she was destined to one day be your closest friend. Your subconscious senses that, and you feel the loss."

"What happened to her?"

"Sylvia was captured by the enemy and held prisoner in one of their strongholds."

"A *stronghold?*" Erin asked. "What's that?"

"A stronghold is an area the enemy controls, where powerful Archon warriors dominate the territory. In this case, it was a neighborhood near the South Bronx called Tremont Point. They knew we couldn't operate openly there to rescue her.

"We tried repeatedly to warn her, but we didn't have sufficient strength to gain her release. In the end they took possession of her body and turned her into a walking bomb. They used her to further their plans."

"They can do that?' Erin recoiled in horror. "Control our bodies against our will?"

"Only when your will has been weakened. If you become hopeless enough they can overpower you and control your every movement."

He paused and looked at her intently. "Erin, you must remain alert. I believe the enemy has formed a plan to eliminate you as well. You must not let that happen."

Erin looked at him and their eyes met for a long moment. She suddenly realized that Araton was the only person in the world she really trusted. He was watching over her and seemed to genuinely care what happened to her. Though he wasn't even human, she felt protected, and totally secure in his presence. That was something she had not felt for many years.

It may have been the wine, be she couldn't stop herself from asking the question that came to her mind. "Araton... We both know my marriage is a sham. I have no one. I'm totally alone. You're the only person in the world I trust right now. Please forgive me for asking, but… is there any possibility of … a *relationship* between us?"

"I'm sorry Erin," he said firmly, "but that would violate our strictest rules. Many years ago, a group of renegade Irin who called themselves the *Grigori*, entered your world and took human wives, but the results were disastrous. I'll tell you the story sometime, but for now, just know that it's not possible for us to be together.

"But I can tell you this." He continued, looking intently into her eyes. "Your destiny does not lie with Rex Vanderberg. There will be another man in your life, a companion you'll fully trust and deeply love. The two of you are destined to be together for many years. Be patient. It won't be long before your paths cross."

Erin paused for what seemed like an eternity, looking at Araton and fighting back tears. Finally, in desperation she said, "Araton, you said I'd receive a phone call... that there'd be a group of people, others to help... When will that happen?"

"Soon, Erin..." He said gently, "Very soon."

*The Lake House*

PART THREE:  SYNAXIS

# Chapter Ten:  Piper and Holmes

## THE LAKE HOUSE--IN THE PINEY WOODS OF EAST TEXAS

Holmes guided his Mercedes CLS550 Coupe onto the Interstate 635 exit ramp.  The Friday-afternoon Dallas rush hour had been a parking lot, but they were now clear of the congestion.  Gently depressing the gas pedal, he accelerated smoothly onto Interstate 30, headed toward the Piney Woods of East Texas.

Derek Holmes was a clinical psychologist in private practice with an office in the city of Frisco on the northern edge of the Dallas-Fort Worth Metroplex.  Tall and ruggedly handsome, Holmes had a perpetual five o'clock shadow and piercing green eyes with black hair tousled casually.  He had always been athletic, and at 41, worked out an hour a day to stay in shape.

Beside him in the passenger seat was Ginny Ann Piper.  Called *Piper* by most of her friends, she was 36 and attractive with an infectious smile and sandy-blonde hair worn in a casual style.

Piper was a psychologist also, with an office a few doors down from Holmes'.  The two had been in a relationship for more than two years, and often weekended together at his house on Cedar Hills Lake.

Their relationship had never really been about passion, although that was certainly part of the picture. The real focus was companionship. Piper and Holmes had both burned out on one-night-stands and shallow relationships in their twenties, and both had been several years without "someone special" in their lives. To put it frankly, they were lonely. Their relationship had begun slowly, meeting for lunch, or for happy hour at *T.G.I. Friday's* after work... but over the course of several months it gradually deepened.

They found they enjoyed being together. They could talk for hours and never run out of things to say, or sit contentedly side-by-side, never saying a word. Sometimes when they walked, they found themselves holding hands like love-struck teenagers. The relationship had surprised them both, and both wondered if marriage was in their future.

Holmes had always looked forward to their weekends at the lake house, but he wasn't looking forward to this one. In fact, he had dreaded this day for months. He knew he had to tell Piper what was happening and wasn't sure how she'd respond.

He wasn't honestly sure what he thought about it himself. He'd dealt with unbalanced people most of his adult life, but now found himself wondering if he had become one.

The trip to the lake house was uneventful, though much quieter than usual. Holmes had been acting strangely for months. Piper knew he was struggling with something and was determined this would be the weekend he opened up.

The lake house was an ideal getaway for two busy professionals. Far enough from the city to feel truly isolated, it was a place they could leave their pressures and responsibilities behind and actually relax.

The main feature of the house was a large "great room" with an eighteen-foot knotty-pine cathedral ceiling and a wall of windows offering a full 180-degree view of the lake. On pleasant evenings, they enjoyed reclining side-by-side on the broad wrap-around deck, watching the sun set across the peaceful waters of the lake. On cool evenings they'd snuggle up on the couch in front of a crackling fire. But this was not a weekend to relax. They both knew this was a time for honesty.

Arriving at the house, they stowed their things in the bedroom and Holmes poured them each a glass of their favorite *pinot noir*. They took seats on the couch facing the large plate-glass windows where the last remnants of a spectacular sunset were still visible across the lake.

They sat for a few moments in uncomfortable silence, sipping their wine and watching the sunset--unsure how to begin. Finally, Piper finished her wine, put down her glass and turned to Holmes. "It's time we had a talk... " She began, her voice tinged with both distress and determination.

"You've been acting strangely the last few months, Holmes. Something's up and I think I have a right to know what's going on."

"You know me pretty well." Holmes responded, meeting her gaze. "There *is* something I need to tell you tonight."

He glanced down nervously, as though checking his watch, then back to Piper. "I'm involved in something,

Ginny…" Holmes used *Ginny* and *Piper* interchangeably, but tended toward *Ginny* when things were getting serious. "I've wanted to tell you about it for months, but it's not easy to talk about. When I tell you, you're going to think I've gone off the deep end. In all honesty, I sometimes wonder if I have also."

"What is it?" Piper asked, her tone softening.

"A few months ago something very strange happened … and since then I've had a number of unusual encounters."

"You're not having sex with a patient?"

"No, it's nothing like that," he assured her. "It's something…*different*… Something totally removed from what we normally think of as reality."

Piper smiled broadly, "Holmes, are you trying to tell me you've got *religion*?"

"I wish it was that simple." He answered uneasily. "No, this is … I'm trying to find the right words and I can't think of any that don't sound totally insane. So, I'll just say it…"

Holmes took a deep breath, looked directly into her eyes, and said, "Ginny… I'm in contact with aliens!"

Piper stiffened and stared at him angrily. "Holmes, that's *NOT* funny! If this is your idea of a joke…"

"If there was any better way of saying it…" he interrupted, fumbling for words. "…but it's *real*, and it's *important*. And it affects you too. And dammit, you need to know. … and you *do* need to believe me."

"So, let me see if I've got this right…" she taunted, still assuming it was a joke. "You're being abducted nightly by little green men … and you want me to run away with you to the planet Vulcan."

"No, they aren't aliens from another *planet*," he protested. "They're aliens from a different dimension. And they've been visiting me almost every week."

"Holmes… do you realize how *crazy* this sounds?"

"Yes… I know it sounds crazy, but either someone's pulling the most elaborate practical joke in history or I'm involved in something straight out of the X-Files."

"You're really *serious* about this, aren't you?"

"Absolutely."

"And you expect me to *believe* you?"

"No, I don't… not yet. But I think I can convince you."

Piper looked indignant, "I'm listening."

Holmes glanced down, checking his watch again, then began. "Last December, while you were in Minnesota visiting your mom, I came to the lake house for the weekend to catch up on some reading. That's when I met them.

"They didn't come to the door; they were just… *here*… two of them, a male and a female. Since then there have been several others.

"I was sitting here, laptop open, about eight o'clock at night, when I heard a noise and looked up. The aliens were standing right there, in front of the window. They looked fairly human, but with some obvious differences.

"After a brief exchange, they explained their reason for coming. They said our world is facing imminent disaster, and they need our help to mount a defense."

Piper's patience was wearing thin. "Why don't these aliens contact the government … or the military?"

"That's not how they operate," Holmes shot back.

"And the military doesn't have anything that would be useful against the kind of force they're dealing with. But we do.

"The aliens have been watching us, Piper. They chose us--*both* of us--because we have special abilities they need. They said if we work with them, we can save the human race from terrible devastation."

As Holmes spoke, warning flares were exploding in Piper's mind. His story sounded all too familiar. In her practice, Piper was accustomed to hearing patients tell bizarre tales... It's a hazard of the profession for a clinical psychologist.

Just last week a used-car salesman had confided--in all seriousness--that he was receiving coded messages from outer space on his car radio. Two weeks earlier there was an overweight, middle-aged schoolteacher, paralyzed by fear that the CIA was tapping her phone. Then there was the elderly man, distraught because he was certain his equally elderly wife was having an affair with Brad Pitt. Over the years Piper had trained herself to listen to these delusions calmly, without showing surprise.

But she wasn't prepared to hear it from Holmes. Holmes had always been rock-solid, dependable. Her relationship with Holmes had brought a sense of stability to her life she'd never known. The thought that he'd somehow gone off the deep end was almost more than she could bear.

As he continued speaking, she felt panic rising within her. Every word he spoke was leading her closer to a diagnosis she couldn't let herself admit. Finally it was too much...

"That's *enough!*" She snapped--almost in tears-- cutting him off.

"But Ginny…"

"Not another *word!*" She blurted angrily, then studied him for a moment in obvious anguish, biting her lip.

"Please." she pleaded, her tone softening. "I can't listen to any more of this."

Piper turned away, unable to face him. As she stared at the fading sunset reflecting on the peaceful waters of the lake, she remembered a phrase she'd learned in grad school: *The neurotic builds dream castles in the air… the psychotic moves in.* Everything Holmes had said told her that he had "*moved in.*" He had totally embraced his delusion.

Her mind raced, frantically trying to think of another explanation, but she couldn't escape the inevitable: *Holmes has suffered some kind of psychotic break… he's lost contact with reality.* She was fighting back tears now. *This can't be happening.*

She turned and looked pleadingly into his eyes. "Please tell me this is all a joke."

"I wish I could, Ginny, but it's not." He answered. "This is *real.*"

Tears were now trickling down her cheeks. "Holmes, you're my closest friend, my soul-mate. I… *love* you," she stammered. "Why are you *doing* this?"

Holmes glanced at his watch one more time, then back to Piper. "I know that nothing I can say will convince you. But the aliens believe the time has come to meet you in person. In fact, one of them is coming here now."

"*WHAT!*" Piper almost screamed.

Before Holmes could reply, a flash of brilliant light filled the room. There was a sound like distant thunder and a change in the atmosphere that made her ears pop.

(Holmes had suggested a dramatic entrance might be most effective.)

As the flash faded, Piper saw a beautiful young woman standing in front of her. She appeared to be in her early twenties, slender, with shoulder-length, dark brown hair and haunting silver-grey eyes. She was dressed in a flowing knee-length dress of an incredibly light material Piper couldn't identify. But Piper barely noticed any of those details. What captured Piper's attention were the wings. For arching gracefully above the young woman's shoulders were two beautiful, living, white feathered wings.

"Piper," Holmes said calmly. "I'd like you to meet *Eliel*. She's an alien."

At that moment, Piper did something she had never done in her life. She fainted.

\*\*\*

## ISLE OF IONA, ARGYLL, SCOTLAND

*Why am I here?* Patrick asked himself as he stretched out on the soft heather between the giant upright slabs of stone. At this point he was willing to admit, at least to himself, that angels, or whatever they were, had planted the dream in his mind. They *wanted* him to be here. The question was, why?

In some ways Patrick felt like Roy Neary, Richard Dreyfuss' character in the old *Close Encounters* movie. In the movie, Neary had responded to a picture the aliens planted in his mind and followed the vision all the way to Devil's Tower, Wyoming, not knowing why he was going.

But when he finally reached the Devil's Tower, an alien "mother ship" landed and took him away.

Only in Patrick's case, he'd made it to his destination, but apart from gorgeous scenery, nothing was here. No aliens. No mother ship. Not even any angels.

He had to admit the place *was* beautiful. He felt relaxed for the first time in recent memory. The turmoil and frustration of the divorce was finally beginning to fade. It was incredibly healing.

But what was he supposed to *do* here? Where was he supposed to go next?

In the days following his discovery of the Hill, Patrick explored every part of the island. He toured the museum and gift shops. He found the local pub and discovered to his delight that it carried *Velvet* also. He toured the medieval abbey and other historic sites but never felt a supernatural presence.

In all of his exploration of the island, he didn't see one angel. And apart from breakfast, he rarely saw Michael. Michael sat in his room before the open window, laptop on the desk, furiously pouring out the words of his latest book.

As days passed, Patrick fell into a routine. In the mornings he would hike, revisiting his favorite parts of the Island. Near the southern tip of Iona he found an old marble quarry and the bay where Columba first set foot on Iona. On the western shore was a rock formation he dubbed *the blowhole*, where incoming waves churned through narrow channels until they exploded skyward in a dramatic imitation of "old faithful." On a particularly clear morning he climbed *Dun I*, the highest point on the island. From that vantage point, he could see *Ben More*, the highest mountain on Mull, far to the east. In the shadow of Dun I, Patrick found a small ring of standing stones not mentioned on the tourist map.

Following his morning explorations, Patrick would grab a light lunch at the pub and a brief nap at the Saint Columba Hotel.

In the evenings he always retreated to the Hill. On clear nights he'd bring a blanket from the hotel and stretch out on the soft heather between the stone slabs, watching the stars wheel past in their slow, nightly pilgrimage.

As days went by, he felt he was absorbing the island. It was penetrating his body with a sense of peace and contentment he had never known.

But always in the background was the question… *what next?* Surely the angels had not lured him here for scenic hikes and relaxing naps. Sooner or later, Patrick reasoned, they would contact him.

And Patrick was determined to stay on Iona until they did. In reality, he had no place else to go.

# Chapter Eleven:  Revelations

## THE LAKE HOUSE--IN THE PINEY WOODS
## OF EAST TEXAS

After the initial shock, Piper seemed to adjust to the idea of aliens with incredible ease.  When she "came to," Holmes was seated by her side.  Eliel had pulled up a chair and was seated opposite them about a foot away.

Piper stared at Eliel for several minutes.

Her first comment was, "Where are your… wings?  Didn't you just have *wings*?"

Eliel smiled, a gentle smile that lit up the room.  "Yes, they're still here.  But when we visit your world we usually fold them back into a dimension you can't see.  We find it's less distracting for humans."  As if to demonstrate, two large shining wings appeared out of nowhere, and then folded back into an unseen realm.

The sight of the wings made Piper feel woozy again.  She leaned up against Holmes for security.  "So you really *are* an alien?  I mean, you're … you're *NOT* a human being?"

Eliel shrugged and smiled playfully.  "Do you want to see the wings again?"

"Point taken.  Okay… so you're *not* a human… but at least you've got a sense of humor."

The exchange lightened the atmosphere a little, but it was clear neither was sure what to say next.

"How about a drink?" Holmes offered.

"Yes, I could use one." Piper gasped. "Something strong. How about a scotch and soda, light on the soda."

"And for you?" Holmes nodded to Eliel.

"Thanks, I'd love a beer… or better yet, do you have *Guinness*?" She glanced at Piper, "I developed a taste for *Guinness* a few years ago in Ireland."

"*Guinness* it is," Holmes replied, "I knew it was your favorite, so I stocked up for the weekend."

Piper sat with her mouth open in amazement for a moment, then caught herself and tried to regain her composure. "I'm sorry, Eliel. I hope you realize this is a bit much for me. I just never thought I'd be sitting around drinking with an alien."

Then she added, "By the way, has anyone ever told you, you look like an *angel*?"

"That's one of many things we've been called over the years."

"Oh great," Piper groaned, "Now I'm drinking scotch with an angel."

"An angel who drinks *Guinness*," Holmes interjected, as he returned, bearing drinks.

Piper groaned again, rolling her eyes,   "My Baptist grandmother is rolling over in her grave."

Holmes distributed the drinks…  A scotch for Piper, with just a touch of soda.  For Eliel, a *Guinness*, and an English ale for himself.

"To multidimensional friendships." He said, raising his glass.

"To good friends, *wherever* they're from." Piper joined in.

"*L'chayim.*" Eliel said, raising her *Guinness* in her favorite toast--one she'd learned among the Hebrew exiles in Babylon more than two thousand years earlier, "To *life!*"

Recognizing the Hebrew toast, Holmes glanced at Piper. "So, *who knew* angels were *Jewish?*" he quipped. They all laughed, and Piper took a big gulp of her scotch, emptying nearly a third of the glass.

It was definitely the most surreal evening in Piper's life. She had several billion questions, and frankly could not think of how to start.

"So… Eliel," she took another gulp of scotch and stammered, "Let me see if I understand this. You're an alien… an *angel*… yet you come and go freely among human beings. You visit our world, you eat, you drink *Guinness*, you look just like one of us, apart from the *wings*… I mean, this is *incredible!*

"I have so many questions. How long have you been doing this? How did you get here? What is your world like?" Piper reached out and fingered the soft fabric of Eliel's dress and added with a twinkle in her eye, "I mean… do you have shopping malls?"

Without waiting for an answer, Piper tilted her head back and finished the scotch in one gulp. Thrusting her glass in Holmes' direction, she gasped, "I need more scotch!"

When Holmes returned with the scotch--he wisely brought the bottle along--he could see that Piper was already more relaxed. "Eliel, before you begin answering Piper's questions, perhaps a little background would be in order."

"Certainly," she smiled, and took another gulp of her *Guinness*.

"Piper," she began, setting her glass down on the floor beside her chair, "the universe is a little different than what most of your race has imagined. Your world is part of a multi-dimensional universe. Your physicists are only now beginning to recognize this.

"My world, which we call *Basilea*, is not in some far off galaxy. It's right here. It occupies the same 'space' but in a different dimension. Many parts of our worlds are surprisingly similar. In my world, for example, there's a lake here, but it's in the midst of beautiful parkland. We have houses and buildings, but with our physical differences our architecture tends to be quite distinct.

"Unfortunately for you, your world is sandwiched between two warring realms. We, of *Basilea*, are what you might call the 'good guys.' We call ourselves the *Irin*. We're ruled by a council of twenty-four Ancient Ones who've committed us to the protection and welfare of the human race.

"The other world is a realm known in your legends as *Hades*. It's occupied by a powerful race known as the *Archons*.

"The war between our worlds began long before your written history… about 20,000 years ago."

"20,000 years is a long time to be at war." Holmes interjected.

"You forget, Holmes…" Eliel glanced at him, "We don't die… at least, not easily. I was here at the beginning of the battle and, hopefully, will still be here at the end, which, I believe, is coming soon."

"You're twenty *thousand* years old?" Piper gasped, looking at Eliel as if for the first time.

"Actually, much older," Eliel said casually. "The beginning of this battle was fairly recent from our perspective."

"20,000 years ago," she continued, "the ruler of Hades set out to conquer the other inhabited worlds, and establish himself as supreme lord.

"He began by invading your realm. The invasion force was massive, a thing never before seen… not in all the cycles of history. His forces included many legions of Archons, as well as a large number of renegade Irin who called themselves the *Grigori*. Joining this force was a horde of earth-born *Nephilim*--monstrous half-breed warriors, the product of *Grigori* fathers and human mothers.

"Terrible things were done…" Eliel shuddered as she recalled the battle, looking from Holmes to Piper. "The devastation was unimaginable… Whole continents disappeared beneath the seas. Your race was decimated. It was from that era that your legends of Atlantis and the great deluge were born.

"The Human Race was nearly obliterated, but in the midst of the destruction, your leaders appealed for help. In those days, there were still individuals among the humans who could travel between realms. So, fearing their battle was lost, the remaining human princes sent a heroic delegation to Hi-Ouranos, realm of the Ancient Ones who rule the inhabited worlds. The Ancient Ones responded to their appeal and raised up a force to stop the invasion.

"A massive portal was constructed on what is now England's Salisbury plain, and tens of thousands of volunteers poured through. They came from every inhabited world: Winged Irin from *Basilea*, Gnomen from the great crystal caverns of Alani, Mermen from Taverea, and the tall Elvin warriors of Ayden.

"In a bitterly contested battle lasting centuries, the Archon advance was weakened, but the Archons refused to retreat. Finally, the Ancient Ones authorized a direct assault on Hades.

"After nearly a thousand years of fighting, the armies of Hades were finally vanquished. It was a time of inexpressible horror…" Eliel faltered. She seemed almost at the point of tears as she envisioned the scene. "In the end, the Archon forces were devastated, and the once-beautiful realm of Hades became a burned-out wasteland."

"I suppose that explains the legends of Hell," Piper said quietly.

"Yes," Eliel continued, struggling to recover her composure, "but living in a burned out wasteland has only reinforced the Archons' determination to seize your world. They've sent many of their number here to prepare the way. Because of their immense lifespan, the Archons plan their strategies in terms of generations--forming plans within plans, centuries in advance--carefully plotting and preparing for their final assault. There have been several attempted invasions down through your history, but each time they've failed. Unfortunately, they learn from their mistakes. I fear we're rapidly approaching a climactic battle.

"Piper, if their invasion can't be turned back, the Human Race, as you know it, will be destroyed. Your world will be conquered, and those of you who remain will be tortured and enslaved.

"To protect you, the Ancient Ones have enlisted us, the watchers--what your people have called *angels*--to patrol the shadow realm on the edge of your world."

"So... where do *we* fit into all this?" Piper said, "I mean, Holmes and I, personally?"

Eliel looked at Holmes, then back to Piper. "That will take a little while to explain. I think I'd rather get into that tomorrow, when you're a little fresher.

"Right now," she said, picking up her nearly empty glass and staring at it wistfully, "I'd like another *Guinness*, and then I'll try to answer some of your questions."

\*\*\*

## BRENTWOOD MEMORIAL HOSPITAL, BOULDER, COLORADO

The evening Lys's parents returned to Dallas, Roger Johnston showed up in her room later than usual. Lys was standing, gazing out the window.

"Well, look at *you!*" Roger laughed in surprise, "I *heard* you were finally on your feet!"

Lys turned and coolly acknowledged his greeting, "Hi, Roger. I'm still feeling shaky, but it feels good to be out of bed."

"You know, Sis, the other doctors call you the walking miracle. They've no explanation for how you survived that crash. They claim the force of the impact alone should have killed you instantly. After a shock like that, it's no wonder you've been a little confused."

Ignoring his comment, Lys turned back to the window. She moved awkwardly, still unsteady on her feet.

Boulder was beautiful at night. Brentwood Memorial was perched on a low rise at the foot of the Colorado Front Range. From her window, Lys could see a panorama of the city spread out before her. It looked like a galaxy of billions of stars at her feet.

"And I have some good news for you," Roger continued, taking a step closer. "Barring any complications, you're due to be released from the hospital next week. Mom and Dad already made your plane reservations. Mom's getting your old bedroom ready. She'll be flying up next week to take you home. You'll be back in Texas… away from all the craziness. Mom and Dad will be there to take care of you…"

*"Stop it!"* Lys snapped, cutting him off sharply. Without turning to look at him, she continued, "I *hate* this. You're all treating me like I'm an *invalid*. Nobody believes anything I say. Everybody thinks I'm crazy. And you all think you have to figure out how you can take care of poor little mixed-up Lys."

"Listen, Lys, no one wants to treat you like an invalid."

He walked to Lys and stood behind her, putting his hand on her shoulder. "You're a strong and independent woman, and in six months you'll be pretty much back to normal. Just don't rush it. You *will* need some help. Right now they're keeping you pumped full of pain medication. But you have several damaged disks in your back, and you're going to be in a lot of pain for a while. Believe me, when they start weaning you off the pain meds, you'll be thankful for all the help you can get."

Lys swung around to face him, but as she turned, the window in front of them exploded. There was a loud crash, flying shards of glass filled the air, and they were both knocked to the ground. When Lys opened her eyes, Roger was lying unconscious on the floor beside her. Then she saw the blood welling from a wound in his chest and pooling on the floor around him. Ignoring her pain, Lys stumbled to the door and screamed for help.

# Chapter Twelve: More Revelations

THE LAKE HOUSE – IN THE PINEY WOODS
OF EAST TEXAS

When Piper returned from her morning run, Holmes was in the kitchen making coffee.

"Did you work out already?" she asked, still trying to catch her breath.

"Yes, and showered," Holmes looked up. "You had a long run this morning."

"It helped me think." Piper said, dabbing the perspiration from her face with a white towel. "There's a big part of me that says none of that last night was real… that I dreamed it. Holmes, this whole thing makes me question my sanity."

"I still struggle with that myself, even after all these months," Holmes said. "When I'm talking with one of the Irin, it can seem the most natural thing in the world. But when the sun comes up the next morning, none of it seems real."

"When did Eliel say she would get here?"

"She said she'll be here at 10:00. She wanted to give us plenty of time. Turns out the aliens don't sleep, either."

They'd already cleaned up from breakfast when Eliel arrived. This time she chose a less dramatic entrance, landing on the broad deck outside the great room windows and actually knocking on the door before entering, precisely at 10:00 AM.

Holmes poured everyone some coffee, and they took comfortable seats in the great room.

"Eliel," Piper began, "I want to thank you for giving me the strangest night of my life. I don't think I slept a wink."

"I *guarantee* you'll have stranger nights than that." Eliel smiled, "Things have just *begun* to get interesting."

"That's comforting," Piper said nervously.

"So, Eliel…" Holmes interrupted, "why don't you explain to Piper how the two of us fit into this whole thing."

"Certainly, Holmes."

Eliel turned to Piper, taking a quick sip of her coffee. "First of all, Piper, you need to understand the danger confronting your world.

"In the last fifty years, your world has experienced some remarkable changes. Many of those changes have been positive: You've recognized the equality of your races. You've made improvements in communications and technology. Your progress in the area of medicine has greatly improved your quality of life.

"But other changes have *not* been positive. In fact, within the last fifty years, trends have developed that threaten to destroy all you've accomplished.

"An obvious example is the rise of terrorism. Terrorism was unheard of fifty years ago. Even in your parents' day, you could walk into any airport and board a plane without passing through a single security check, and no one questioned your safety. Now increasing threats bring more oppressive security measures every year. But terrorism is just the tip of the iceberg.

"Every nation on earth is being inundated by a rising tide of violence. Look at your own country. In your grandparents' day, Americans slept with their windows open and their doors unlocked and felt totally secure. Violent crime was rare.

"Piper, when your grandmother was your age, she could walk down almost any street in any city--even at night--with little fear of harm.

"Yet today you have 20,000 murders every year in America. That's like having 40 jumbo jets, loaded with 500 people each, crashing every year; yet few are even aware of the problem."

"I had no idea there were so many." Piper said, genuinely appalled.

"It's worse than you think," Eliel continued. "In the nineties your politicians tried to slow the rising tide of violence by imprisoning more and more of your population. Since 1987 your prison population has tripled. Almost two and one-half million Americans now live their lives behind bars. If they were all consolidated in one location, it would form your fourth largest city, bigger than Philadelphia or Houston.

"Yet, they haven't been able to build prisons fast enough to keep up with the rise in violent crime. So your chance of being assaulted, murdered, or raped increases every year."

"What's caused all of this?" Piper asked.

"In the last fifty years, the Archons have launched a massive offensive against your world. Because of the destruction that occurred 20,000 years ago, the Ancient

Ones won't permit them to attack you in force. So they come covertly, working behind the scenes. Their goal is to create such widespread disruption that there can be no resistance to their invasion, and they're very close to success.

"Even now, Archons are moving among you. Sometimes they choose human victims to ensnare and destroy. Sometimes they find individuals weak enough to possess and use as tools. More frequently, they use their mental powers to plant suggestions, perverting your natural desires and ambitions. They stir up lust and greed and plant thoughts of violence. Their goal is to cause you to destroy yourselves.

"Your situation becomes more perilous with every passing month. The number of Archons in your world is overwhelming--tens of millions--and their numbers are increasing rapidly. This build-up of enemy forces is something we've not seen since the Great Wars, and it's taken us by surprise. We're now badly outnumbered."

"How has this happened?" Piper pressed, with increasing concern.

"In the last century, the Archons implemented a new strategy," Eliel explained, "They've used their mental abilities to enlist large numbers of Human allies. They gave promises of power and offered tantalizing experiences with the supernatural. They worked through your media to make their sinister path seem exotic and exciting.

"As a result, many of your people are now flirting with some very dark powers, not truly understanding what they're doing. A few have even become willing allies of the Archons and are opening doors of great destruction for your world. The Archons are using these unwitting allies to create entry-points--momentary wormholes between the earth-realm and Hades. With each new entry-point, more Archon warriors pour into your realm.

"There have always been humans who chose the path of darkness, but we weren't prepared for the sheer numbers of your race that have now given themselves to the Archon cause. If this Archon buildup continues, the fragile web you call civilization will soon disintegrate, and your world will be plunged into chaos."

"But, how could *that* happen?" Piper objected. "I mean, I don't see our society in danger of imminent collapse."

"Don't you?" Eliel gave Piper a questioning look. "What about the sense of dread you sometimes feel when you read the news? ... the unspoken fear that your world is headed in the wrong direction ... rushing headlong toward some unthinkable calamity? Are you telling me you've not sensed an approaching disaster?"

"Well, I know things are bad... but surely there's still time to find an answer!"

"You don't understand how fragile your civilization is," Eliel persisted. "The world you know is inherently unstable. You go to the grocery store and the shelves are full. You take abundance for granted.

"But introduce a disruption in the supply chain and those shelves go empty within days. What happens then? A few weeks later people are starving. Gangs go from house to house stealing what food they can find. Police are overwhelmed. Transportation and communications break down. All the things you took for granted are destroyed within weeks.

"Your society is hauntingly similar to the final years of the Roman Empire. To the Romans, the idea that Rome could collapse was unthinkable. They looked at their monumental architecture, their proud history, and their mighty legions, and assumed Roman civilization would last forever. Yet Rome did fall.

"For now, your governments are keeping the crisis contained, but you'll soon reach a tipping point where your ability to maintain order is overwhelmed. When that happens, things will unravel quickly."

"What can we do about it?" Piper asked.

"The source of your problem lies in a realm you can't see..." Eliel said, "an unseen world populated by beings you've only read about in myth and legend. Yet a very real war rages in that realm and it affects every member of your race. To avoid destruction, you must join in that battle.

"You've accepted the reality of angels," she continued. "You need to see that the creatures you've called *demons* are also real. And you'll have to learn to fight them."

"Wait a minute," Piper raised her hands in protest, feeling suddenly overwhelmed. "This is getting *way* over my head pretty fast."

She paused a moment, trying to collect her thoughts, then continued, "Okay... I suppose it *is* logical to admit that angels exist... since I'm sitting here talking to one. Though to be honest, I don't think *you* are exactly what they sing about in Christmas carols!

"And if angels are real, then it's not a huge leap to believe in demons... But even if demons do exist, Eliel, how could we ever *fight* them?"

"Piper," Eliel's voice softened, "the Creator of all

worlds placed incredible powers within you, but you've lost the ability to use them.

"In the warfare that raged before your history began, the Archons inflicted genetic damage on your entire race. Your lifespan was drastically shortened and your life-force nearly extinguished. Your race became a mere shadow of what it once was.

"The Ancient Ones assure us that your race will one day be restored. That's a time all the realms look forward to with great eagerness. That's why we volunteered to come here and fight... we remember what you used to be."

Eliel paused a moment, looking intently into Piper's eyes. "The human race was always the highest of the races. Your abilities were amazing. It was once common for humans to exercise powers you'd now call supernatural. If you can recover even a small portion of these lost powers, you'll easily be able to stand against the Archons."

"What kind of powers are you talking about?"

Eliel hesitated, as if uncertain how much to say. "Your race had abilities on many levels. Some were gifted to be healers. Some had the second sight--the ability to see into the future. Some could see beyond your own dimension. Some could alter matter by the sound of their voice."

Then, choosing her words carefully, Eliel added, "And there are *other* abilities, far beyond those... abilities you remember now only in your dreams."

"All of those abilities are still there, locked up inside you. You still have the potential... every member of your race secretly senses that."

"Why can't we use these powers now?"

"Part of the problem is fear...

"The Archons know what lies dormant within you, so they've used their influence to hold you in ignorance. They planted superstition and suspicion and filled you with irrational fears. For thousands of years, any human who tapped into even a small portion of his potential was burned at the stake.

"The other problem is the weakening of your life-force. Your life-force is what the Greeks called the *pneuma*. It's the part of you that goes beyond physical existence, and it's what energizes all your abilities. Because of the damage inflicted on your race, your life-force is greatly diminished... almost non-existent."

"So, how can we regain those powers?" Piper asked.

"The key is what we call a *synaxis*."

Seeing her puzzled look, Eliel explained, "The word *synaxis* is an ancient human term. It was coined by the Greeks to describe the union of two worlds--the natural and the supernatural realms meeting together. The Greeks believed when a synaxis took place, humans could mingle freely with angels, receiving hidden knowledge and gaining miraculous powers. That's why the earliest Christians used the word *synaxis* to describe their secret gatherings in the Roman catacombs.

"More accurately," she continued, "a synaxis is a group of humans who are brought into a special relationship with the Irin. In that relationship, a portion of our life-force is transferred to you and the damage inflicted on your race is partially reversed. Over the course of time, as you meet in synaxis, your dormant powers begin to awaken.

"In that process a *synergy* develops. The abilities of each member strengthen and reinforce the abilities of the others. Eventually, the members of the synaxis learn to function together, almost as a single living organism, exercising powers far greater than any of the individuals possess.

"There have been a number of times in your history-- at times of great crisis--that we've entered into synaxis with your race. Each time, as humans regained their lost powers, the Archon forces were overcome."

Eliel glanced at Holmes, then back to Piper. "Piper, you need to understand the importance of what I'm telling you. We're about to initiate the first synaxis in the Human-realm in more than a thousand years, and it's truly the only hope for your race. As your life-force is restored and your lost powers are energized, you *will* gain the power to confront the forces of Hades and drive them from your world.

"That's why we chose you." Eliel said, looking at Holmes again, then resting her gaze on Piper. "You've been chosen to lead the first synaxis... *both of you.*"

*"Us?"* Piper and Holmes both blurted.

"Wait a minute, Eliel..." Holmes objected. "For weeks now, you and the other Irin have been telling me about this group you're forming to save the world... I thought you were recruiting Piper and me to be *part* of it. You never said we'd be the ones to *lead* it."

"I'm sorry, Holmes," Eliel responded. "I thought you understood... That's why you and Piper were chosen. You *both* possess the necessary abilities to lead a synaxis."

"Of course, we don't expect you to fight the battle alone," she continued, "There are others we must draw together with you. But our time is short. The Archon forces are strengthening rapidly and war is almost upon us. I fear we may be caught unprepared."

Eliel tilted her head slightly, as though listening to a faint sound. "Rand is coming now... and Araton is with her."

Piper could see, far out above the lake, what appeared to be two great white-winged birds soaring in their direction. Approaching the house, the aliens spread their wings and floated gracefully down to a soft landing on the deck. As their wings faded from sight, Eliel opened the door to welcome them inside.

\*\*\*

## ISLE OF IONA, ARGYLL, SCOTLAND

It was now more than a month since Patrick arrived on Iona.

He felt he'd always been there. There were few parts of the island he had not explored. It amazed him that he felt more at home on Iona than he'd ever been in Dallas.

As spring merged into summer, the pilgrim hordes came. During the day, the tiny island was overrun by pilgrims of every variety--Catholics, Protestants, Orthodox, Neo-pagans, Druids, New Agers, history buffs, and a few retired couples from Michigan on a bus tour of Scotland. It seemed like everyone wanted a piece of Iona.

With inquisitive strangers hiking all over the island, Patrick stayed close to the hotel during the day. But with just two small hotels and a handful of bed-and-breakfasts on the island, most pilgrims retreated to the mainland for overnight accommodations. When the last ferry departed for Mull in the evening, life on Iona returned to normal.

So Patrick continued his nightly vigil on *Cnoc nan Carnan*. It was much warmer than when he first arrived, and the summer sun lingered late in the sky. Patrick purchased a used sleeping bag from a departing pilgrim and often spent the night on the hill. He'd discovered a book on astronomy in the bookcase of the hotel dayroom and could now identify almost every constellation as they wheeled overhead.

Patrick had just stretched out the sleeping bag for his nightly vigil when a shooting star flashed overhead... a *bolide*, or fireball, by the look of it. The astronomy book had mentioned an annual meteor shower, the Lyrids, occurring about mid June, but that was over a week away. He wondered if he was seeing an advance guard of the Lyrids.

Patrick relaxed and savored the crisp night air. The night was crystal-clear. The great cloud-like band of the Milky Way marched majestically from horizon to horizon. *How often did Columba sit on this same hill, a millennium and a half earlier, watching these same stars?* Patrick mused.

Sometime later, Patrick closed his eyes and was about to drift off to sleep when he heard a faint sound on the road below. Looking up, Patrick saw, by starlight, someone approaching up the hill.

A few pilgrims made their way up the hill by day, but none had yet disturbed his vigil at night. "Hello," Patrick called, hoping the intruder was seeking an isolated place and--finding this one occupied--would choose to look elsewhere.

But the stranger continued in his direction, responding to his call with an answering, "Hello."

By the faint illumination provided by the stars, Patrick could see that his visitor was a man, probably in his mid-forties. His hair appeared to be prematurely grey, actually white.

The man stopped a few feet away from Patrick and stood, looking at him, as if waiting for a response.

"Can I help you?" Patrick asked.

"Yes," the man replied, "but I can also help you, Patrick of the *Ui Neills*."

Patrick sat up, suddenly wide awake. "How did you know my name?"

"My name is Khalil. I knew your ancestors when they lived on this island and your namesake Patrick in Ireland as well. I've been assigned as your defender."

Every hair on Patrick's body was now standing on end.

His initial skepticism about Michael's "angels" had faded with his discovery of the Hill. Patrick's first glimpse of *Cnoc nan Carnan* convinced him that these creatures, whatever they were, had called him to Iona. He'd resolved to remain on the island until he found out why. But he suddenly realized that all of that was merely a mental exercise. He was totally unprepared to actually encounter one of these ancient beings.

"Are you really an…" He could not even bring himself to say the word. "Are you really one of *them*?"

"If you're referring to the beings your ancestors called *angels*, yes, I am. Although we prefer to call ourselves the *Irin*."

Patrick was strongly tempted to go into a "doubting Thomas" mode, demanding some proof of the unknown visitor's claim. Three weeks ago, he would have. But not now. Somehow he knew Khalil was speaking the truth.

"Patrick, I have something to tell you, and it is very important. A great war is about to take place, and much of it will take place right here. But the Irin don't yet have sufficient strength in this realm to assure victory.

"To gain the strength we need, a portal must be opened between your world and ours, and it must be done here on Iona.

"Your ancestor, Columba, opened a portal in his day, but it was later allowed to close. Because of your ancestry, you have the authority to reopen Columba's portal. But you can't do it alone.

"Your time on Iona must end, for now. You must return to Dallas. We have others waiting for you there. They'll show you what must be done."

Something in Khalil's tone left no room for discussion or argument.

"Who am I supposed to meet in Dallas?"

"Don't worry. Just go," Khalil replied. "We'll contact you there."

Patrick was surprised by his willingness to accept the angel's direction. Independent by nature, Patrick usually resisted being told what to do. Yet he never had a second thought about obeying Khalil's instructions.

"I'll make preparations tomorrow for the trip home," Patrick agreed, "but first, I need to ask you one favor. I have a friend here who *must* meet you. He's studied angels his whole life but has never spoken to one. Can I bring him here to meet you before you leave?"

"You mean Michael Fletcher, of course," Khalil said, smiling. "I'm quite familiar with Michael, and his books.

By all means, bring him here.  But go quickly.  I have very little time."

The Saint Columba Hotel was only a few minutes' walk south of the Hill, and Patrick made it in record time. Michael was sitting at his desk furiously typing on his laptop when Patrick bounded up the stairway and pounded on his door.

Not waiting for the door to open, Patrick called out breathlessly, "*Michael!*  Come quickly, there's something you MUST see."

Michael did not hesitate, and a few minutes later they were both making their way up the steep slope to the top of *Cnoc nan Carnan*.  As they entered the sheltered area between the ancient monoliths, Patrick felt panic rising within him.  The place was deserted.

Then, Khalil walked around one of the huge stone slabs and stood before them.   But Khalil had changed.  As he stepped into view, Patrick saw that Khalil's wings were now unfurled, and his whole being glowed with a brilliant white light.

"Good evening, Michael." Khalil said with a knowing smile, "It's been a long time.  The last time you saw me, you were only nine years old."

Michael's mouth dropped open, and his eyes widened in recognition.  For the first time Patrick could remember, Michael Fletcher was speechless.

# Chapter Thirteen:  The Shades

## THE LAKE HOUSE--IN THE PINEY WOODS
## OF EAST TEXAS

Holmes welcomed the newly-arrived *Irin*, and introduced them to Piper.

At the sight of Rand, the new female alien, Piper's
mouth fell open in amazement.  There could hardly have
been more of a contrast between Eliel and Rand.  Eliel was
small and delicate in appearance.  While she possessed great
strength and intelligence, it was tempered by an aura of
gentleness and an almost childlike playfulness.

Rand, on the other hand, was a stunning beauty--tall
and slender, yet with an intensity about her that was more
than slightly intimidating.  Dressed simply in a black belted
tunic and leggings, Rand's piercing brown eyes, coupled
with the long dagger strapped to her right thigh, gave her
the unsettling appearance of an Amazon warrior.  Her lithe
body was crowned by a long flowing mane of dark auburn
hair.

The male Irin was equally striking.  Araton was tall
and muscular, with rich, dark-brown skin and closely
shaved head.  He wore a multicolored, two-piece garment
reminiscent of a West African *dashiki*, with a metallic mesh
belt cinched tightly around his waist.  Attached to the belt,

the hilt of a scimitar protruded from a three-foot-long steel scabbard. Piper somehow knew the sword was not for ceremonial purposes.

As the newcomers entered the room, Piper leaned close to Holmes and whispered, "I think I need a *drink*."

"A little early in the day for that, don't you think?" Holmes chided, "How about some more coffee?"

"Let's compromise," Piper urged with a subtle smile, "How about coffee with *Baileys*?"

"Compromise accepted!" Holmes laughed. Piper knew it was his favorite Saturday morning beverage. "Coffee with Baileys coming right up."

Holmes took orders for coffee, and was surprised that the *Irin* chose the coffee with Baileys as well.

Holmes brought in the coffee, along with a bottle of Baileys Irish Cream, and the five sat down in a cluster before the unlit fireplace of the great room.

Rand spoke first, looking from Piper to Holmes, "Has Eliel explained the synaxis?"

"Yes," answered Holmes, "But I must confess, I'm a little overwhelmed. Are you sure Piper and I are the ones you want to *lead* this?"

"I agree with Holmes," Piper cut in. "If our world is falling apart we want to do what we can, but I don't see that the two of us have the ability to head up a secret group to save the world."

"I understand what you're saying..." Rand came back, "Your problem is, you don't see who you really are, or what you could become."

"What do you mean?" Piper asked.

"Surely, as psychologists, you recognize that most

humans use only a tiny fraction of their true abilities. Your literature is full of examples. Are you familiar with the case of Kim Peek?"

"I remember hearing the name, but I don't recall any details," said Piper.

"Kim Peek was born with brain damage, yet developed almost superhuman mental skills. He could, at will, recall detailed information from any page of the twelve thousand books he'd read. He could read a new book in about an hour, and remember ninety-nine percent of its content. Peek also had perfect pitch, and could remember every tune he ever heard."

"I read an article about him just a few months ago," Holmes interjected. "A few years before his death, NASA scientists ran a series of tests on Mr. Peek to try to discover his secret."

"He's just one example," Rand continued. "The blind American savant Leslie Lemke never had a piano lesson, yet could play Tchaikovsky's Piano Concerto No. 1, after hearing it only one time.

"There are people who can fluently speak dozens of languages, multiply multi-digit numbers in their minds as fast as they can be written down, figure out cube roots faster than a calculator and recall the value of *pi* to 100,000 decimal places. There was even a boy who could recite all six volumes of Gibbon's *Decline and Fall of the Roman Empire*... backwards or forwards. And their brains are not significantly different from yours. But they've tapped into abilities most humans have never used. And those are just the *mental* abilities."

"What are you saying?" Holmes asked.

"I'm saying that both of you have gifts and abilities you don't comprehend at this point. If you allow those powers to be activated, you'll be able to do things you never dreamed possible."

"So, if you activate my gifts," Holmes grinned, "you're saying I might finally be able to remember where I left my keys?"

"Holmes, I can see the abilities that lie dormant within you and Piper. Allow them to be activated, and you'll have everything you need to turn back the destruction that faces your world."

Holmes and Piper looked at each other.

Piper shrugged, "What do we have to lose?"

"I agree…" Holmes said, turning back to Rand, "but you'll need to walk us through this step by step."

"Don't worry," Rand responded with a reassuring smile. "We won't take your training wheels off too soon. Right now, all we ask is that you assemble the group. We'll do the rest."

"How do we begin?" Holmes asked.

"Here is a list of those you need to contact." She handed him a folded piece of paper. "We've already contacted these individuals, and they're expecting your call. It's imperative that you gather the group quickly."

Holmes accepted the paper and glanced at it. It was a list of four names along with phone numbers. He skimmed the list and noted that all of the numbers had Dallas area codes.

As he read the last name he hesitated a moment and smiled.

"Do you see someone you know?" Rand asked.

"Not exactly," Holmes said. "Though I've met her a few times. But everyone in Dallas knows the name Erin Vanderberg. Seems like Erin gets involved in everything sooner or later."

"Erin's a special woman," Araton said. "And she's crucial to the future of your world, though she doesn't yet understand her true value. You must keep an eye on her, though. The Archons have targeted her for destruction, and won't give up easily."

Rand continued, "In addition to these four, there are two other humans vital to our success. You need to be on the lookout for both of them."

"The first is named Patrick O'Neill. He's in Scotland now but should return to Dallas within the week. He'll bring a friend with him who is also part of our plan. We'll direct them both to you.

"The other human essential to our success is a woman named Lysandra Johnston. There hasn't been a human born with her level of ability in over a millennium, though she has no inkling of her potential. She'll also be coming to Dallas in the near future. We believe we can influence her to contact one of you as a patient. She's vital to our plan, and the enemy knows it."

"They've tried to kill Lysandra twice." Araton interjected. "They've also released the shades against her."

"What are *shades*?" Piper asked.

Rand took a long sip of her coffee, then explained. "On the edge of your dimension is a region we call the shadow realm. It's part of your world, but invisible to you, shifted slightly out of the plane you can access.

"There are creatures in the shadow realm. We call them shades. They're an artificial life form created by the Archons during the Great Wars. They're normally invisible to you, although you sometimes perceive them as a faint cloud of darkness. Shades are mental and emotional parasites. They attach themselves to susceptible humans, distorting their emotions and feeding on their pain. They often drive their hosts to destruction.

"As psychologists, you've dealt with shades many times without knowing it," Araton added. "When a shade tries to attach to a human, the human feels something 'come over' him. It feels like an inexplicable, yet powerful, wave of emotion.

"A person may suddenly be overwhelmed with anxiety, without being aware of anything to be anxious about. Shades come in many forms. Some produce anxiety, some unreasoning fear, some depression, some lust, and some rage."

"Most humans are able to simply shrug them off," Rand said. "But if you're susceptible--and Lys *is* at this point--they can attach themselves. It can be overpowering.

"The Archons are using the shades to try to drive Lys to suicide. If they succeed, I see little hope for your world."

Araton drained the last of his coffee and put the empty cup on the coffee table. "I hate to cut this short," he said. "But our time is limited. This is Saturday. Holmes, can you call the first synaxis for next Wednesday night?"

"I don't see why not, if the others are able to come."

"Good." Rand cut in, "Then Eliel will meet you at your home at 7:14 Wednesday night."

The *Irin* stood to their feet and thanked their hosts. To Piper's amazement, the three turned and walked right through the plate glass windows of the great room, onto the deck. Without a word, they unfurled large, white feathered wings, seemingly from nowhere, mounted the deck rail in a single step, then stepped off and flew.

Watching the three rise effortlessly into the air, it struck Piper that, while the Irin used their wings to fly, they didn't operate on aerodynamic principles. They didn't flap their wings, as a bird would. Rather their wings seemed to be interacting with invisible flows of energy, gracefully angling against unseen forces like a sail adjusting to the wind.

The three circled the house, gaining altitude, then banked into a gentle glide down, almost to the surface of the lake. Near the center of the lake, they spread their wings wide and shot upward with incredible speed. In a few moments they were lost from sight.

***

## BRENTWOOD MEMORIAL HOSPITAL
## BOULDER, COLORADO

Morgan Johnston was no pushover. Although married to a prominent Dallas attorney and maintaining an active social life, she had still found time to raise two children and earn acclaim as a fashion designer for *Metro Designs International*, even developing her own line of boutique sportswear.

In her mid-fifties Morgan was as slender, blonde, and

nearly as active, as her daughter, Lys. Morgan had always been fiercely protective of her children, earning her the nickname "Mama Bear" in their younger years. God help anyone who tried to harm her kids. She was justifiably proud of both.

But the last two months had left her daughter r ecovering from a near-fatal automobile accident--apparently the object of attempted murder--and her step-son in ICU with a gunshot wound to the chest. Morgan couldn't help Roger at the moment, but she was determined to get Lys out of Colorado.

Lys had spent most of the past week in bed. Since the doctors began to wean her from the heaviest of her medications, the pain was almost constant. The only way she found relief was lying flat on her back. Even then, however, there were twinges of pain that grated on her. The slightest movement could bring agonizing torment.

Yet pain wasn't the worst part. Lys felt she was losing her mind. For days she'd battled waves of depression.

She knew part of it was her appearance. With her light ash-blonde hair, trim body, and captivating steel-blue eyes, Lys had always enjoyed being considered an attractive woman. But when the doctors removed her bandages, the mirror revealed a swollen mass of bruises and lacerations where her face had been. Her first thought was, *I look like Frankenstein's monster!* Though the doctors assured her that she would eventually heal up "almost as good as new," the sight of her face still brought tears to her eyes.

Then there was Roger. She didn't know why anyone would fire a high powered rifle at a hospital window, but she was certain of one thing. They had not been aiming at her brother. They were aiming at her. Twice now someone had tried to kill her, and she had no idea why.

Along with the depression came waves of fear. Someone had tried to kill her twice. Would they try again? Would someone burst into her room? Would they poison her food? She knew it was insane to follow that line of thought, but it seemed no more insane than what had already taken place.

A police lieutenant interrogated Lys three times, trying to discern why someone would want to kill her. When she had no answers, he didn't seem to believe her.

Finally Morgan Johnston arrived from Dallas to take her home. Physically, Lys no longer required hospital care, but the hospital was concerned enough about her mental condition that they resisted her release. But Morgan Johnston was not to be deterred. A forty-five minute confrontation with the hospital administrator, coupled with a call from her husband's law firm, produced the desired result.

Morgan checked Lys out of the hospital at 2:00 PM and headed south to Denver, taking State Highway 470 across the northern edge of the city. At the Denver Intercontinental Airport exit, Morgan swung the silver Lexus onto Pena Boulevard, and followed the signs to rental car return.

They'd just made the turn from Pena onto Gun Club Road when Lys noticed three figures standing at the side of the road. Dressed in black, they had the appearance of hitch-hikers but they weren't trying to catch a ride. They simply stood beside the road, studying each car that passed, as if watching for someone.

And then they were looking at *her*. Their eyes followed her as the car approached. Lys found herself returning the gaze of the tallest figure. It was a woman--a thin, unattractive woman, with long black hair. The woman was staring at her. Lys's mouth fell open in unbelief. It was *Kareina*. As the car swung past, Kareina smiled at her--a look of twisted satisfaction.

Only then did Lys notice the two young men standing beside Kareina.

"Mother!" she screamed, *"Stop the car!"*

At the sharp cry from Lys, Morgan Johnston jammed her foot on the brake and steered for the shoulder. Even before the car ceased its forward motion, Lys had thrown open the door. Ignoring her pain, she jumped out, ready to confront the three figures.

But the three were no longer in sight. They had disappeared. Lys looked around franticly. She had an unobstructed view in all directions--wide fields of mown grass, with the towering, white, tent-like roof of the Denver Intercontinental Airport terminal in the distance. But the three figures were simply not there.

# Chapter Fourteen:  Synaxis Begins

## FRISCO, TEXAS (A SUBURB OF DALLAS)

The intercom function on his phone gave its usual irritating chirp.  Holmes looked up from the journal he was reading and tapped the speakerphone button.  "Yes, Shersti?"

"Dr. Holmes, there's a Donald Johnston on line one. He says he knows you and needs to speak with you urgently."

"Sure, put him through."

A second later his phone gave a gentle buzz, and Holmes picked up the receiver, "Yes?"

"Derek, thanks for taking my call.  This is Don Johnston.  We've played golf together several times out at Preston Lakes Country Club."

"Sure, Don, I remember you.  What's up?"

"Derek, I'm in a desperate situation and need to ask a big favor.  My 26-year-old daughter has experienced a severe trauma.  I believe she's suffering from depression and also appears to be delusional."  He paused, then continued, "…I also fear she may be suicidal."

"I talked to your receptionist, but she said you were booked solid for the next three weeks.  Is there any way you can see her sooner than that?"

"Sure, Don, I'm sure I can find a time. Let me check my schedule and call you back. We may be able to work her in later this week... What's her name?"

"Her name is Lys--short for Lysandra--Lysandra Johnston."

Holmes froze.

After a brief pause, Holmes continued, "Don, I just remembered I have a cancelation later today. Can Lys come in this afternoon at 3:30?"

Holmes gave a lame excuse for ending his three o'clock appointment twenty minutes early and gave Shersti instructions to send Lys into his office as soon as the disgruntled three o'clock appointment left.

Lys hobbled into the office with a limp, obviously in a great deal of pain. She forced a gallant smile and introduced herself. "Hi, I'm Lys Johnston."

Holmes stood and greeted her, hoping his face didn't register the shock he felt at her appearance. A few weeks earlier, Lys might have been described as an attractive blonde with a cute face and pleasing figure. But the woman who entered his office now would get no votes for anyone's pin-up calendar. Her once-pretty face looked like it had been run over by a truck. Large areas were bruised, swollen and discolored with a number of cuts and abrasions in various stages of healing. She walked bent over with pain and the lines of stress on her face added years to her appearance.

Worse than any of that was the almost visible cloud of darkness that surrounded her. She gave the appearance of someone who was fighting a determined battle with depression, and losing.

Holmes thought to himself, *this woman still possesses an incredible reserve of strength. Only sheer determination could have brought her here in this condition.*

Holmes motioned for Lys to sit down and took a seat across from her, notebook in hand. He made some introductory remarks, laying down the ground rules for his counseling sessions, and explaining that he always devoted his first appointment to taking a "case history." He asked Lys to give him some background on her life, and the events that led to her present condition.

As Lys poured out her story, Holmes jotted down some notes and made a few comments. For most of the session, however, he just let her talk.

Piper had gotten a call from Holmes, and was sitting in the waiting room when his appointment with Lys ended.

Holmes accompanied Lys into the waiting room and introduced her to Piper. "Lys, let me introduce you to a good friend, Ginny Ann Piper. Piper's a psychologist also. I asked her to meet us here after your session.

"Piper and I have a group meeting at my house tomorrow night. There are six members so far, and we just began meeting last week. We'd like to invite you to come. I believe it may help you."

"Some kind of group therapy?" Lys asked.

Holmes hesitated, not certain how to answer. "Not *exactly*…" he finally replied. "It's not part of our normal professional treatment, but I believe in your case, it can be very helpful."

Lys was instantly suspicious, and it showed in her expression.

Before she could object, Piper cut in, "Believe me,

Lys, it's totally safe. It's a new approach, but I believe it holds great promise."

Lys looked from Piper back to Holmes. Both seemed trustworthy. And Lys was aware that Holmes had a well-deserved reputation as one of the most effective counselors in the Dallas Metroplex.

"Okay," Lys said, still obviously cautious. "I'll come."

"Good," Holmes smiled. Pulling out one of his cards, he added, "Let me write down the address. The meeting starts at seven, but feel free to get there early for drinks."

The next evening as Lys prepared to leave for the group, she found herself battling increasing waves of depression. Several times she picked up the phone to cancel, but each time resisted the temptation.

Her back was in agony. Lys had been up most of the day, and every muscle in her back was tied in knots. Her mother offered to drive her, but she firmly refused. *No one's going to make me an invalid.* She limped to her car and struggled to pull the door open without wrenching her back.

Something told her this was a stupid decision. She ought to go back to her room and lie flat on her back; then the worst of the pain would subside. She needed to relax and rest. That's what the doctor had told her. She could wait a few months, and when her back was feeling better, she could visit the group.

Then her determination kicked in. Maybe it was stubbornness, but the depression and pain made her angry. She hated the way people treated her now. She hated being limited. She hated being dependent, and she wasn't going to let this thing beat her.

As she drove, she felt an almost physical resistance. Waves of apprehension crashed against her. *What was this new treatment?* They hadn't really told her anything about it. What could they do at a group session that could possibly help her?

Then came the fear. *Was this new treatment really legitimate?* She was foolish to go to a stranger's house without getting more information. *Was this really a treatment at all?* Maybe Holmes and Piper were part of a religious cult. When she got there, they would kidnap her... brainwash her. Make her do... *what?*

She continued on. At each intersection she battled the temptation to turn back. She felt she was pushing through a tangible cloud of opposition, and had to muster all her resolve to keep moving.

Nearing the address, Lys slowed to a crawl. She pulled to the curb two houses away and cut the engine. The neighborhood was a typical affluent North Dallas neighborhood. Large custom homes with distinctive architecture were set on beautifully landscaped lots and surrounded by carefully manicured lawns.

It all looked legitimate, yet she hesitated. She watched several others park and walk up to the door. *Who were these people? Why did they come here?*

Lys finally forced herself out of the car. She hobbled up the walk, driven by a sheer determination not to be beaten. She rang the doorbell. As the door swung open, Piper greeted her with a gracious smile and escorted her in.

The exterior of the home was designed to suggest a medieval castle with rough-hewn stone walls, leaded glass windows, and a cylindrical turret rising near the right-hand side.

The interior mirrored the same theme. Entering the house Lys crossed an expansive flagstone entry with a small formal sitting area on the right and leaded glass doors leading to a paneled study on the left. A curved staircase led to the second floor.

Passing through the entry they came to an immense great room where the gathering was evidently to be held. The furnishings here were massive, and in a Mediterranean style, with a great deal of rich leather and wrought-iron. Great wooden beams supported the ceiling high above them. A balcony overlooked the room on three sides, while directly ahead, on the fourth side, a massive rock wall was highlighted by an equally massive walk-in stone fireplace that could have been borrowed from a medieval castle keep. A well-stocked wet-bar occupied the southwest corner.

Most of the group were already present. Trying to be sensitive to Lys's back problems, Piper had reserved the firmest chair for her. Lys carefully eased herself into the seat, her face contorting as a stab of pain shot from her spine all the way to her feet. Lys looked around warily.

Most of the guests were already caught up in conversation, sipping drinks and laughing. *How could she tell if this was a religious cult?*

Holmes walked over and greeted her warmly.

Lys was clearly nervous but gave her very best imitation smile.

"Is this when you break out the Kool-aid?" Lys asked, suspiciously.

Holmes smiled, "Sorry, we're all out of Kool-aid. How about a nice Shiraz?"

His good-natured response relaxed her considerably, "Thanks," she said. "I'd love it."

Holmes returned a few moments later with a paper-thin crystal glass half-filled with a rich dark liquid. Lys swirled the Shiraz, sniffed, and took a sip. It was outstanding. "Thanks," she said again, with a more genuine smile this time, "This really helps."

"Just what the doctor ordered," Holmes smiled in return. "One of my favorite prescriptions."

While Lys nursed her drink, Piper brought a steady stream of people over to her chair and introduced them. It was quite a diverse group. The youngest was Ron Lewis, a large, barrel-chested man with a close-cropped beard.

The oldest, named Michael Fletcher, looked like a college professor. He was accompanied by a young businessman named Patrick, who apparently had just returned from an extended trip to Scotland.

Next, Lys met a young black woman with a willowy figure who introduced herself as Reetha Shire. She explained that her parents had been big Aretha Franklin fans.

There was Marty Shapiro, a medical doctor, slender with wiry hair, a neatly trimmed mustache, and mischievous smile.

Finally Piper introduced her to Erin Vanderberg, a stunning brunette, impeccably dressed. Lys recognized Erin from the society blogs. Erin was a wealthy Dallas socialite, married to Rex Vanderberg, one of the richest men in Texas.

The introductions were almost finished when the last member of the group arrived. The late arrival was a slender brunette wearing a simple, knee-length dress of a material Lys didn't recognize. She was introduced simply as Eliel.

After Piper refreshed everyone's drinks, Holmes opened the meeting. "Welcome to the second gathering of our synaxis. I believe you've all met our newest member, Lysandra Johnston. Since Lys wasn't with us for our first meeting, I want to begin by giving her a brief explanation of why we are here.

"Lys, one of the purposes of our group is to unlock the latent abilities within each one of us. Locked away in each of us are some incredible powers, but most of us never learn to use them. Fortunately, our friend here, Eliel, has the ability to help us tap into those powers. We worked on that briefly last week and saw some interesting results.

"We'd like to begin our meeting tonight with a 'lab' session, and with your permission, Lys, I'd like to use you as the guinea pig. I promise nothing we do will hurt or embarrass you, and if you feel uncomfortable at any time, just let us know and we'll stop immediately.

"Is that okay with you?"

Lys looked around, wondering if she should bolt for the door. But no one looked very threatening, and she wasn't sure she could "bolt" very well in her condition in any event.

"Sure," she said, "go for it. I'm afraid I'm a pretty pathetic guinea pig right now, but if I can help, I'll be glad to."

"Okay," Holmes smiled, "just sit back and relax."

Turning to the late arrival, Holmes smiled, "Eliel, I'll now turn the meeting over to you..."

Without a word, Eliel walked over to Lys and studied her for a moment. She then began giving instructions to several members of the group.

"Reetha," she began, "come over here and stand behind Lys."

Reetha smiled broadly, then walked nervously to the center of the room, taking a position directly behind Lys.

"Now... lay your hand gently on Lys's back and tell me what you feel."

Reetha followed Eliel's instructions. As her fingers rested lightly on Lys's back, her face contorted in pain for a moment, then relaxed. She shifted the position of her fingers several times, each time with a similar response. Finally she glanced up at Eliel, "It feels like her back is damaged--here, here, and here," she said, softly touching Lys's back in three places.

Lys was impressed. *Three for three isn't bad.* Reetha had touched exactly the points of the damaged disks.

"Thank you, Reetha," Eliel said, then looked at Lys.

"Reetha's what we call an empath," Eliel explained. "She has the ability to feel what someone else is feeling. She just discovered how to use her powers last week, but she's already very good."

Eliel next turned to Piper, "Now, Piper, it's your turn. Come and stand here with me."

As Piper took her position, Eliel explained, "Piper discovered last week that she's a healer. She's had that gift all her life, but never recognized it... or understood how to use it. Tonight will be her first real test.

"Okay, Piper," Eliel instructed. "Put your hands gently on Lys's back right here--no, a little higher. That's it."

147

Sensing Lys's apprehension, Eliel explained, "Lys, you're about to feel some strange sensations. Don't be afraid. This won't hurt, and when it's finished, you'll feel a great deal better."

As Piper's hands rested lightly on her back, Lys was surprised by a sensation of warmth that began at the top of her spine and slowly extended down her back.

"Lys, tell us what you're feeling." Eliel prompted.

"It feels strange," Lys responded, nervously. "I feel heat flowing down my spine. It's not a bad feeling, just unusual."

Eliel continued, "Now, Piper... move your left hand slightly lower--just *there*--and put your right hand here."

Piper shifted the position of her hands.

"Now, let's wait a few minutes."

The feeling of heat continued its spread, but Lys now began to notice other sensations. She felt lightheaded. There was a tingling in her hands, then a trembling, finally an uncontrolled shaking. Waves of energy seemed to be surging through her body. She felt she was plugged into a power outlet and her body was being overloaded. After a few minutes, Eliel directed Piper to remove her hands.

Every eye was on Lys. The heat, and the other sensations, slowly subsided.

"Now," Eliel asked, "How do you feel?"

"I feel relaxed... and refreshed," Lys responded. "That was amazing."

"What about your back?"

Lys straightened up, and got a puzzled look on her face. The sensations had been so overwhelming that, for a moment, she'd forgotten about her back.

She carefully twisted her body to the right, and then to the left... but felt no pain.

"This is incredible.  I'm not feeling the pain."

"Try standing up and moving,"

Lys stood up, still being careful how she moved. Slowly she bent over, stretched, and then moved from side to side.  With each movement she expected the usual twinge of searing pain, but the pain never came.

"This is impossible." Lys looked at Piper in amazement.  "I have three damaged disks in my back.  I've been in agony for weeks.  But I don't feel it now."

Eliel reached out and took her by the hand.  "Lys, I have good news for you.  Your disks are no longer damaged.  But there's more...

"Piper, now place your hands on Lysandra's face."

Piper gently cupped Lys's face between her hands, and again a sensation of heat enveloped her.  The atmosphere of the room seemed to subtly shift.  Her whole body relaxed, and she began to breathe deeply.

"I don't know what's happening, but it feels good," Lys said.

Lys began to feel lightheaded again and found it hard to remain standing, but Eliel held her hand and steadied her.

And then it was over.

As Piper removed her hands, a collective gasp went up from everyone in the room.

"Lys," Eliel said, "there's a mirror over there on the wall.  Go and look at your face."

Lys walked over to the mirror and almost collapsed. She put out one hand to steady herself against the wall.  "Oh my God!" she cried in unbelief. "Oh my *GOD!*" Tears began flowing down her unscarred cheeks. The bruising, the swelling, the lacerations were gone.

"This is impossible!" Lys gasped, unable to look away from her face in the mirror. She reached both hands up and gently stroked her face, then began to press and mash on her cheeks to make sure it was all real. "My God!" she cried. "This is a *miracle!*"

As she turned to face Eliel, Lys again realized that her back pain was gone. She gingerly bounced up and down, then stretched her hands up, and bent down to touch her toes. For the first time in weeks, she didn't hurt.

The tears were still flowing as she glanced around the room. Her eyes again focused on Eliel. "How did you *do* this? I mean... *this is impossible!"*

Holmes interrupted, "Lys, there are some things you need to know, and it's difficult to explain. We're here at this meeting because we've each had a strange encounter. We've all had something unusual happen to us--something that, for each of us, was just as surprising as what you've just experienced.

"But before we can explain it, you need to know something about Eliel."

Lys glanced around again, not sure of how to respond. Everyone was still looking at her, but she no longer felt fear.

Eliel walked over and calmly stood in front of her, a few feet away, smiling mischievously.

Standing face to face, Lys was surprised by how small Eliel was. She was slender and not more than five feet tall. Every feature of her face was incredibly delicate, yet she was clearly not frail.

Eliel looked her straight in the eye. Lys tried to return her gaze, but found she could not. Lys had never met anyone quite like her. There was something unearthly about her--she bore a childlike gentleness and innocence, yet with an aura of great power and authority.

Looking at her face-to-face, Lys was surprised to see that Eliel wasn't wearing makeup. She didn't need any. Her skin was clear and flawless. It appeared to glow.

Lys looked closer and her mouth dropped open. Eliel *was* glowing... *literally.* Light was coming from her, and it was gradually increasing in intensity. Lys stepped back and almost fell over backward onto a chair.

The glow emanating from Eliel was almost blinding now. And suddenly her wings unfurled. Eliel extended her wings horizontally and without effort rose into the air to float six inches above the floor.

Unable to remain standing, Lys dropped awkwardly to the floor, never taking her eyes from Eliel. Her body began to tremble uncontrollably.

The look on her face was one of awe, almost of worship. "Who *are* you?" she stammered, "*What* are you?"

Holmes came behind Lys and put a hand on her shoulder to steady her. "Okay, Eliel, I think she gets the point."

Eliel's glow faded quickly. Holmes helped Lys to the nearest chair, and when Lys looked again, Eliel's feet were firmly planted on the floor and her wings had vanished.

"Now," Holmes said, "I think we have some things to explain."

# Chapter Fifteen: Before the Storm

## FRISCO, TEXAS (A SUBURB OF DALLAS)

As the rest of the group listened, Holmes and Piper gave Lys an overview of the ongoing battle between the Irin and the Archons, and the crisis confronting the human race. Then Eliel shared a brief explanation of the synaxis.

She concluded, "To put it simply, Lys, a synaxis is a group of ordinary humans who choose to align themselves with the Irin. In the context of that synaxis, their depleted life-force is renewed and their lost abilities recovered. Through this, they gain the power to stand against the forces of evil that threaten your world."

Eliel glanced around at the members of the group, then smiled warmly at Lys. "That's why we're all here tonight. This is our synaxis. It's the first synaxis to meet in your world in more than a thousand years.

"The Archon's goal is the total destruction of the human race, and they won't settle for less. But through this group, and others to follow, you will gain the power to resist them and drive them from your world."

Lys was still in shock. "When will all of this begin?"

"It's already begun," Eliel responded. "Last week we began the process of activating your gifts. Last Wednesday night, Piper learned she's a healer. We discovered that

Reetha's an empath and that Marty has the ability to see into other dimensions. They're just beginning to learn how to exercise these gifts, but as you saw tonight, the gifts are already powerful."

"In the coming months we'll continue this process. For this synaxis to be fully functional, *all* of you need to be equipped to use your gifts."

Eliel glanced again at the members of the group. "Michael, we never got to you last week, but you have the ability to dispel shades. Patrick and Erin, you both have the gift of second sight--the ability to sense future events before they happen.

"Just by being here--being part of the synaxis--these gifts will begin to stir. As you continue to meet with the Irin, your life force will grow stronger. Each of you will learn to recognize your gifts, and discover how to use them.

"Over the next few months we'll also add new members to the group. In a synaxis, each member draws on the abilities of the others. Each of your gifts strengthens the gifts of the others. Because of that, there's a power that comes when you're gathered in synaxis that you can never have individually. It's generally felt that the minimum number for a fully functional synaxis is ten. The ideal number is twelve.

"But beyond unlocking your gifts," Eliel continued, "this synaxis has a second purpose. And that's to open a portal between *Basilea* and the earth-realm."

"A *portal*?" Lys asked, looking genuinely perplexed. "What's that?"

"A portal is a passageway between dimensions," Eliel explained. "Your physicists would call it a *wormhole*. It's

an open doorway that allows free movement from one
world to another.

"The Archons have been able to open many portals
between the earth and Hades. Through these they've
assembled a massive force in your world. Thousands more
are added each month. As a result, the Irin here are greatly
outnumbered. If we're to successfully resist the Archons,
we must open a portal to *Basilea*."

"What prevents more Irin from coming now?"
Michael interrupted.

"Only a few of us can travel freely between
dimensions as I do." Eliel explained, "It's a unique ability,
even among the Irin.

"A few more are able to cross over at 'thin places' like
Iona, where the barrier between our worlds is more easily
traversed.

"But to stand against the overwhelming power of the
Archons, we must create our own portal… a doorway
connecting your world to *Basilea*. When that wormhole is
established, many more Irin can enter your world. With
their help we can establish many groups like this.

"This synaxis is just a prototype," Eliel continued.
"To overcome the Archons, you'll need thousands of groups
like this one, all over your planet. You who are here tonight
will one day lead those groups and train many thousands of
your people to use their gifts. Together you will drive the
Archons from your world."

As Patrick listened to Eliel, he had a flash of insight.
"That must be what Columba did!" He blurted, "There must
have been a *synaxis* on Iona!"

As everyone turned to Patrick, he looked at Michael.

"Michael, you once told me that--according to the ancient legends--the angels came to Iona and revealed secrets hidden since the beginning of time. Columba and his followers then went out with miraculous powers throughout Europe, all through the dark ages. Everywhere they went, a new group of twelve was created. A new *synaxis*. *That's* how the Irish saved civilization."

"That's exactly right, Patrick." Eliel affirmed.

Seeing the puzzled looks on the faces of the group, Eliel added, "This may sound like ancient history, but it's vital that you understand what happened on Iona.

"By the sixth century the Archons had so undermined the Roman world that Roman civilization collapsed. The legions deserted. Rising violence brought commerce to a standstill. Thousands starved. Many times that number were slaughtered by the roving gangs and warlords who rose up to seize power. Into that chaos rode barbarian hordes from the east to loot, rape and kill.

"The Archons had hoped to bring human society to such a place of devastation that they could easily seize control, and they almost succeeded.

"But in 563 a man named Columba, with a group of twelve followers, sailed from Ireland to a small rocky island off the western coast of Scotland--a place called Iona. There a synaxis was formed and a portal opened. Through that portal, thousands of Irin were released into the earth-realm; and with their help, the monks of Iona went out by twelves across Scotland and England. Every group of twelve formed a new synaxis.

"During the dark ages, emissaries from Iona traveled throughout Europe and beyond, driving back the Archons and restoring ancient knowledge. Slowly order was re-established. From that one small island, the powers of destruction were turned back for the whole planet.

"Yet forces of superstition eventually came, even to Iona. The power of synaxis was replaced by religion and ritual. The portal was allowed to close, and the Archon powers began to rebuild.

"If your world is to survive, the Iona portal must be re-opened. That's the other goal of this synaxis. When your synaxis is complete, you must all travel to Iona and re-establish the ancient wormhole to *Basilea*.

"That's where Patrick comes in..." Eliel explained, "Patrick is a direct descendant of the line that first established that gateway. Because of his ancestry, Patrick has the authority to reopen the Iona portal."

Listening to Eliel, Lys was feeling overwhelmed. It seemed like a whole new world had opened to her, but she wasn't sure how she fit in.

"Eliel," she finally asked, "This is all incredible, but it's a lot to process at one time. Are you saying that *every* human being has the potential to do the kinds of thing Reetha and Piper did tonight?"

"Yes, Lys," Eliel answered, "every human being has that potential and more. In fact, what you saw tonight was just their *first* level of gifting. You each have *many* gifts. And you're each unique... each one has a different *set* of abilities. That's why you need each other. As you learn how your gifts work together you'll see things far beyond what took place tonight."

"Can you tell what *my* gifts are?" Lys asked.

"Lys, you have one of the most powerful gifts, and it's

why the enemy has targeted you. You're what we call a *singer*."

Lys was puzzled. "My gift is *singing*?"

"It's not a matter of music," Eliel explained. "Something in your life-force produces a sound that can resonate between the dimensions."

Lys was still puzzled. "How does *that* work?"

"Remember as a little girl, you liked to sing 'made up' songs?

"You'd begin to sing nonsense syllables, and suddenly words you never learned began to flow from your mouth. It was a beautiful melody, and you sang and sang. You thought it was silly, but that was your gift beginning to stir. You're a singer of songs. The sound of those songs has power.

"The sound of your song can alter reality. It can change the structure of matter. And most importantly, it can open a portal to a different world. That's why the Archons have tried to kill you. Patrick has the *authority* to open the Iona portal, but only *your* gift can make it happen."

Lys was shaken. "You're saying I have the power to open a doorway to another world?"

"You not only have that ability, Lys," Eliel smiled reassuringly. "It's your *destiny*. It's part of what you were created for. You're the only one on earth right now who can open the Iona portal."

While Eliel and Lys were talking, Erin was pondering the comment Eliel had made about her gift. "Eliel," she ventured at last. "You said I have the second-sight--that I can sense things before they happen.

"The last few nights I've had another recurring dream,

and I haven't been sure what to do with it. I wonder if it can be significant."

"What was the dream?" Eliel asked.

"It was a very pleasant dream at first," Erin glanced nervously around the room. "We were having a picnic at a beach. It was a beautiful sunny day. We were talking and laughing. It was a wonderful time, and all of us were enjoying the afternoon. Then we heard a sound behind us."

"As we turned around, we saw that, just behind us, massive storm clouds had gathered. Huge thunderheads towered over our heads. Wind-driven rains were rapidly approaching. The storm was almost upon us. We quickly scrambled to pick up our things and find a shelter. That's where the dream ends.

"I've had that same dream the last three nights," Erin said. "Each morning as I wake up, I hear the words, 'It's the calm before the storm.'"

Eliel looked around at the group and then at Erin. "You can't imagine a how accurate that dream is, Erin. The storm *is* coming, and your world has no idea how close it is."

After the meeting ended, Eliel waited until everyone but Holmes and Piper had left and then gave Holmes an unusual instruction. "Holmes, don't go to the lake house this Friday. Stay close to home. You'll be needed. And be alert. You must be prepared to leave at a moment's notice."

\*\*\*

Saturday morning at 3:00 AM, Holmes' cell phone rang.

"Hello... Dr. Holmes?" a breathless voice gasped, "This is Erin Vanderberg. *Please help me.*" There was a brief hesitation. It sounded like Erin was sobbing. "I'm at a convenience store on Highway 380, just north of Dallas." In a weak and faltering voice Erin described her location, then pleaded, "I'm sorry to call at this hour, but there's no one else I can turn to. Please *come!*"

Within minutes, Holmes and Piper were headed north on the Dallas North Tollway. They turned west on Highway 380 toward the convenience store Erin had described.

Piper and Holmes rode in silence. They'd both heard the desperation in Erin's voice and sensed the tension of the situation, though they had no idea what they'd find.

The Mercedes pulled into the convenience store's parking lot at 3:37 AM. The place looked deserted.

Pulling to a stop well away from the building, Holmes and Piper got out of the car and glanced around. The night was humid and hot--over 80 degrees even after midnight, with no discernable breeze. The asphalt under their feet seemed to radiate with the built-up heat of the scorching Texas summer.

Two rusty gas pumps stood near the west side of the building, their nozzles covered with black plastic bags. A hand-scrawled "out of order" sign was taped across the front of each.

Broken glass from long-smashed beer bottles and the bodies of dead crickets crunched under their feet as Piper and Holmes approached the building. The only other sound was the occasional *whoosh* of cars speeding past on Highway 380.

The store exuded a musty aura of dirt, faded paint and disrepair. The long-unwashed windows served as a bulletin board for hand-lettered signs seeking the return of lost puppies and offering well-used pickup trucks for sale. A long crack in one window had been inexpertly patched with a strip of now-peeling duct-tape. *A fine establishment specializing in cheap beer and fish bait,* Holmes thought.

He tried the front door, but it was firmly locked. The faint illumination provided by two security lights revealed no one inside the store. *Where is Erin?*

They continued around the building, seeing no one. Finally, from the shadows along the east side of the store, they heard a faint noise.

By the light of the full moon, they could just make out something dark crumpled on the ground between the side of the building and a broken-down pickup truck.

As they approached, they realized it was a woman, but she was scarcely recognizable as Erin Vanderberg. The Erin Vanderberg they knew was an elegant and beautiful woman, the envy of Dallas society.

What lay on the ground before them looked more like a homeless derelict clothed in rags. Erin's silken, chestnut-brown hair was now a dark, tangled mass, caked with blood and dirt. Her once-elegant clothing hung in filthy shreds from her bruised and lacerated body.

Seeing them approach, Erin struggled weakly to get up but fell back to the ground.

Piper knelt down and checked her vital signs. Erin was in bad shape but didn't require immediate medical attention.

As Holmes and Piper helped Erin to her feet, she

looked at them with terror in her eyes. "Quickly," she gasped, clenching Holmes' arm in a claw-like grip. "We must get away from here. *Now!* They may come at any moment!"

# Chapter Sixteen:  Erin's Story

*EN ROUTE* FROM DALLAS TO EAST TEXAS

Piper helped Erin into the rear seat of the Mercedes and climbed in beside her.

Holmes and Piper quickly discussed where to take her.  Not knowing the situation, they didn't want to risk going to Erin's home.  They needed a secure location.   They glanced at each other and both knew--*the lake house.* Holmes headed south on the Tollway to pick up Loop 635 around the northeastern corner of Dallas.

It was too early for morning traffic and the drive around the city went smoothly.  Erin was trembling from trauma and pain, barely able to talk, but she leaned back into the Mercedes' plush leather upholstery and slowly began to pour out her story.

"Our marriage was always a joke," she began.  "I was just a kid, 22 years old, working as a waitress to put myself through college.  I was swept away by the glamour and power.  Who wouldn't be?  The man was a billionaire.

"Rex was 31 at the time, and already one of the richest men in Texas.  It was a whirlwind romance… a classic Cinderella story.  But I soon discovered what he was behind the façade.

"For our honeymoon he flew me to his beachfront house on Hawaii's Big Island in his private jet. But the dream quickly turned into a nightmare. Our second night in Hawaii, he left me alone in bed while he slept with another woman. I found out later that's his pattern. He doesn't sleep with the same woman two nights in a row. Rex even keeps his own harem in one wing of the ranch house--a private one-man bordello for his personal use, and for entertaining his clients. He calls them 'his girls'."

Erin hesitated for a moment, looking down at her lacerated hands, streaked with dirt and blood. "Rex only married me because I had the right 'look' for his public image. He needed someone 'respectable' to accompany him to social functions, but no respectable Dallas family would let their daughter near him.

"When I finally realized the kind of man he was, I demanded a divorce, but he exploded in rage and threatened to kill me. He said he would 'lose face' if I left him. That was the first time he hit me," she said, her voice faltering, "… the first of many."

Erin took a deep breath as she struggled to fight back the welling tears. Regaining her composure, she continued, "So I chose to make the best of it. At the same time, I did everything I could to distance myself from him. I poured my life into worthwhile causes. I joined the Junior League and put in volunteer hours at Ronald McDonald house. I joined the Dallas Arts Council. I served on committees for the Arboretum and the annual charity ball. I was involved in many philanthropic projects and always gave big.

"Over the last twenty years I developed my own reputation. I gained the respect of everyone in Dallas society.

"Of course, Rex loved it. It made the Vanderberg name look good. But he hated *me* because I refused to be the kind of person he was.

"But I never realized *how much* he hated me," she muttered tonelessly, "not until... "

Erin's voice faltered again as she finally broke down and wept, allowing the tears to stream down her battered face. Her whole body was quaking.

Piper gently brushed a clot of bloody hair from Erin's face, then held her hand until the sobbing subsided.

After a long pause, Erin clumsily wiped the tears from her eyes. "Of course, it hasn't been all bad," she said, rallying strength. "After the first few months I rarely saw Rex apart from social events. We've lived separate and very different lives. I stay in the 'city' house in Plano, while Rex lives at the ranch. In exchange for making appearances with him I've enjoyed many benefits.

"Rex satisfied my appetite for the good life. I had an unlimited budget, and I spent big--thousands each month for clothing and jewelry. I could use the private jet and travel when he didn't need me. Of course, there was always someone watching, making sure I didn't do anything that could make him lose face.

"He's always been a hard, cruel man. You could never cross him. Ever. I learned that quickly. But I never realized how truly evil he is until yesterday."

She paused a moment, as if summoning her resolve. Finally she spoke again, "I discovered last night what Rex Vanderberg really is. He's linked with *them*... with the Archons. They have their own version of a synaxis... their own portal... but it's..." She shook her head and looked down at the floor, not able to finish her sentence.

Gaining a little composure, she continued, "They know all about us… about you and the Irin. And they're furious. There's nothing they won't do to stop us."

Just east of Dallas, Holmes pulled into a convenience store and got Erin some food, along with a bottle of Gatorade to replenish her electrolytes. They also bought a first-aid kit so Piper could begin to dress Erin's wounds.

As they pulled back onto the interstate, Erin's story continued to unfold…

At 10:45 Friday morning Rex called Erin and ordered her to meet him at the ranch immediately.

Erin had spent Friday morning getting ready for the Dallas Arts Council luncheon at the Hilton Anatole. She'd been preparing for the event for weeks. The dress she was wearing, purchased for the occasion, would easily have set most families back a month's salary. And that didn't count the diamond earrings.

But she knew better than to refuse Rex. *I'll definitely be the best-dressed woman at the ranch today,* she thought to herself. Erin flipped her phone shut and, with a sigh, picked up her purse and headed for the garage.

She took the Tollway north and made a left on Highway 380, finally turning north again into an area of sprawling estates. Huge ranch houses sat far from the road surrounded by expansive fields bordered by neat, four-rail, white board fences.

This was horse country. The rich, loamy soil in this part of Texas made it an ideal place for running horses, and the horses raised here are elite athletes, both Arabians and Thoroughbreds. Though Kentucky is better known to most laymen, some of the racing world's best-known champions have originated in this small corner of Texas.

And raising them is a profitable business. A single brood mare can sell for twenty thousand dollars, and a sire for over a million. Those who care for these magnificent animals treat them with great respect, catering to their every need.

Horse people are usually good, hard-working people. They believe in God, mother, and apple pie, and go to church every Sunday. But that was not the case with Rex Vanderberg. Erin was about to discover that beyond the long driveway, the neat white fences and the cavernous barns, something unspeakably evil lurked at Vanderberg Hills Ranch.

Arriving at the ranch, Erin turned up the long, arching driveway and pulled her vapor-grey, Jaguar XK convertible to a stop in front of the main building. Leaving the keys in the ignition, she nodded to the security guard and walked purposefully to the door.

The structure could easily have been mistaken for a country club. Double glass doors opened onto a spacious lobby, and then into a well-appointed living-room-like area for clients.

Erin strode briskly through the lobby and out the double doors on the far side. She followed a brick path through carefully tended gardens to the private quarters, a sprawling 23,000 square foot house overlooking a private lake.

But she wasn't expecting what came next.

As she walked confidently into the main reception area, Rex was standing with his arms crossed and a look of utter contempt on his face. Rex Vanderberg was a tall, muscular man with closely cropped black hair. He stood just under 6'2" and weighed-in at 260 pounds. Never one to pay attention to style, Rex was dressed in typical cowboy fashion--Levi jeans, a plaid shirt, and cowboy boots.

Three of his top hands--or perhaps it was more accurate to say, *thugs*--Reno, Bryce and Grat were with him. All three were bad news, but the worst was Grat. Grat Dalton was a descendent of Gratton Hanley Dalton, a train robber and murderer in the late 1800's, one of the infamous Dalton gang. Grat didn't have to work hard to keep up his outlaw persona. He had a reputation for ruthless violence throughout the region.

As she walked toward Rex, Erin noted that Reno and Bryce were circling around behind her. Not to be intimidated she walked up to Rex and looked him in the eye. *"What?"* she demanded.

His answer was a forceful, tooth-rattling slap across her face. "You *BITCH!*" he roared, as Erin struggled to remain standing. "You stupid, good-for-nothing *bitch*." He struck her again, harder, then began pacing around the room. "You worthless whore… you *traitor!* You were never good for nothin'." He screamed in fury, "But now you've joined *them!"*

"Joined who?" Erin demanded, trying to control the quiver of fear in her voice. She had seen Rex enraged on many occasions, but never like this.

He whirled on her. "You didn't think we'd *know?* We know all about you… about the *Irin*… about your little synaxis meeting. *Damn,* you're stupid!"

"You're trying to mess up everything." He raged, coming closer. "The Archons came here to save us. This country's been run by the stupid, the weak and the lazy long enough. No wonder it's falling apart.

"The Archons are going to end all that. When they take over, I'll be a *king!*"

Rex lowered his voice and leaned down until his face was only inches away. "Well, I've decided to let you in on what we do in the *real* world while you live in your fancy house and go to luncheons. We have our own little *synaxis*--some of my girls, along with some carefully chosen ranch hands. We open our own doorway to another world every month at full moon. It only opens for a brief moment, but it gets the job done. Every month, hundreds of Archons come through. Every month we gain strength. It's quite a show. The Archon's methods are, shall we say, very entertaining.

"And I'm going to show you how it's done. *Our* way! In fact, I'm going to give you a front row seat tonight so you won't miss a thing."

Rex slapped her again. Then, feeling that wasn't enough, he reared back and gave her a roundhouse punch to the side of the face that sent her sprawling across the room.

He turned to Grat and barked, "Take her out."

Grat and Reno each took an arm and literally drug her outside. As Erin struggled to get her feet under her, they drug her down a long path to an isolated area behind the main barn. There, concealed in a thicket of waist-high brush and mesquite trees, was an old storm cellar. Bryce undid the padlock, lifted the heavy steel door, and swung it aside.

Without warning, Grat grabbed Erin by both arms and roughly threw her down the stairs. She landed in a shallow pool of fetid liquid.

The place smelled of urine and blood. She glanced around in horror to see that the storm cellar had been re-fitted into what looked like a torture chamber. Manacles were fitted to the reinforced concrete walls, and blood was splattered everywhere.

Fastened to one set of manacles was a pitiful derelict. He was filthy, unshaved, and reeked of alcohol. He hung with his head down, unconscious.

"We're calling this one Joe," Rex sneered, following her down the stairs. "Grat and Reno picked him up in Dallas last night."

Rex watched as the men slammed her body against the far wall. Reno and Bryce held her hands in place while Grat clamped manacles around her wrists.

Rex continued, "Old Joe was going to be the main event tonight, but he just got demoted. Now he's just the warm-up act. We're going to have a double feature tonight, and we're saving the main event for *you*," he spat in her direction, "Honey!"

When the men left and the steel door slammed down, Erin was left in total darkness. Her head was swirling. She heard the click of the padlock closing and conversation fade into the distance. She struggled with the shackles for a few minutes but knew Rex well enough to know they'd be secure.

In the brutal heat of Texas summer, the storm cellar quickly became a sweatbox. Perspiration poured down Erin's face and saturated her clothing. The derelict never awoke but snored noisily from time to time. As the long hours crept past, there was nothing to do but wait.

Just after sundown, the door opened again. They took Joe first, unfastening his manacles and roughly dragging his still-unconscious form up the stairs. The doors slammed shut and Erin was left in darkness again. She longed for something to drink, but at least it was cooling off slightly.

Twenty minutes later they returned. Without saying a word they released her hands from the manacles and threw her roughly to the floor. Pulling her arms behind her back, they shackled her hands tightly in handcuffs. As the cuffs clicked into place they jerked her to her feet. Grat led the way up the stairs while Reno and Bryce forced her after him.

Holding her arms in a vice-like grip, they loaded her into the rear seat of an extended cab pickup. Bryce climbed in beside her while Grat and Reno took the front seat. In the gathering dusk, they lurched and bounced across the open fields toward a distant grove of scrub oaks. Erin's head was swimming. She feared she was going to be sick.

Passing through the trees, they entered a large, open area lit by generator-powered quartz-halogen lamps mounted on tall poles.

Around the perimeter of the area a crude circle had been painted on the ground in white spray paint. At the center of the circle, the still-unconscious derelict lay spread-eagled on a concrete dais with chains firmly attached to his wrists and ankles. On either side of the dais stood a large pile of dry brushwood.

The pickup stopped just outside the circle. Erin was rudely shoved out and dragged to the rear of the truck. While Bryce and Reno held her arms, Grat opened one handcuff and slipped it through a hole in the pickup's rear bumper. They worked quickly and with precision. There was no emotion. She was being handled like a sack of feed or a side of beef.

Grat clicked the shackle into place, checked to make sure both cuffs were secure, then left without saying a word. Erin slumped onto the ground in total exhaustion and pain, numbly observing the preparations taking place before her.

More trucks were arriving and equipment unloaded. A crowd was gathering.

A few minutes later Rex drove up in his classic 1962 Rolls Royce Silver Cloud II. Rex exited the car and began a heated conversation with a tall, slender black-haired woman. Rex was still enraged and kept gesturing wildly and pointing in Erin's direction.

As the two finished their conversation, Rex approached Erin and stood, staring at her in silent contempt for several moments. Finally he leaned down and softly said, "Don't be impatient, Honey. We don't want to rush Joe in his big part. It'll be the performance of his life. But he's just getting things warmed up for you. It'll be *your* turn soon enough."

Rex stood glaring at her a moment longer, then kicked her, driving the pointed toe of his eel skin boot forcefully into her ribs--taking her breath away. Then he spat and strode away without looking back.

Preparations were continuing around the dais. Thirteen drums were set up around the perimeter of the circle, and drummers in black robes took their positions.

When it was fully dark, a pretty, black-robed woman with long blonde hair came into view, carrying a torch. With quick, yet deliberate movements, she lit both of the piles of brushwood. As the fires began to blaze brightly, the quartz-halogen lamps were extinguished.

A circle of thirteen young women in black robes formed around the dais, staying about twenty feet from the derelict. Beyond them gathered a circle of hooded men, also in black robes. The drums began to sound a slow, deliberate cadence.

The derelict was finally stirring. Looking from side to side, he shouted frantically, "Hey... what's going on here? Who are you people?" He struggled futilely against the chains that bound his arms, then cried, "Somebody let me go!"

Ignoring the derelict's pleas, the black-robed men and women began a slow, rhythmic dance around the dais.

The terror of the scene before her caused Erin's adrenalin to begin flowing. Finding new strength, she sat up and tried pulling against the chain that bound her, but the handcuff was firmly secured.

She looked around for something, anything, to use as a tool or weapon, but Grat had done his job well. There was nothing within reach but bare, hard-packed earth. She could see no possible way of escape.

Erin sat crouched in an ocean of darkness, illuminated only by the full moon. Her attention was captured by the horror steadily unfolding around the dais. Rex had come into view again. He was wearing a black robe trimmed in gold. Walking calmly through the lines of dancers, he stood before the dais observing the terrified derelict. At a motion from Rex, two figures dressed in black entered the circle and quickly ripped open the derelict's shirt, exposing his heaving chest.

The drummers increased their speed.

Slowly, from within his robe, Rex withdrew a seventeen-inch serrated-edge bowie knife and brandished it in the air. A cry went up from around the circle.

Sensing what was about to happen, Erin frantically examined the shackle that gripped her wrist, running her free hand along every surface, searching for some way to release its hold. But there was none.

She twisted her wrist in the cuff, pulling against it with all her might, yet it held firm.

Rex began a slow circuit of the dais, holding the knife over his head. The firelight gleamed on its polished surface. The dancers were chanting now, though Erin couldn't make out the words.

Erin's struggle against the manacles grew more desperate. She hammered the cuff against the pickup's bumper, jerking it, thrashing it back and forth, but it would not yield.

The drums were louder now... the drummers had been steadily increasing their speed and intensity. The dancers matched the quickening pace with even more grotesque moves. It was all building to an inevitable climax.

Erin was hysterical now. She put both feet on the pickup's chrome bumper and pulled against the chain, straining against the stainless steel shackle until blood flowed down her arm, but the cuff remained tightly locked around her wrist.

She was in agony, tears pouring down her face. Though she'd never believed in God, Erin found herself praying desperately for help.

And then, seemingly from nowhere, a hand reached out and touched hers. It was a woman's hand, and the touch was gentle. She looked up, incredulous, and saw a woman dressed in black kneeling over her. The woman bent down, and by the flickering light of the distant infernos, Erin caught a glimpse of her face. *"Eliel!"* she gasped through the tears, "what are *you* doing here?"

"Be quiet!" Eliel ordered. Eliel's hand reached out and rested lightly on the stainless steel shackle. With a slight click, the handcuff fell open.

Eliel spoke quickly, "You must *run!* I'll try to divert them when they come for you, but I can't hold them back for long. Run! Run and don't stop. Run toward the east. That bright star up there… follow it! It will lead you to the road. Araton is waiting for you there with a car. No matter what happens, you *must* not stop. Now *GO!*"

Erin didn't need to be told again. She ran. Out across the dark field. Away from the unspeakable terror unfolding in the island of light behind her. She stumbled and fell, but got up and ran again, keeping the star in view. In the distance the drums continued to build to a crescendo. As Erin climbed over the white board fence marking the edge of the ranch, she heard the drums stop. A bloodcurdling cry split the air, then a flash of light, like distant lightning, and the sound of thunder.

Erin didn't need to look back. She knew exactly what had happened. The portal had opened. A sound like the rasp and clatter of hundreds of leathery wings filled the air overhead. Then it died away, and there was silence.

By then she was over the fence and stumbling across the next field.

In the distance she heard shouts. Angry shouts. The sky behind her lit up as the quartz halogen lights flashed on. They'd discovered her escape.

Erin was running across open farmland now with only the light of the full moon to show the way. As she clawed her way through tangles of brush, she felt thorns ripping her flesh but didn't slow down. She clambered over a barbed-wire fence and was out across the next field.

Running across a mud flat at the edge of an old cattle tank, she sank into mire up to her ankles. She fell, landing on her hands and knees. She was covered in ooze and fought to free herself. Both of her shoes were lost in the dark mud, and there was no time to retrieve them. She scrambled to her feet and kept running

On dry ground again, her feet were soon torn and bleeding. She fell several more times. Every muscle in her body was screaming in pain, but she didn't dare stop. She kept on, knowing her life depended on it.

Erin struggled through more dry brush and up over a low rise. Coming down the other side, she tripped, landing hard with her face in the dust. She lay there, breathing in ragged gasps, her chest heaving. If only she could rest. If only she could stop.

She struggled to stand, but her limbs would not cooperate. In the distance she could hear more shouts… and then the barking of dogs.

She forced herself to get up, and again she ran.

Through more bushes… inch-long thorns stabbed at her hands and legs as she stumbled on. *Was every bush in Texas a thorn bush?*

The dogs were getting closer. They'd found her scent.

Over another rise… and then another barbed wire fence blocked her path. Her hands were covered in blood and her fingers trembled uncontrollably as she depressed the top strand and clambered over.

Making it over the fence, Erin attempted to run, but stumbled in the darkness, falling hard on her face.

The dogs were much closer… just beyond the last rise. They'd be upon her in minutes. She couldn't bear to think what would happen when they caught her.

Overwhelmed with exhaustion, Erin steeled herself to rise one more time. She pressed her palms firmly against the ground, and willed herself to get up. Then she stopped... perplexed. Something about the surface under her hands arrested her attention. She tried to dig her fingertips into the soil, but could not. *What is this?* It wasn't the dry dirt of Texas farmland. It was rock-hard and solid. And it extended in every direction.

And then Erin knew... she had found the road.

*What had Eliel said? Araton would be here with a car.* Erin thought of her first meeting with Araton on the brink of *Halema'uma'u* crater. He'd already saved her life once. If only he were here.

Ignoring the pain, she stood and looked around frantically. She didn't see a car.

Then, above the sound of the approaching dogs, she heard an engine start up several hundred feet down the road. With no lights visible, an old pickup truck slowly approached and pulled to a stop next to Erin. The windows were open, and she heard Araton's voice. "Quickly... get in.

"I can't stay with you long, but I can take you to a place where you'll be safe for a few hours. You must call Holmes and Piper. You'll be safe with them."

# Chapter Seventeen:  Mendrion

## THE LAKE HOUSE – THE PINEY WOODS
## OF EAST TEXAS

When they arrived at the lake house early Saturday morning, Erin had a glass of brandy and a hot shower, then slipped into one of Piper's softest nightgowns.  She was asleep within minutes and slept fitfully through the day.

Saturday evening she got up long enough to eat and quickly fell asleep again.

Before dawn on Sunday morning, Holmes and Piper were awakened by a bloodcurdling scream.  Running to the guest room, they found Erin sitting up in bed sobbing.  From the look of terror in her eyes, Piper knew she had been revisiting the nightmare in her sleep.

Piper sat down beside her and gently touched her forehead.  Erin's whole body was quaking, and she was running a high fever.

Looking up in alarm, Piper said, "She's not doing well.   Do you think we need to take her to a doctor?"

"Piper…" Holmes smiled.  "Have you forgotten last Wednesday night?  You're a *healer*.  Did you try to use your gift?"

"Do you think that would work *here*?  Outside of the synaxis?"

"I'm not sure, but it's worth a try."

Piper looked at Erin's trembling body. "I'm not sure where to put my hands. I know she probably has infection all through her body... along with who knows what else. I wish Eliel was here, or even Reetha... "

Then Piper had an idea. "Erin, I want to try the healing thing we did for Lys last Wednesday. Is that okay?"

Erin nodded weakly.

"I'm not sure how to do this, but I have an idea. I'm going to sit here beside you..." Piper inched closer to Erin. "Now lean up against me..."

Erin carefully leaned forward until she was resting against Piper. Like a little girl snuggled against her mother, Erin Vanderberg, the pride of Dallas society, rested her head on Ginny Piper's shoulder. Piper put one hand on Erin's back and another behind her head, and held her gently. Within a few seconds, Piper felt the now-familiar sensation of heat flowing through her hands.

The trembling gradually subsided, and she sensed Erin's body relax.

"This feels good," Erin murmured. Within minutes she had fallen into a deep sleep.

After a few minutes, when the sensation of heat in her hands ceased, Piper gently lowered Erin to the bed and stood up to evaluate her condition. Many of Erin's bruises and lacerations were visibly improved, and the fever seemed to be gone.

Holmes and Piper were relaxing in the great room on Sunday afternoon when Erin came limping down the hallway. The bruising on her face was greatly improved, but she still looked like she'd been run over by a truck. *She walks like a crude automaton,* Piper thought. *Her body is functioning, but something in her personality has shut down. She looks numb.*

Piper went to her and gave her a gentle embrace. "Are you ready for some food?"

"Yes. Thank you," she said weakly. Seeing the afternoon sun shimmering on the lake, she added, "I know it's afternoon, but is there any possibility of breakfast?"

"Breakfast it is," Piper smiled.

Piper fixed a big plate of bacon and eggs, along with toast, coffee and OJ. Erin thanked her, and silently devoured every bite.

Erin was just finishing the meal when Eliel arrived.

Eliel landed on the deck, and without bothering to knock, walked right through the door.

Seeing Eliel, a brief flicker of life came to Erin's eyes. Erin went to her and embraced her, weeping. "Eliel, I never got a chance to thank you. If you hadn't been there…" But she could not say more. She just held Eliel.

Eliel gently stroked her hair. "I'm sorry I wasn't able to do more, Erin.

"I was able to lay a false trail that diverted them for a short time, but when they brought in the dogs, there was little I could do. The number of Archons gathered at the ranch was overwhelming. If I'd tried to stand against them, I would have been destroyed. I could only hope you'd be able to reach Araton in time."

Eliel helped Erin to a seat on the couch and sat beside her, then looked to Piper and Holmes. "What are your plans now?"

"We were just discussing that," Holmes replied.

Piper asked, "Is it safe for Erin to return to Dallas? Or would it be better for her to stay here in the lake house?"

"I believe the best plan would be to return to Dallas tonight." Eliel responded. "But stay together. There's strength in numbers.

"Stay with Holmes," Eliel added, glancing at Piper. "Rand has assigned Araton and Khalil to guard the house. And one of you must be in the house with Erin at all times. The shades will be after her.

"I'll meet you again on Wednesday night," she said. "We're nearing a critical hour. We'll need to speed our training process."

Eliel carefully examined Erin's wounds and turned to Piper, "Piper, your gift is growing stronger. You can never experience the full power of your gift outside the synaxis, but your gift will always be there. Keep using it."

\*\*\*

## FRISCO, TEXAS (A SUBURB OF DALLAS)

Piper and Holmes both canceled most of their appointments and worked out a schedule that allowed one of them to be in the house with Erin at all times. Despite their best efforts to encourage her, Erin became more withdrawn, spending much of her time in bed staring blankly at the wall. From time to time Piper could hear her sobbing.

By Tuesday evening, Piper sensed an almost palpable darkness settling over Erin. Entering the room, she found

Erin curled in a fetal position with her eyes tightly closed, her whole body trembling.

Piper pulled a chair next to the bed and sat down beside her. Sensing a presence in the room, Erin's eyes slowly flickered open.

"How are you feeling?" Piper asked quietly as their eyes met.

"I've had better days..." Erin mumbled, trying to force a smile.

"Tell me what's happening..."

Fighting back another round of sobbing, Erin looked at Piper in anguish. "Piper... I keep reliving the horror of that night... It all just replays, over and over in my mind.

"I see Rex pacing the room and feel the pain of his blows. I smell the stench in the storm cellar. I feel the manacles on my hands. I hear the scream of that derelict as Rex ripped the life from his body. I feel like I'm still *there*.

"I hear the dogs pursuing... the knowledge that agonizing death is just minutes away. And I'm truly thankful that I survived, but then I wonder if I really did.

"Piper, my life is over!" Tears were beginning to flow again. "The life I've known is gone... Nothing I was can ever be again. I can't go back to my home... I can't be seen in public... Rex and his thugs are looking for me and they'll kill me when they find me. I have no future."

She pleaded, "Piper, what can I do?"

Piper leaned close and held her hand.

"Erin, I don't know what lies ahead," she answered gently. "It may be that none of us survive this time, but we can't focus on that right now. There's a battle ahead, and the stakes are bigger than all of us.

"If we succeed, I believe there'll be an incredible future for you... for all of us. But that time is so far distant it's hard to see what it will be like. All we can do right now is take things one step at a time and keep moving forward.

"The life you knew in the past was bound up with Rex and the Archons and everything you saw at the ranch. You didn't understand what you were part of, but it had to end. I believe your destiny is beyond all of that."

"Piper, I know you're right..." Erin sobbed. "But it's so *hard*. I feel like I'm dying."

By Wednesday evening, Erin seemed much improved, though a tangible darkness still hung over her. Just before seven o'clock, the synaxis members began to arrive. For once, Eliel was there early. With her was Araton, and a male Irin Piper hadn't seen before.

Most of the synaxis member had not yet heard of Erin's ordeal. They followed their normal pattern of breaking up into small groups, talking and laughing about the experiences of the week.

Reetha and Michael got their drinks and sat together. Reetha listened attentively as Michael launched into a monologue on the nature of the universe. Eliel and Holmes retreated to the kitchen, quietly discussing Erin's condition.

Seeing Patrick and Araton without drinks, Piper walked over to take their order.

"Whiskey and soda, please," Araton smiled, "*Irish* Whiskey if you have it."

"Angels drinking *whiskey*?" Patrick blurted.

"Check your history, Patrick," Araton laughed. "In your world, whiskey was first distilled by ancient Irish monks. They even named it. In Columba's day they called it *Uisce Beatha.* That's *Gaelic* for 'water of life.' The English shortened the name to *whisky.* But..." He added with a twinkle in his eye, "Who do you think taught the monks to make it?"

"That's good enough for me," Patrick laughed, turning to Piper. "I'll have the 'water of life' also... on the rocks with soda."

Returning to the room, Holmes allowed the conversation to continue for a few minutes. Then, while Piper went to the guest room to retrieve Erin, Holmes asked the group to be seated.

Piper helped Erin to her chair. She was dressed simply in one of Piper's casual outfits, but her hair had been restored to its former glory. As she took her seat, Araton came and stood at her side.

Holmes began, "Most of you haven't heard that Erin was almost killed Friday night. Tonight I've asked her to share her experience with the whole group. It's important that we all understand what we're facing."

Haltingly, Erin began her story. There were long pauses, and several times she broke down in tears, but finally made it through. By the end, several members of the group were weeping with her. When she finally finished, both Reetha and Lys went to her and embraced her. There was a long silence in the room.

Holmes looked quietly from person to person before continuing, "I asked Erin to share this, because I want you to have a clear picture of the battle that lies ahead. This is not a game."

"You must understand that to move forward with us

from tonight, you're committing your life. If you stay with us, it's likely some of us won't survive."

"But if we *don't* succeed..." he added, "*none* of us will survive."

"So before we go any further, I want to give anyone who's not ready to be part of this a chance to back out. You know where the door is. If you can't do this, you're free to leave now, no questions asked."

Holmes again looked from person to person, awaiting a response. An uneasy silence hung over the group as each one looked at the others.

Finally Reetha broke the silence. "I'm in this thing for the duration!"

Marty joined in, "Me too!"

Patrick looked Holmes in the eye, "Holmes, I never chose to be in this. I was drafted. But you can count on me to the end."

One by one, they all made their commitment.

Holmes motioned to Eliel, who took the floor. "Tonight," she began, "I want to introduce a powerful Irin prince."

Gesturing to the tall alien standing next to Araton, Eliel smiled. "This is Mendrion. He's come to assist us in something unusual. Because of the urgency of our situation, we need to abandon our normal procedure. We'd normally prefer to work with each of you individually, gradually energizing your life force as we train you to recognize and use your gifts. But time won't allow that. So Mendrion has consented to come.

"As I explained last week, in the wars of your distant

past, the Archons inflicted genetic damage on your entire race. Your life force--what the Greeks called your *pneuma*--was weakened, almost extinguished. When that happened, an important part of you died. You lost the use of many of your abilities, and your normal lifespan was drastically shortened.

"Mendrion has the unique ability to repair crucial elements of your DNA, undoing--at least in part--the damage that was done, and reawakening your life force. This is a highly invasive process and it's not done lightly. It means going into the shadow realm, and actually changing portions of your DNA sequence on a cell-by-cell basis. The time involved varies, depending on the severity of the damage present in your individual DNA.

"When the process is complete, you may or may not notice an immediate change; but gradually, sometimes at unexpected times, your gifts will begin to activate. Hopefully, we'll be close enough to assist you when that happens. If not, there can be some confusion when your new abilities begin to function.

"Because this process is so invasive,' she added, "the Ancient Ones won't allow us to do this without your express permission."

Eliel paused, looking from face to face, awaiting a response. There was a moment of uncomfortable silence as the members of the synaxis glanced at each other, uncertain what to think.

"Does it... *hurt?*" Reetha asked finally.

"You'll feel no pain," Eliel answered, "though there are often physical sensations. Sometimes strange things happen in your emotions, but that's only temporary. Some won't feel much at all."

Piper looked around at the others, then back to Eliel, "This all seems a little crazy," she said nervously, "but *somebody's* got to be the guinea pig… I guess it might as well be me."

Without saying a word, Eliel nodded to Mendrion, who walked over and stood before Piper. He studied her for a moment and she returned his gaze, smiling uneasily. Then he reached out his hand and gently touched her forehead.

Piper continued to watch him intently, uncertain what to expect. To her amazement, Mendrion silently faded from view.

Every eye was now fixed on Piper. At first it seemed nothing was happening.

Then, as if responding to inaudible instructions, Piper closed her eyes, leaned back in her chair, and allowed her body to relax. Her breathing deepened. She looked totally at peace.

Several minutes passed. Almost unnoticeably at first, a slight tremor appeared in her eyelids, as though the tiny muscles in her eyelids were rapidly twitching. The tremor grew in intensity. Piper's fingers began to quiver also. Then her whole body tensed and began to tremble. She was breathing deeply in ragged gasps.

Without warning, Piper broke into a childish giggle, which quickly gave way to uncontrolled laughter. Then, just as suddenly, she quieted.

The shaking gradually subsided. Piper sat motionless for several more minutes, breathing slowly, in and out. Finally, she took a deep breath and her body again relaxed. Thirty seconds later, her eyes blinked open and her face lit up.

"Oh, wow!" she laughed, smiling broadly and

glancing around at her anxious friends. As Mendrion reappeared beside her, she looked at him with a twinkle in her eye and said, "Mendrion, thank you. That was fantastic!"

Holmes was the first to speak, "Piper, what just happened?"

"I don't know how to describe it," Piper answered. "It wasn't like anything I've ever experienced. It felt like something penetrating through layer after layer of my personality… reaching down to the core of my being… and when it got there, there was an explosion of light."

"How do you feel now?" Eliel asked.

"At a loss for words," Piper smiled again, looking down at her body, then back up to Eliel. "I feel …lighter. It feels strange, but it's a good feeling."

Seeing Mendrion already glancing around for his next volunteer, Michael raised his index finger eagerly, "I'm next!"

One by one they took their turn. Each one had a different experience. Some wept. Some trembled and shook. Ron Lewis collapsed to the floor and lay, apparently unconscious, for about five minutes. But each one ended their experience reporting an overwhelming sense of wellbeing.

As they worked their way around the room, Michael noticed the darkness resting upon Erin appeared to increase. There was an unmistakable look of fear in her eyes. Then, as he watched her, he saw the faint outline of what appeared to be several dark, fuzzy, amoeba-like creatures attached to her body. They varied in size from three inches, to more than seven inches across. One of the creatures was attached to the left side of her face. Another was on her side. Still more were fastened to her arms and legs. From each of the creatures, dark tentacle-like limbs extended and wrapped around Erin's body.

He was about to go to Holmes and tell him what he was seeing, when Marty Shapiro let out what could only be described as a cowboy *whoop*. The whole group broke into laughter as Mendrion reappeared beside Marty, who had opened his eyes and was looking around, smiling sheepishly.

Mendrion then turned to Erin, who was next in line. But Erin looked down for a moment, then shook her head, and said simply, "I'm sorry… I'm not ready yet."

Piper leaned closer, "Erin, are you sure?"

"Look, I'm in this thing with you, but I'm just worn out. I don't want to have any new experiences just yet. You go ahead. I'll join in next time."

When the synaxis ended, Eliel drew Holmes and Piper aside.

"Things are developing much faster than we anticipated," she said. "I need to see what takes place this week, but by Friday our direction should be set.

"Piper, someone needs to stay with Erin at all times. Ask Lys to come and stay with you to help. Erin must not be left alone.

"Holmes, plan on meeting me Friday night at seven at the lake house. By that time I should be able to give you our plan of action."

# Chapter Eighteen: Angel Dance

THE LAKE HOUSE – THE PINEY WOODS
OF EAST TEXAS

Friday afternoon, Holmes left directly from the office for his 7:00 PM meeting with Eliel but the trip did not go smoothly. Heading south from Frisco, Dallas North Tollway was a virtual parking lot, with stop-and-go traffic creeping along at 10 MPH.

Swinging onto Loop 635--the broad, multilane highway encircling Dallas--Holmes breathed a sigh of relief, thinking the worst of the traffic was behind him. But in less than a half-mile, traffic came to a complete standstill. An eighteen-wheeler had overturned on the road ahead, blocking the interstate and backing up traffic for miles. It took almost an hour for crews to reopen the road.

Finally clearing the blockage, Holmes exited onto Interstate-30 east and mashed the accelerator. The Mercedes responded smoothly as he transitioned from gear to gear until he was cruising at 80 MPH. He was finally on the way to East Texas almost two hours after leaving the office.

As he drove, Derek thought about Eliel. He had been surprised to detect the note of fear in Eliel's voice when she described the horde of Archons at the Vanderberg ranch.

What had she said? *"If I'd tried to stand against them, I would have been destroyed."*

That was a new revelation for Holmes about the Irin. While the aliens don't naturally deteriorate and die as humans do, they *could* still be destroyed.

That meant the battle ahead was as real for Eliel as it was for him. Victory was not assured, and neither was survival. Holmes had asked the members of the synaxis to be prepared to lay down their lives. For the first time Holmes realized that Eliel had made the same commitment.

Exiting the interstate in the gathering dusk, Holmes noticed a shooting star streaking across the sky from the north. He glanced at his watch and frowned. It was almost seven o'clock. He was running late.

The night was clear, and traffic on Texas Highway 37 was light. As Holmes took the turnoff to Cedar Hills Lake, he lowered the windows and opened the moon roof, savoring the feel of the wind in his hair as he traced the winding road through the cool pine forest. Finally arriving at the lake house, he walked through the great room and out onto the deck. And there he saw Eliel.

She was dancing. But it was a dance no human had ever seen. Eliel was dancing in the air, out over the middle of the lake. Holmes stood transfixed by the sheer beauty of what he was witnessing.

As Holmes watched from the deck, Eliel skimmed horizontally across the lake, just feet above the surface, then rose into a graceful pirouette, twirling rapidly with arms extended, poised fifty feet above the water. Then she broke for the shore and flew along the edge of the lake, flying a high-speed slalom through the pine trees. Her whole body was glowing as she flashed smoothly in and out among the trees, not even rustling the branches as she sped through.

Next, she veered to the left and up, climbing without effort. She banked and flipped, and then flipped again.

Holmes had never seen anything more graceful. He couldn't help laughing out loud at the sheer joy of it. It was the joy of freedom. The joy of flight. The joy of life.

Angling her wings to catch the edge of the currents that constantly flow between the dimensions, Eliel began executing a series of graceful twirls and loops, each one rising higher, as she compassed a great circle around the lake.

Like some surreal figure skater, Eliel spun around and jumped from current to current, then swooped again toward the center of the lake and shot upward, all the while twirling in another pirouette. As she rose, she drew her arms and wings close to her body, and her spinning accelerated until all that was visible was a blur of white light. Finally, when she was almost out of sight, she broke her upward momentum and, extending her wings, made a long, triumphant spiral back down to the lake.

Holmes suddenly understood what Eliel was expressing in her dance. She was heading into battle and--perhaps for the first time in her long existence--faced the real possibility of death. But this was her protest against the powers of darkness. In the face of unthinkable destruction and death, her dance was an extravagant celebration of life.

Eliel whirled effortlessly, executing a graceful loop that flowed into a series of aerial somersaults, then swung into a smooth arc across the lake that brought her to a stop

directly over the deck.  Extending her wings horizontally,
Eliel allowed herself to descend, drifting to a stop mere
inches above the deck's surface.

Breathless, Eliel noticed Holmes and broke into a
broad smile.

He couldn't resist breaking into applause.  "Eliel, that
was beautiful!"

Holmes sensed a slight embarrassment that her dance
had been seen.  "I used to dance before the twenty-four
Ancient Ones in Hi-Ouranos," she ventured, trying to catch
her breath, "But that was before the Great Wars.  When the
Archons invaded, I volunteered to come here to defend your
world."  Then she added, "But I still enjoy dancing."

She drifted gently down to the deck surface and
folded her wings into the unseen plane.  She looked up at
him and smiled again.  "You're late," she said quietly.  It was
not a rebuke, just an observation.

Holmes opened a *Guinness* for Eliel, and an English
ale for himself.  They took seats opposite each other in the
great room.

Taking a sip of the *Guinness*, she began, "Holmes, our
worst fears have been confirmed.  The Archons have
amassed great numbers and are on the move.  We believe
they're preparing to take Iona, and if they do, our cause is
lost."

"Why is that?" Holmes asked, sipping his ale.

"Iona is crucial," She replied, looking at him with an
intensity he'd never seen in her.  "It's the only place on earth
we can open a lasting portal with our present level of
strength.  Our forces in your world are now greatly

outnumbered. If we can't open the Iona portal, I fear we'll all be destroyed.

"So we must make a drastic change in our strategy. You must make plans immediately for the entire synaxis to travel to Iona. The time for battle has come. Most of our forces are already there."

"But Eliel," Holmes protested, "you said our training would take months. We're not ready! Most of us have never even had a chance to use our gifts.

"*I'm* not ready!" He continued, "I don't even know what my gift is!"

"I understand that, Holmes, but our time has run out. I know you don't feel you're prepared, but we must go with what we have. It's our only chance. We must try to open the portal before the Archons seize Iona."

"But you *do* need to know your gift," she acknowledged, "and that's why I've asked you here tonight. Your gift is vital."

"What *is* my gift?"

"Your gift is to be what we call a *sent-one*. There's no word for it in your language. It means something like an envoy or ambassador, but much more.

"It's a gift you share with Piper. Piper's a healer, but she also has the gift of a sent-one, though her ability isn't yet as strong as yours. That's why we chose the two of you. It's unusual to find two together with such a high-level gift.

"To be a sent-one means you have the ability to act as an Irin, in some respects, at least. With regard to the synaxis, you'll be able to do what we do. You can activate the gifts of other members. You'll know how to set the group in order, even if an Irin is not present. It's a high calling, and a great responsibility. You may be called on to lay down your life for the others."

Eliel hesitated a moment, then continued, "And there's something else… a sent-one is a citizen of two realms. As your gifts develop, you and Piper will both develop the ability to move between worlds as I do. You'll live in the earth-realm, yet there will always be a part of you that feels more at home in *Basilea*. *Basilea* will always call to you.

"Mendrion has activated your life force. But before your gift can begin to operate, you must visit your other home."

Holmes was confused, his head swimming. "I don't think I understand." He protested.

"There's no need to understand, Holmes. Just come." She stood and extended her hand to him.

Still uncertain what was about to happen, Holmes followed her lead and stood also.

"Give me your hand," she beckoned. "It's okay."

He reached out and cautiously placed his hand in hers. Even though he'd interacted with the Irin for months, this was the first time he could recall actually touching one. He was surprised that her hand felt totally human. Her flesh was *real*. It was soft and warm, and living.

As she clasped his hand in hers, he was also surprised at her strength. "Since this is your first journey," she directed, "be careful not to let go of my hand."

He responded by holding her hand more firmly. Then he felt a tug on his hand. There was a sensation of movement, but not in a direction he could identify. Fighting vertigo, Holmes glanced around in confusion. They hadn't moved, but the room around them had somehow faded. It seemed like a ghostly outline of the room he knew.

"This is the shadow realm." Eliel said. "To the eyes of someone in your world, we just winked out of existence. We're now invisible."

Holmes noted that he could still see every detail of the great room, although the colors were severely muted.

"There's nothing material in the shadow realm," Eliel continued, "apart from the shades." She nodded in the direction of a dark, fuzzy amoeba-like creature that was slowly drifting toward them. Three tentacle-like arms extended in their direction, slowly undulating.

Reaching out her free hand, Eliel casually batted the thing away. Its tentacles immediately retracted and it drifted off in another direction.

Holmes felt another tug on his hand. They began to move. He realized for the first time that there was nothing solid under his feet. They hung suspended in mid-air. It was the sensation of floating in a crystal-clear pool of water.

"In the shadow realm the effect of gravity is greatly reduced," Eliel explained, sensing his surprise.

They drifted through the rear wall of the lake house and found themselves hovering several inches above the deck, gazing out across the lake.

"Time is greatly expanded in the shadow realm," Eliel added. "Virtually no time has passed in your world. This is all taking place in a fraction of a second.

"But that's enough of the shadow realm," she said with obvious enthusiasm. "Now let me show you *Basilea*!"

She grasped his hand more tightly. There was a firm tug, and again a sensation of movement, but greater this time. The vertigo was greater also. Holmes felt he was losing his balance and squeezed Eliel's hand more tightly. Powerful currents of energy surged around him, tugging at him, tossing him, stretching him in several directions at once.

The scene around them had vanished. In its place was a fog of nearly-blinding white light. Holmes closed his eyes against the brightness. There was a sensation of rapid acceleration, though again, not in a direction he could identify.

Finally the sense of movement ceased. He opened his eyes, and at first glance, it looked like he was still in Texas. The lake was still spread out before him, though it now extended much further to the west. The shore was still lined with trees and vegetation. The biggest difference was the sky. Though the sun had recently dipped below the horizon, the light of two large moons brilliantly illuminated the entire landscape. It felt like a late summer afternoon.

"Welcome to *Basilea*," Eliel said with delight. "the most beautiful of all realms!

"As a sent one, this is now your second home," she continued. "You'll one day learn to come here on your own. And Piper will come also when she's ready."

Holmes glanced down and gasped involuntarily, clenching Eliel's hand more tightly. The lake house, and with it the deck beneath them, had vanished. They were suspended in mid-air, twenty-five feet above the ground.

Sensing his alarm, Eliel looked up at him reassuringly. "Don't worry, Holmes. As long as you hold my hand you'll be fine. We're in my world's version of the shadow realm so the effect of gravity is almost non-existent."

Still clasping her hand firmly, Holmes scanned the horizon. Far to the north a line of majestic, snow-capped mountains rose to impossible heights.

In the south stood a city like no city he'd ever seen. It reminded him of the fanciful "cities of the future" drawn by artists in the nineteen-fifties. A myriad of incredibly tall, slender towers reflected rainbows of pastel colors. Between the beautiful towers Holmes could faintly see hosts of winged creatures flying from building to building. *No need for flying cars in this "city of the future,"* Holmes thought. *The inhabitants have wings.*

Remembering a comment Eliel made back in the lake house, he said, "You mentioned a place called Hi-Ouranos where the twenty-four Ancient Ones rule. Is that near here?"

"Hi-Ouranos is another dimension entirely," Eliel answered. "A higher dimension even than *Basilea*. It's the highest of all dimensions.

"But it isn't just another dimension, Holmes," she continued. "It's a realm beyond realms… a separate reality. You aren't yet able to go there yet. But one day you will."

They drifted slowly to the ground and experienced another shift--a sensation of movement without moving. The colors around him intensified. Holmes again felt solid earth beneath his feet. They'd left the shadow realm and were at last standing on the soil of *Basilea*.

"I *must* be dreaming…" Holmes said quietly to himself as he glanced around in wonder, trying to take it all in. "This can't be real!"

"I can assure you it's *very* real…" Eliel smiled. "It's my *home!*

"But come…" she added, "the others are waiting for us."

Beckoning for him to follow, Eliel led him along a path to the east--heading away from the lake, walking through the space occupied by the lake house in his world.

The parkland around them reminded Holmes of a carefully tended botanical garden. It was alive with colors and scents, almost overwhelming in its beauty. Flowering plants of all shapes and sizes had been arranged to perfectly complement each other, as though an artist had created a complex work of art using a living palette. A few of the plants were familiar to him, but others were like nothing he'd ever seen.

The path sloped gently uphill and entered the surrounding forest. It was cooler under the trees, and slightly humid, but still pleasant.

Beneath the forest's overarching canopy, the path wound through a lush carpet of multi-hued moss and lichen, punctuated by delicate fern-like vegetation. Splashes of light from the two large moons seemed to prance and skip, chasing each other among the trees.

Further into the forest, the path wound along the edge of a shaded pool. The pool was crystal clear and more than fifty feet across. And it was alive with fish... iridescent, multicolored creatures that flashed and darted among the rocks. At the far side of the pool Holmes noted a small horse pausing to drink.

Holmes caught a brief glimpse of the horse, then did a double-take. The horse was a classic palomino--the distinctive gold coat paired with a flowing white mane and tail--yet it stood less than sixteen inches tall at the shoulder. Seeing them approach, the tiny horse shook itself and unfurled beautiful golden wings. Like a miniature Pegasus, it broke into a gallop, spread its wings, and gracefully ascended into the forest canopy.

Each new experience in this world increased Holmes' sense of astonishment. Everything here seemed dreamlike, ethereal... almost too perfect. It was Utopia, Shangri-la, and Paradise rolled into one. He expected to wake up at any moment.

"Eliel," he said finally, trying to put words to his feelings, "this placed is unbelievable. My brain is on overload just trying to process it all. If I was a religious man, I'd say I'd died and gone to Heaven."

"You haven't died, Holmes," Eliel responded with a gentle smile as they walked side-by-side through the forest. "But in a sense, you *are* in Heaven... or at least one part of it."

Seeing the incredulity on his face, Eliel continued. "Stop and think where your concept of Heaven came from. We said in the synaxis that some members of your race have a gift to see beyond your own dimension. When your race wasn't trying to burn them at the stake, you've called these people prophets and mystics and seers.

"Over the centuries, your seers have had many visions of other worlds. Many of them saw with surprising clarity, yet not one of them had a framework to understand what they were seeing. They viewed scenes of astonishing beauty and unobtainable perfection--worlds untouched by the Archon revolt--and gave them names like *Heaven, Paradise, Valhalla, or Elysium.*

"Over time, your concept of heaven developed--an idea that now pervades almost every religion on your planet. While some of the accounts have been greatly embellished, what they saw was very real. They were viewing realities beyond your world. Many of their descriptions of Heaven, for example, can be identified with real locations here in *Basilea*. At other times, they described places in Hi-Ouranos, Ayden, Alani, or Taverea.

"As your legends developed," she continued, "your seers' descriptions of *Basilea*, Hi-Ouranos, and the rest, tended to meld together, becoming the various levels of the paradise you call Heaven. So in coming to Baseila, you *are*, in a very real sense, *in Heaven.*"

Holmes looked thoughtful.

"So here I am…" he mused, "Dr. Derek Holmes: Respected psychologist and confirmed agnostic… three-time president of the Texas Psychological Association, no less… And I'm walking around in *Heaven*, conversing with an *angel*… and preparing to do battle with the *demonic hosts* of darkness?"

"That's pretty much it, Holmes," she nodded, smiling.

Holmes shook his head in wonder. *There's no need to worry…* He laughed to himself. *The alarm's about to go off. I'll wake up any minute.*

Holmes was still trying to process this latest revelation when he caught a glimpse of one of *Basilea*'s large moons through a break in the trees. The moon was huge: at least four times the apparent size of earth's moon, and seemed to glow with a cool blue luminance. As the shining sphere captured his attention, Holmes was amazed to note that more than half its surface was covered with white clouds.

It took him a moment to recognize the significance of what he was seeing. Finally the reality struck… *That huge moon hanging close overhead is not a dry airless rock… it's a living world!* Between its clouds, he could just make out what appeared to be areas of green vegetation and the outlines of large bodies of water. *And could that lighter area near the river delta be a city?*

But the forest canopy closed in overhead, and the moon was lost to view.

Holmes felt numb. It was too much to process. He truly was in another universe, and the categories he'd learned on earth simply did not apply. He stopped trying to figure it out, and just enjoyed walking with Eliel along the cool forest path.

After a few more minutes, the path took a jog to the right and led them into a broad clearing.

Entering the clearing, Holmes saw a large pond fed by several crystal-clear streams. On the far side of the pond, a huge stone gazebo soared majestically above the surrounding landscape. Eight massive columns of gleaming white marble towered thirty feet into the air, where they were joined by marble arches intricately carved with flowers and pomegranates. Above the arches rose a solid dome of polished white marble. The splendor of the structure seemed to be a reflection of the skill and beauty of the beings that created it.

Eliel and Holmes followed the path across a small bridge and into the gazebo. As they entered, Holmes found a number of Irin waiting for them. He recognized Araton, Rand, and Khalil, but there were others he didn't know. One of the Irin was of a breed he hadn't yet encountered--an imposing figure almost nine feet tall. Unlike the Irin who frequented the human realm, the large Irin made no attempt to hide his wings.

Seeing him, Holmes leaned close to Eliel and whispered, "I hope he's on *our* side."

Eliel laughed, and introduced the giant as *Uriel*, who

smiled graciously and reached down to shake his hand. It was an awkward handshake. Holmes sensed Uriel didn't interact much with humans, but seeing how the others deferred to him it was obvious he was a person of some importance.

"In your tradition," Eliel explained, "Uriel was known as an *archangel*. He's one of the most powerful of all Irin. Only the twenty-four Ancient Ones have more authority. I've brought you here to meet him.

"Preparing a sent-one requires a higher level of power than most Irin possess," She explained. "That's why Uriel is here. He'll activate your gift, just as he did for Columba, and many others throughout your history."

As Holmes was introduced to the other Irin, it struck him that he'd always thought of the Irin as *aliens*. But he was now in *their* homeworld. In this world, they were the natives, and *he* was the 'alien being' from another dimension.

Eliel said something to Uriel in a language Holmes hadn't heard before.

Uriel came near and knelt down on one knee, looking at Holmes face-to-face. Their eyes met. "Eliel has explained your gift?" he asked.

"Yes… a little," Holmes answered tentatively, still uncertain what was about to happen.

"Good!" Uriel said. "Then let's begin…"

Without explanation, Uriel placed one huge hand on Holmes' chest, and another firmly on his back. Uriel's hands felt every bit as "real" as Eliel's, but much more powerful. Holmes felt his chest tightly clamped in the jaws of an iron vice, making it difficult to breathe.

Suddenly a surge of energy began to flow from Uriel's hands. It was hot and not entirely pleasant.

The heat poured into his chest and then outward to engulf his body, flowing even to his hands and feet. Holmes was getting lightheaded. If Uriel had not been holding his body firmly between his powerful hands, he would have collapsed to the ground.

The level of power continued to increase, and with it, Holmes' discomfort. The heat passed a threshold and became pain. His body was on fire. Holmes gasped, struggling to catch his breath. Every nerve in his body was screaming in protest.

*Something's not right.* Holmes thought in alarm. He'd never known the Irin to willingly inflict pain.

He struggled to pull away, but Uriel kept his massive hands firmly in place.

Holmes had never experienced anything like this. For the first time since meeting the Irin, he experienced raw terror. His body was trembling uncontrollably. He felt he'd been plunged into the heart of a nuclear reactor, at the mercy of forces that were ripping him apart.

Finally the sensation eased. Uriel withdrew his hands, and Holmes collapsed onto the polished marble floor of the gazebo.

Holmes lay there, dazed, for several minutes. He felt weak. Shaken. Unsure what had just happened.

He looked around warily. The Irin still surrounded him, but he sensed no malice in any of them.

"How do you feel?" Uriel asked.

"I'm not sure..." Holmes said, struggling to speak. "Better, I think... now that it's over."

Sensing his distress, Uriel explained, "We probably should have prepared you better for that. We sometimes forget that becoming a sent-one isn't always a pleasant experience… but there's no other way."

Holmes felt strength slowly seeping back into his body. "Thank you… *I think.*"

Uriel extended a huge hand to help him up.

Holmes hesitated at the thought of making physical contact with Uriel again, but finally accepted the help, and stood shakily to his feet.

His body was still trembling. His legs felt week. He looked in confusion at the Irin gathered around him.

"What just happened to me?" he asked.

"Your gift has just been activated," Uriel said. "You're now a sent-one, a citizen of two realms. Eliel tells me there's no time to teach you about your gift at the moment, but at the right time, it will begin to manifest. It may take years for the full expression of your gift to surface, but know that you are now a new kind of creature. A sent-one is human, but also more than human. You're not an Irin, yet you're now like us in many ways.

"In your own realm, you'll be--in some ways at least-- more powerful even than the Irin. Unless the Archons attack in force, the Ancient Ones won't allow us to enter openly into battle. We're limited in what we can do, but you are not. You can directly confront the powers of Hades. There's a saying among the Irin, 'Those with the gift of *sent-one* have an interesting life.'"

*"Interesting?"* Holmes laughed. "In my world, to wish someone an interesting life is sometimes considered a curse."

"It's not always an easy path," Uriel agreed. "But when you see the Archons driven from your world, you'll find it's worth all that it costs."

"When does this interesting experience begin?"

Uriel laughed again. "It's already begun," he said. "Look where you are!"

"When you return to the human-realm, don't expect to notice much difference at first. Just do what's before you and at the right time, your gift will manifest.

"You must now return to your own world," Uriel said, smiling, "but we *will* see you here again."

With that, the meeting in the stone gazebo was apparently over.

Holmes felt a little bewildered as the Irin gave a few parting words, spread their wings, and abruptly departed, leaving him alone with Eliel in the gazebo.

Eliel looked at him reassuringly. "Are you okay?"

"I'm feeling much better now, thanks," he replied, still shaken. "That just took me by surprise."

She reached out and gently grasped his hand again. "It's time to return to your world, but there's one more place I need to show you."

She clasped his hand firmly, and the scene before him winked out of sight, replaced by a fog of white light and more vertigo.

He felt he was falling now … a long fall through ever-darkening skies.

At last the sensation of movement ceased and the fog cleared. Holmes glanced around, trying to orient himself. They were floating several hundred feet above the ground, but this was neither Earth nor *Basilea.*

The place was unbearably hot, and in this reality there was no lake. A dry lakebed lay parched under an overcast sky that slowly pulsed with a dull, red light. The crumbling ruin of an ancient structure stood just to the East. From the heaps of rubble on the ground, it must have once stood as tall as the rainbow towers of *Basilea*, but no part of the ruin now rose more than three stories. It reminded Holmes of the World Trade Center following the terrorist attacks of Nine-Eleven.

No vegetation was visible anywhere. In all directions, a hot, barren wasteland extended to the horizon. Far to the west, a volcano was erupting. Clouds of yellow, sulfurous dust scudded across the southern plain.

Holmes could see no life on the ground, but leather-winged, pterodactyl-like creatures wheeled slowly high above.

"This is *Hades*," Eliel explained. "In this dimension, the entire planet is a burned out wasteland. For twenty thousand years, the Archons have lived in this barren world. For twenty thousand years, they've blamed the human race for their suffering. They'll stop at nothing to destroy you. That's why you *must* get to Iona."

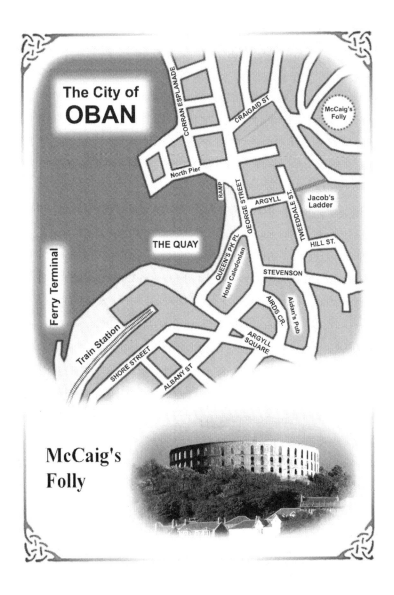

The City of
**OBAN**

CORRAN ESPLANADE

CRAIGAID ST

McCaig's Folly

North Pier

RAMP

GEORGE STREET

ARGYLL

TWEEDALE ST.

Jacob's Ladder

THE QUAY

QUEEN'S PK. PL.

Hotel Caledonian

HILL ST.

STEVENSON

Ferry Terminal

AIRDS CR.

Aidan's Pub

Train Station

SHORE STREET

ARGYLL SQUARE

ALBANY ST

McCaig's
Folly

PART FOUR: PORTAL

# Chapter Nineteen:  Haggis

## THE PORT OF OBAN, ARGYLE, SCOTLAND

Two weeks later, the entire synaxis flew from Dallas to Glasgow by way of London's Heathrow Airport. Deplaning at Glasgow, they collected their luggage and met at the rental car counter where Holmes had reserved two Mercedes C220 five-passenger sedans.  Since Patrick and Michael had the most experience driving UK fashion--on the "wrong" side of the road--they were unanimously selected to drive.

Heading north from Glasgow they drove along the "bonnie banks" of Loch Lomond, then followed the A82 highway on its long climb into the Scottish Highlands, driving through some of the most spectacular scenery on the planet.

The Highlands are often described by phrases like "majestic loneliness" and "wild grandeur."  It's a place where towering mountain peaks stand vigil over desolate moors, punctuated by scattered flocks of sheep and the ruins of ancient castles.  Every turn of the road brought new wonders into view.  Golden eagles soared above shimmering lochs, while shaggy highland cows roamed the glens.

At Crianlarich they turned west on the A85.

Following the shore of Loch Awe, they passed the magnificent ruins of Kilchurn Castle, former home of the Campbells, and finally descended into Oban, the gateway to the Western Isles.

The synaxis arrived in Oban on Tuesday evening, thoroughly exhausted, almost twenty-four hours after leaving Dallas. It was the height of tourist season, and Oban was thronged with visitors from all parts of the world.

Holmes had booked rooms for them at the Caledonian Hotel. The Caledonian is one of Oban's landmark buildings, located directly on the waterfront. Built in 1882, it proudly boasts that it was the first hotel in the Highlands with "a motorised lift and central heating." Almost every room offers breathtaking views of Oban Bay and the distant mountains of Mull.

After an hour in their rooms to freshen up, Holmes called everyone to the lobby to formulate their plan for the evening. Eliel had asked to meet with them at ten o'clock for a final briefing, leaving them just four hours to see the sights of Oban.

Ron, Reetha, and Marty elected a quick snack in the hotel bar, followed by a nap.

Michael and Patrick, however, were ready to explore. Their plan was to visit one of the city's famous pubs, and the remainder of the group enthusiastically chose to go along.

They exited the hotel, and walked north along the waterfront to the city's main shopping district. Crossing George Street, Michael pointed up at McCaig's Folly, the huge coliseum-like structure perched like a giant tiara on the cliff above the town, and related the history of the landmark to Holmes and Piper.

"You really should go up there some time," he said. "There's a public garden inside the hollow shell, and an observation platform offering one of the best views of the Western Isles. It's a steep climb to the top of the hill, but the view is worth it."

Michael and Patrick had compared notes on the pubs they'd sampled on earlier visits, and finally agreed on Aidan's.

Aidan's is a quintessential Scottish pub, situated in the centre of Oban on a short, curved street called Aird's Crescent, not far from the Hotel.

Entering the pub, the Americans immediately fell in love with its Celtic warmth and charm. The well-stocked bar was situated prominently in the center, with the taproom on one side and a cozy dining room on the other. The surrounding walls were awash with maritime prints honoring Oban's centuries-long seafaring heritage.

Though popular with tourists, Aidan's is primarily a local watering-hole, famous throughout the region for its friendly staff and menu of home-cooked highland faire. During soccer season, the place is often packed with loudly cheering fans, all crowded around the big-screen televisions. There was no game this night, however, so the locals had found other forms of entertainment. A group of younger Scotts were enjoying a game of darts near the back, while some older patrons shared a few pints over a cutthroat game of dominos.

As they took their seats, Michael passed out the menus. "This place will give you a good sampling of traditional Scottish food," he said.

"I seem to remember a line from a Mike Myers movie…" Lys interjected, "something like 'All traditional Scottish food is based on a dare'."

"That accusation is sometimes made," Michael smiled. "But most Scottish food is really quite good." Pointing to the menu, he added, "Take Scottish eggs, for example. Not something a vegetarian would choose, but quite delicious."

"What are Scottish eggs?" Piper asked.

"Scottish eggs," Michael explained, "are not like any eggs you've ever eaten. To make a Scottish egg, you take a hard-boiled egg and encase it in a thin layer of ground sausage meat, then roll it in breadcrumbs. The entire concoction is then deep fried until the outside layer is golden brown. It's usually served with hot German mustard along with a chilled spinach and bacon salad."

"That really does sound good," Lys agreed. "What are some other Scottish foods?"

"Well, the quintessential Scottish food is *haggis*," Michael answered with a mischievous smile. "And the Scots have discovered an amazing variety of ways to eat it. Sometimes it's battered and deep-fried and served with chips. It's even sliced and eaten in a bun as a 'haggis burger.'

"More traditionally it's served with 'neeps and tatties'-- that's mashed turnips and potatoes--and a 'dram' … a glass of Scotch whisky. You should try it."

"Be sure to ask what's in it before you order it," Patrick cautioned with a smile.

"I disagree, Patrick," Michael laughed, "It's really best to taste haggis the first time without knowing the ingredients. You tend to enjoy it more."

That, of course, brought an immediate demand from the women at the table that Michael reveal the ingredients of Haggis.

Finally surrendering, he explained, "To make haggis, they grind up a sheep's heart, liver and lungs, mince it with onion, oatmeal, and spices, then stuff it all into the sheep's stomach, and boil it for several hours. It has an excellent, nutty texture and is really quite delicious."

Seeing the expressions on the women's faces, Holmes couldn't help laughing out loud. Lys, in particular, looked like she was going to be sick. Screwing up her face, she said, "Now I know why they always serve it with whiskey. I think I would need to down a good many of those drams before I could force myself to put *that* in my mouth."

While only Michael ordered the haggis, they loved the Scottish food, and thoroughly enjoyed the atmosphere of Aidan's, talking and laughing long after the plates had been cleared away.

They left the pub a little after nine, crossed Aird's Crescent and turned north on George Street. Being the height of the tourist season, the sidewalks were crowded, even at nine at night. They walked slowly, enjoying the evening. The time at Aidan's had given them a chance to relax from the stress of the trip, and for a brief moment they were able to put out of their minds their reason for coming.

As the group continued down George Street, Erin suddenly grabbed Lys's arm and pulled her back into the shadows. Lys glimpsed the look of horror on her face.

"Erin, what is it?"

"Look, over there," Erin whispered, "in front of that pub… just across the street."

Turning to look, Lys saw four men just exiting a small pub. All four were dressed in blue jeans, western shirts, and cowboy boots, and definitely looked out of place in the Scottish Highlands. All four were drunk. They staggered along the sidewalk, loudly cursing, and roughly shoving each other and anyone else that got too close.

Lys had never seen the men before, but their presence made her blood run cold. "Who are they?"

Erin leaned close and, in a faltering voice, whispered, "The three shorter ones are the thugs that manhandled me at the ranch. The tall one leading the way is my *husband*, Rex Vanderberg."

Lys nudged Erin further into the shadow and tried to shelter Erin with her body, hoping the men would not look in their direction. Neither had any doubt that the men would kill Erin there on the street if they saw her.

But the four men continued to stagger down the sidewalk, shouting and cursing, oblivious to Erin's presence.

Grat turned and leered as two young girls in short skirts walked past, then glanced at Rex, "Hey, Rex... you think your *wife* will show up tomorrow?"

"Hell, Grat," came the reply, "I don't even give a damn! With the Irin gone, she's dead meat, no matter where she tries to hide. We'll get that traitorous bitch sooner or later, and next time we'll have some fun with her." They all laughed.

Grat started to turn in at the next pub, but Rex grabbed him by the shoulder and roughly swung him around. "That's enough for tonight, Grat," he barked. "Time to bed down. The Archons want us on board the ferry at seven in the morning."

As the men disappeared around the corner on Argyle Street, Lys enfolded Erin in her arms and held her close. Erin's body was trembling, and tears were streaming down her face. With one hand she still clenched Lys's arm in a vice-like grip.

None of the others had noticed the incident and had continued down the street, turning left on Queen's Park Place, heading back to the hotel.

Lys held Erin close for a few moments more, then gently tugged on her arm. "Come on, Erin, let's get back to the hotel."

Just before ten, they gathered on the open promenade next to the quay, just across the street from the hotel--an area once known as the Queen's Park. Oban Harbor lay quiet in the cool night air. The tourists were still laughing and talking in the busy pubs and restaurants along George Street, but here the darkened fishing boats gently bobbed in the swells while the lights of the north pier shimmered and danced across the water.

Lys and Piper stood close to Erin, who was still visibly shaken, while the others talked quietly, pondering this most recent development.

And then Eliel was there. No one had seen her coming. She was simply standing in their midst. The group quickly huddled around her while Piper described the evening's events.

"The Archons recognize the importance of the battle ahead," Eliel responded, "and have gathered many forces. We've now entered a desperate time.

"Individually, we Irin are much stronger than the Archons, but their numbers have overwhelmed us. Over the last few years, many portals have been opened between the earth and Hades, bringing hundreds of thousands of the Archons into this realm.

"There are many thousands of Irin waiting in *Basilea*, ready to come to our aid, but they can't come without a portal. Our only hope is to re-open the Iona portal, and only *you* can open it. You must get to Iona as soon as possible.

"A vast army of Archons now surrounds Iona," she continued. "All Irin have been called to the island to defend it until you get there, but we can't hold it for long. I must leave now to join them.

"Make every effort to get to Iona quickly. All of you. The enemy will have a plan to keep you away, so be on guard. Make use of your gifts, as much as you're able. I won't see you again until you get to Iona."

And with that, Eliel simply faded from view and was gone.

Holmes paused a moment, then looked around at the group. "We leave for Iona in the morning. Rest well tonight. If Rex and his thugs are taking the first ferry, we'll take the second. No need asking for trouble. The second ferry leaves at 9:50. Let's meet in the lobby at 8:45. We want to be on board by nine-fifteen."

# Chapter Twenty:  The Search

THE CITY OF OBAN, ARGYLE, SCOTLAND

On Wednesday morning, Holmes' cell phone rang at 8:15 AM.  It was Erin, and she was frantic.

"Dr. Holmes?"

"Yes, Erin, what is it?"

"I just went to Lys's room.  She's gone!"

"I wouldn't worry," Holmes answered, "She's probably just gone down to breakfast."

"No. I checked the dining room," Erin came back.  "In fact, I've looked all over the hotel and even outside on the promenade.  She's not here.  Anywhere. *She's gone!*"

"Where are you now?"  Holmes asked.

"I'm downstairs, in the lobby."

"Stay there.  I'll call the others.  We'll meet you there in five minutes."

Holmes hung up the phone and turned to Piper.  "Lys is gone."

"Are you sure?" Piper said.  "Erin's still not herself, you know, especially after last night."

"Even allowing for Erin's panic, it's not like Lys to leave and not tell anyone where she's gone."

Holmes quickly called the other members of the group and asked them meet in the lobby.  After a brief consultation, they split up and searched the hotel.

At Holmes insistence, the desk clerk sent someone to unlock Lys's room. Holmes and Piper searched her room thoroughly. There was no sign of violence or forced entry, and Lys's luggage, purse, wallet, cell phone, and even passport were still in the room. But Lys was nowhere to be seen, and there was no indication where she had gone.

Resisting panic, Holmes regathered the group. "It's almost nine o'clock. We have to be in line at the ferry by nine-twenty, at the latest." Holmes thought for a few seconds, then knew what he had to do.

"Patrick," he began, "It's imperative that you get to Iona. You're the only one with the authority to open the portal. Take one car and get on the ferry now.

"Reetha, Ron, and Marty, go with Patrick. Patrick knows the way across Mull. You can just make it if you leave now, so get your things and head out. I'll check you out of the hotel."

Patrick asked, "What about you?"

"Piper, Michael, Erin and I will stay here and search for Lys. We'll follow you as soon as we find her."

"What if you *don't* find her?"

Holmes shook his head. "If we haven't found Lys by this evening, we'll head to Mull on the last ferry of the day. We should get to Iona first thing tomorrow morning at the latest."

Patrick checked his watch, then turned to Reetha, Ron and Marty. "Let's meet at the car in five minutes. We need to move."

Patrick put his hand on Holmes' shoulder. "Godspeed, Holmes."

"See you on Iona, Patrick." Holmes answered.

Holmes found a shop with a color copier and made blown-up copies of Lys's driver's license photo. Then they split up two-by-two and covered the city. Piper went with Erin, who was barely functioning after her surprise sighting of Rex the night before. Together they worked their way down George Street and the Coran Esplanade, talking to every shopkeeper and pub owner, but no one remembered seeing Lys.

Holmes and Michael walked along the waterfront and through the industrial areas, talking to fishermen, mechanics and dock workers. But again, no one recalled seeing Lys.

They all met at the Waterfront Pub on the quay at noon for fish n' chips.

After placing their orders, they shared a quick update on the morning's fruitless search. No leads had turned up anywhere.

Piper ventured, "Do you think Lys might have gotten up early and taken the first ferry?"

Holmes shook his head. "Not Lys. She'd never have left without telling us."

Several more suggestions were considered and quickly discarded. In the end they realized none of them had a clue what could have happened to Lys.

When the food arrived, they ate in uneasy silence, each one pondering the mystery of Lys's disappearance, and what their next step should be.

As they finished eating, Michael looked across the table to Erin. "At our second meeting, when Eliel described our gifts, she said Erin's gift is the second sight… she can sense things before they happen. Erin, I know your gift isn't fully activated, but are you getting anything?"

"I have," Erin replied nervously. "I've been hearing a strange phrase all morning... something like 'Look for Ben,' or 'Watch for Ben.' *Do we know a Ben?"*

None of them recalled meeting anyone named Ben in Oban, but having no other leads, they split up again, revisiting every shop in the vicinity of the hotel. Again they came up empty. No one they met knew anyone named Ben.

Finally, in desperation, they checked out of the hotel and boarded the last ferry of the day. "I called and made reservations for the night at the Torosay Inn in Craignure," Holmes said as Michael guided the Mercedes down the ramp and onto the ferry. "The tourist guide said it's just across the road from the ferry terminal."

"Why are we staying in Craignure?" Piper objected, "Why not just head across Mull to Iona tonight?"

"We can't get to Iona tonight." Holmes explained, "I checked the ferry schedule. The last ferry to Iona will have already left before we get to Mull. Besides, we're all exhausted. It's better that we get some rest tonight, and head out at first light to cross Mull. We can still be on the first ferry to Iona in the morning."

As the MacBrayne ferry approached the Island of Mull, Erin Vanderberg stood silently with her companions on the observation deck, leaning against the cold steel rail.

The scene before her was almost surreal in its beauty. To the west, the sky was glowing brilliantly with the last light of day, while the first faint stars of night glimmered over the eastern horizon. Directly ahead, Mull's red granite mountains had already faded to near-black in the dying light.

Though the sky overhead was clear, a stiff offshore breeze had begun to blow. The *Isle of Mull's* deck shuddered continuously as its massive engine thrust the big ship through the rising seas. Erin drew her shawl more tightly around her body against the chill, watching numbly as the darkened island before her grew steadily larger.

But Erin wasn't really focused on her surroundings. In her mind she was revisiting the scene from the night before, experiencing again the horror of seeing Rex and his thugs on the streets of Oban.

Finally looking up from her reverie, Erin noted, far above the glistening lights of Craignure, a strange, dark cloud that seemed to be approaching from the north. *"What the..."* she muttered, but her barely spoken words were quenched by a sudden sense of foreboding.

Tapping Michael's arm, she pointed toward the cloud. "Michael, what do you make of that cloud?"

Michael dug a pair of binoculars from his backpack and scanned the sky. Through the binoculars, the cloud resolved into an army of winged Archon warriors heading in their direction. Thousands of them. Michael's mouth fell open. He shoved the binoculars into Holmes face, "Holmes, you better take a look at this..."

Holmes fumbled with the binoculars, then lifted them to his eyes and adjusted the focus. He studied the cloud in silence for a moment. "They're Archons... " he said uneasily, "And they're headed this way. I thought the Ancient Ones didn't allow them to attack us in force. That sure looks like force to me.

"Wait a minute..." He paused a moment, keeping the binoculars focused on the cloud. "Something new is happening... The leading ranks of the Archon army just went into a crash dive."

He traced the path of the cloud as the whole Archon horde began accelerating toward the earth. "That's one of the damndest things I've ever seen."

He glanced at Michael, then to Piper and Erin, still trying to process what he'd seen, "They were heading straight for us, but at the last minute they took a nose dive. They're diving right into the ground at high speed."

He handed the binoculars back to Michael, who watched in amazement as the vanguard of the Archon army entered the earth at the foot of a tall mountain. "That's Ben More." Michael remarked.

"Ben More?" Holmes asked.

"Yes… that's the name of the mountain." Michael explained, handing the binoculars back to Holmes. "It's the tallest mountain on Mull. The remains of an ancient volcano, actually."

Holmes watched until the last of the Archons disappeared into the ground. "I wonder what that's all about."

"I've a feeling we'll find out soon enough," Michael answered.

They found the Torosay Inn right where the tourist guide had promised. Michael practically drove down the ramp from the ferry into the inn's parking lot. Arriving at the inn, the four checked into their rooms, then met for dinner in the hotel pub.

The inn was originally an 18th century drovers' inn, part of a network of inns built for the benefit of men herding sheep across the island for shipment to Lismore and then on to mainland Scotland. In the early twentieth century, the inn's stables had been converted to a dining room, greatly enlarging the pub, which is now rated as one of the best in Scotland.

Though updated to twenty-first century standards, the pub still retained its historic character, including the stone walls, wooden floor and open fireplace.

As they took their seats, Holmes glanced at the members of the group and commented. "I have more bad news. I've been trying to call Patrick but could never get a connection. The innkeeper just told me all communications with Iona and western Mull went out early this afternoon. We can only hope Patrick made it safely to Iona."

The pub keeper came to the table, handing out menus and taking drink orders.

"I've eaten here several times," Michael commented, studying the menu. "The food is excellent, and home-cooked. Back in the 19th century, Robert Louis Stevenson stayed here, you know. The Torosay Inn was actually featured in one of his novels."

When the pub keeper returned to take their orders, Michael chose the beef steak and Highland ale pie, while Holmes ordered the chicken stuffed with Mull brie and leeks.

Piper closed the menu, looked up at the pub keeper and sighed, "After a day like today, just give me a great big vat of beer and a snorkel and I'll be happy." But she finally ordered the Tobermory salmon filet.

Erin ordered only a salad, and barely picked at that.

Erin had been unusually quiet all day. The darkness they'd seen over her in Dallas was now more pronounced.

When the group finished eating, Erin turned to Holmes in obvious distress.

"Holmes, I'm sorry…" she said haltingly. "I shouldn't have come.

"I thought I could do this. I truly wanted to. But when I saw Rex and his thugs last night, I knew…

"I was going to talk to Lys about it this morning," Erin continued, "but then she was gone. And then I was so focused on finding her that I just couldn't think…

"But I had time to think on the ferry… I can't go to Iona if Rex is there. I just can't." Glancing from Holmes to Piper in desperation, she added, "I have to go back."

Holmes was quiet for a moment. It felt like the synaxis was disintegrating around him.

Lys was gone, and now Erin.

Eliel had said a synaxis needed at least ten people. Now they were down to seven. Could they accomplish anything when they did arrive on Iona?

But they couldn't just abandon Erin.

"Okay, Erin," Holmes sighed. "I trust you know what you need to do. We'll make sure you get on the first ferry back to Oban in the morning."

After dinner, Holmes and Michael walked out into the cool night air. "Michael, you know the way across the island. Tomorrow morning, Piper and I will take the car and head off at first light. We need to get to Iona as quickly as possible to let Eliel know what's happened with Lys and Erin.

"The first ferry to Oban is due to leave at 8:45. Stay with Erin, and get her on the ferry. Then catch the next bus across Mull."

Holmes headed to his room, wondering what would await them in the morning. It had been a long day and an emotional roller-coaster. He felt shakier than he had expected. Even the ground under his feet seemed to be trembling.

Michael re-entered the pub and ordered a pint of *Guinness*.

Erin was sitting at the table weeping. Piper had given up trying to console her. She was just sitting with her.

Michael pulled up a chair. "Piper, let me talk to Erin for a while. You go on to bed. I'll make sure she's okay."

"Thanks, Michael," Piper sighed. "It's been a day."

Michael waited for Piper to leave, then leaned close to Erin and spoke quietly. "Erin, do you remember the night you told your story at the synaxis meeting?"

He waited a moment for a response, but Erin kept her face buried in her arm, weeping quietly. He continued, "Something happened that night, right after Mendrion activated my gift. I looked at you, and I saw something on you. It looked like a strange, black fuzzy amoeba attached to your skin, and it had long, lumpy tentacles extending out and wrapping around your body."

Erin raised her head and clumsily wiped the tears from her eyes, then tilted her head slightly to the side and gave him a perplexed look. "Michael, if you're trying to encourage me, this isn't cutting it."

"It's not encouragement, Erin. I believe it's a sort of diagnosis. Eliel talked about the creatures in the shadow realm, the shades. She said they attach to us when we're susceptible, and can play on our emotions.

"Eliel also said my gift was the ability to dispel shades. I think that's what I saw on you. There were several of them, and they appeared to be attached at the point of your bruises, as though the physical injury you suffered somehow gave them a place to attach."

Erin looked thoughtful. Tears were still trickling down her face, but she remembered how, at various points since her trauma at the ranch, inexplicable waves of emotion had crashed over her. She found she could swing from incapacitating depression through seething rage, and into mind-numbing fear, all within a few minutes. At times she felt she was losing her mind. Her emotions were totally out of control. It did sound like what Eliel had described.

"Michael, I hadn't thought about the shades. I was so focused on what I've been through, I hadn't made the association. If you have the gift to get these things off, I'm all for it.

"What do we do?" she asked.

"I haven't a clue, Erin. I've been pondering it ever since that night, but there hasn't been an opportunity to ask Eliel.

"I do recall that with both Reetha and Piper, some kind of physical contact activated the gift. May I place my hand on your shoulder?"

Erin looked Michael in the eye. If this was a pick-up line, it was the worst in history. But Michael had never struck her as the dirty-old-man type. In his eyes she saw only genuine concern. "Sure, go ahead."

Michael felt a little awkward putting his hands on Erin. He had always been shy around women, and Erin Vanderberg was the most stunningly beautiful women he had ever met.  Carefully moving aside her silken, chestnut-brown hair, he placed his hand softly on her shoulder with his fingertips extending onto her neck.

At first, nothing happened, but as he watched, a shadow seemed to fall across her face.  The shadow darkened and resolved into a large amoeba-like mass that now covered more than half her face.  It had grown since the last time he'd seen it.

The creature was covered in something like dark undulating fur, and from it extended three black tentacles.  Two entwined around her head, while the other coiled around her neck and down her back.

"I can see it, Erin.  It's on your face, but I'm not sure what to do."

"Michael, just do *something*.  I trust you not to get weird.  Get that thing off me!"

Keeping his left hand in place on her shoulder, Michael tentatively extended the index finger of his right hand, and touched at the center of the creature, expecting to be able to feel it as well as see it.  But his finger encountered nothing.  It passed right through the shade, until his finger was gently touching the soft flesh of Erin's face.

"Erin, I'm sorry… this seems quite strange."

Michael's finger traced the path of one of the dark tentacles around to the side of her head, thinking he could pull it free.  But again, there was nothing tangible to grasp.

"I don't know what I'm doing," he continued, "and this probably looks very strange."  Michael glanced around the pub, but all the other guests had gone back to their rooms, and he heard the clatter of the pub keeper washing dishes in the kitchen.

Michael remembered that when Piper placed her hands on Lys, some kind of energy was transferred to release healing.

"Let me try one more thing."

"Michael, just do it. It's okay." She said impatiently.

He placed the palm of his right hand gently across her face, completely covering the dark creature's body, and held it there. At first nothing happened, but then he seemed to feel a tingling, like a flow of energy, in his hand. *Was that just his imagination?*

Then there was movement. The tentacles began to slither from side to side, as though trying to obtain a firmer connection. The creature clearly did not like what was happening.

The creature continued to slither and squirm, but did not dislodge.

"Erin, what emotion are you feeling right now?"

"Fear," she replied, "dark unreasoning fear. Incapacitating fear." Her body was quivering as she spoke.

"My theory is that these creatures are somehow nourished by the emotions they induce." Michael explained. "Try to resist the fear."

"I'm not sure I can. It's overpowering."

"Yes, you can. Remember, that fear is not from you. It's not *real*. It's being placed in your mind by an outside force. Resist it. Stand against it. *Will it* to leave."

Erin closed her eyes, trying to find a way to stand against the engulfing current of fear that swirled around her. She repeated to herself, *This is not REAL. This is NOT REAL!*

Her mind filled with pictures from the ranch. The manacles in the storm cellar. The derelict crying for help as

Rex lifted the knife over his head. Then the pictures changed. She saw herself on the dais with Rex standing over her. Grat and Bryce were holding her arms. Rex was lifting the knife. It was beginning to descend.

*No! This is NOT REAL!* She said to herself again as she struggled to push the pictures out of her mind.

She remembered Eliel, risking her life to save her. She thought of Araton, waiting for her in the beat-up pickup truck. She remembered Holmes and Piper, rushing to her rescue in the middle of the night.

She wasn't alone. She had people and forces standing with her, defending her. She didn't have to give in to this.

"Erin, I don't know what you're doing, but it's working. My hand is burning hot, and the creature on your face is waving its tentacles around wildly. I think it's almost off."

"Now, Erin, tell it to leave. Command it to go."

Erin clenched her teeth. Every muscle in her body was tense and struggling… From deep within her rose something like a growl, and through clenched teeth came one word, barely audible, "Go!"

"Again, Erin."

Again, there seemed to be a titanic struggle within her, a fight to even speak the word. But again she said, *"Go!"*

There was a battle in her mind. Pictures of death and torture and destruction were struggling to hold their position, but scenes of life and hope and strong companions were pushing against them.

"One more time," Michael coaxed.

She leaned hard against his hand and every muscle

again tightened. The word rose from deep within her, and exploded out of her mouth, *"GO!"* And then her mouth opened in a scream that could be heard throughout the pub. She collapsed forward onto the table. But the creature was gone.

"Are you okay, lady?" The pub keeper stuck his head into the room. "Is that man bothering you?"

Erin lifted her head weakly and smiled.

"No, it's okay. I'm fine. It's just a game we're playing."

The pub keeper shook his head, and retreated into the kitchen.

"I really *am* fine," she muttered. "I feel lighter. The fear is gone."

"Now, let me check you over..." Michael said, "The one on your face was the largest one, but there had been others also."

Keeping one hand on her shoulder, Michael quickly looked over her body, feeling a little self-conscious about closely examining the body of a beautiful woman. He was greatly relieved to see that when the creature on her face had left, the others apparently had gone also. No other creatures were visible.

Just then, the glass on the table in front of him began to shake and clatter. The remains of the *Guinness* were sloshing from side to side in the bottom of the glass. The glasses on the shelves behind the bar were shaking also. One tumbled to the floor and smashed.

But before anyone could speak, the shaking stopped.

Both Michael and Erin were looking around in confusion, not certain what had just happened. When no further shaking occurred, they both took a deep breath. "Well, Erin, I believe we just had a small earthquake. I've never encountered one of those in this part of the world. Quite a rarity."

The pub keeper was already at work with a broom and dustpan, cursing under his breath as he cleaned up the broken glass.

"Can I get you anything to drink?" Michael asked.

"No," Erin answered, "I think I'm fine. I'm just very tired."

Michael walked Erin back to her room, and paused briefly at her door. She looked up at him, and for the first time in many days, Erin smiled. "Michael, thank you so much. I can't tell you how much better I feel. I think I can go to bed now and actually sleep."

"Do you still want to turn back... go back to Oban tomorrow?"

"I don't know," she said. "The unreasoning fear is gone, but Rex *is* still on Iona. I know the kind of man he is. If he ever catches me, I hate to think what he'd do." She shook her head. "I just don't know."

Unlocking the door, she turned back to Michael and without saying a word, gave him a quick peck on the cheek. Then she reached out and grasped his hand, just for a moment. "Thanks again." She smiled, and pulled the door closed behind her.

Erin was exhausted, but slept peacefully for the first time in weeks.

# Chapter Twenty-one:  Kidnapped

## THE PORT OF OBAN, ARGYLE, SCOTLAND

At 6:30 A.M. Wednesday morning, Lys Johnston was awakened by a sound outside her room on the third floor of Oban's historic Caledonian hotel.  Cautiously drawing aside the drapes, Lys peered out, blinking her steel-blue eyes against the light.  Dawn was breaking, and from the window she had a panoramic view of the Bay of Oban with the green island of Kerrera just offshore, and the distant mountains of Mull glowing red in the morning sun.

In the harbor, brightly painted fishing boats were already heading out for their day's work.  Further to the south, the massive ferry, the *Isle of Mull*, was alive with activity as crewmen prepared to take on vehicles for the first crossing of the day.

To the north, Lys caught a glimpse of the four men Erin had seen the night before.  They were walking south along the quay on Queens Park Place, heading for the ferry terminal parking area.  As they passed in front of her room, they paused to talk to a woman who was leaning against the concrete railing at the edge of the quay.  The woman was tall and slender with a pallid complexion and long, jet-black hair.  After an animated discussion, the four men continued toward the ferry terminal.  As they departed, the woman turned, looked directly at Lys, and smiled. There was no mistaking her. It was Kareina.

Lys quickly pulled on jeans and a tee-shirt, slipped on a pair of sandals, and ran down the stairs. Exiting the hotel, Lys looked around frantically. Kareina had already reached the corner of Queens Park Place and George Street and was walking north toward the Corran Esplanade.

*Damn!* Lys said under her breath, *I forgot to pick up my cell phone. I should let Holmes and Piper know where I'm going.* But there was no time to turn back. Sprinting to catch up, she reached the corner of George Street just in time to see Kareina turn right on Argyle Street. Lys ran to the corner of Argyle and peered down the street.

Kareina was much closer now. Lys slowed her pace. Moving away from the tourist area on George Street, they walked past rows of plain, three-story tenements. Lys followed as Kareina turned left on Tweeddale Street, passing an old Congregational church and more three-story tenements of grey granite.

Tweeddale was a narrow street jammed up against the base of the mountain. On the right, Lys passed a set of steep stairs known to the locals as *Jacob's Ladder*, leading up the hillside toward McCaig's Folly. Further ahead, the street dead-ended at the rear of the famed Oban Distillery.

Halfway down the street, Kareina turned into a narrow alleyway that passed between two shabby tenements. Peeking around the corner, Lys caught a glimpse of Kareina slipping through the door of a small carriage house at the rear of the tenements.

Lys cautiously approached.

The carriage house had been plain and utilitarian in its

day, and that day was long gone. Its grey slate roof sagged like a sway-backed horse, while its broken windows and crumbling walls confirmed that it had gone unused for many years.

The left-hand panel of the door had been left slightly ajar when Kareina entered. Lys walked quickly to the door and peered through the crack, but could see nothing in the darkness within. She waited a minute, listening, but no sound emerged from the dilapidated structure.

Logic told her that she should turn back, but Lys didn't want to let Kareina get away again.

Easing the door open a few more inches, Lys stepped inside. Pausing while her eyes adjusted to the darkness, she looked around, but could see no one. The building smelled of mold and decay. The bare rafters over the coach area were rotten and badly bowed, and the hay loft over the horse stalls in the back had collapsed many years earlier.

There was no sign of Kareina.

Lys noticed another door at the rear of the structure and was cautiously making her way across the liter-strewn floor when she was startled by the sound of the door slamming shut behind her. She whirled around and found herself face-to-face with Kareina.

Kareina studied her in silence, with lips drawn into a sneer and eyes burning with hatred, then took two steps in her direction.

"So we meet again... my good friend *Lys*." Kareina smirked, then slapped Lys hard across the face.

Recoiling from the blow, Lys felt two sets of hands grab her arms from behind. Turning her head, she found herself looking into the leering eyes of the men from the BMW.

"Let me introduce my subordinates, Botis and Turell," Kareina said. "I know you've seen them before, but you've never been properly introduced."

Lys struggled frantically against their grip, but they held her arms firmly.

Kareina stood back and eyed Lys for a moment, while Lys continued her futile battle to break free.

"You've grown stronger since I saw you last," Kareina finally observed. "When our last attempt to kill you failed, I had hoped to possess you and use you for our purposes, but I see you're beyond that now. What a pity. It would have been interesting to possess a *singer*."

Looking to Botis, Kareina said simply, *"Bind her!"*

Lys was stunned by the superhuman strength Botis and Turell both possessed. Ignoring all her struggles, the two calmly forced her hands behind her back and bound them securely with duct tape. Almost immediately, they stuffed a foul-smelling rag deep into her mouth, wrapping a strip of duct tape around her head several times to hold it in place.

As Lys fought to keep from gagging, they roughly threw her body to the floor and bound her legs as well.

When they finished, Kareina spoke again. "On our first attempt to kill you I spent three long weeks setting up the scenario. It was such an amusing game. You tried so hard to be a good friend to poor, lonely Kareina." Grinning sadistically, she continued, "It's too bad your Irin friend, Araton, spoiled everything by cushioning your impact when the Corolla went off the cliff.

"But I wouldn't count on help from your Irin friends this time," she added, "They're all fully occupied now … on Iona."

Lys looked on in horror as Kareina withdrew a small hypodermic from a pouch and filled it with yellowish liquid from a vial. Plunging the needle into her thigh, Kareina smiled, "This should keep you quiet 'till we're ready to move you."

Lys felt an unpleasant warmth spreading through her body. The carriage house began to swim around her. She caught a glimpse of Botis standing over her, darkened eyes glaring. His lips went taut and he bared his teeth in a demonic grin. Then only darkness.

There was a sensation of motion. Lys opened her eyes and began to struggle back to consciousness. The rag and duct tape had been removed. It was dark, and she was being carried through the crowded streets of Oban. People looked at her as they passed. Some were laughing. She tried to resist, to cry out, but her body refused to cooperate.

Her vision began to clear, and with it came awareness of her situation. Botis and Turell were walking on either side, with her arms draped over their shoulders. Although smiling and laughing, they each held one of her wrists in an iron grip. They'd liberally sloshed a bottle of scotch down the front of her shirt, giving the impression to passersby that they were helping a drunk friend back to her hotel.

They crossed George Street and started down the concrete ramp at the north end of the promenade. By the lights on the promenade above, Lys glimpsed Kareina waiting in darkness at the bottom of the ramp, standing beside one of the tiny fishing boats that crowd the quay.

With no power to resist, Lys was dumped roughly into the back of the boat, face-down on the weathered deck.

Botis and Turell climbed in after her. The pungent aroma of rotting fish made her gag.

Standing on the ramp, Kareina watched as Botis crudely bound her hands behind her back with a length of rope. "Take her out to the middle of the Firth of Lorne," Kareina ordered, "... well away from the town, and drop her overboard. Make sure the anchor line is secure around her when you do. I want no mistakes this time."

Kareina shoved the boat away from the ramp and Lys felt the engine rumble to life. The tiny craft swayed for a moment, rocking from side to side, then began moving across the harbor.

The ride out to the Firth of Lorne was long. A stiff offshore breeze had sprung up, and once outside shelter of Oban harbor, the seas were rough. Lys was still battling the effects of the drug. She passed in and out of consciousness several times. Once she vomited.

But the cool night air was gradually reviving her. She tried to formulate a plan of escape. Gaining strength, Lys struggled with the rope binding her hands. Botis hadn't anticipated much resistance from her, and the bindings were not tight. She quickly loosened them enough that she could slip her hands out when the time came.

*Now, if they would only attach the anchor line that loosely.*

She knew there was no hope of escaping her captors in the boat. Her only opportunity would come after she was in the water. If she could free herself from the anchor line and somehow swim to shore...

Lys decided her best strategy was to feign unconsciousness.

After plowing through the rough seas for almost an hour, the boat finally came to a stop. Leaving the engine idling, Botis and Turell came back to Lys and quickly wrapped the anchor line around her limp form. They looped the line around itself several times and pulled it into a knot, then lifted her up and calmly tossed her into the churning water.

As they hoisted her body from the deck, Lys began to hyperventilate--breathing rapidly in and out--trying frantically to build up the oxygen supply in her bloodstream. Then, as they released her, she took one more deep breath and hit the water.

It was *cold!* Much colder than she'd anticipated. Thousands of pins and needles were jabbing at her, all over her body. Then she felt the anchor line tighten around her with a jerk, and begin pulling her down. She knew she had mere seconds to free herself.

Slipping her hands from the rope bindings, she began to fumble frantically with the anchor line, but the weight of the anchor had pulled it tight and her fingers were already growing numb.

She fought the rising panic. *I must stay in control. I must think clearly. Now... where is the end of this line?*

She felt along the coil of rope that was tightly wrapped around her waist. One end was taut, leading downward to the anchor, pulling her steadily into the depths, but the other end hung free. She grasped the loose end with numb fingers and traced it back to the knot. Then she began to pick at the knot to loosen it.

Her chest was burning. Her body demanded to exhale, to take a breath...

She continued to fumble with the line in total darkness... working to pull the loose end out of the knot. She sensed the line loosening, sliding further down her body. And then the line slipped free. It was gone! The weight of the anchor pulled the remaining line from around her torso as it plummeted into the depths of the Firth.

Lys sensed she was rising, but there was no light above... only darkness in every direction. She was disoriented. *Which way is up?* She could only wait for the buoyancy of her body to bring her to the surface.

Her lungs were screaming to exhale, but she forced herself to resist. The air in her lungs was the very thing pulling her upward. She didn't dare release it.

And at last, she was *there!*

Breaking through the surface, Lys exhaled explosively, then gasped--her chest heaving--drinking in huge gulps of the crisp night air. She'd never realized what a luxury it could be just to *breathe.*

As she began to catch her breath, Lys glanced around in the darkness.

Her plan had worked so far... she was free... but which direction to go now? She knew she wouldn't last long in the frigid water. Her teeth were already chattering and her body shuddered in the cold.

The boat was nowhere in sight, but she didn't dare scream for help. Not yet. Not 'till she was certain Botis and Turell were gone.

She bobbed up and down in the churning sea, trying to catch a glimpse of shore.

The stars overhead gave her a rough sense of direction. To the northeast she saw a lighthouse, but it was much too far away. There were faint lights along a distant shore to the west, but she couldn't tell how far. She set out toward the lights, knowing her chances weren't good.

It was difficult swimming through the heaving water. Wind-blown swells surged under her, propelling her skyward, only to smash her down, thrashing her body violently.

Lys was growing disoriented. Every muscle ached, but the waves kept coming.

She tried diving under the swells. *That's better.*

Lys established a ragged rhythm: popping to the surface to gulp air, swimming one or two strokes, then diving again before the next wave struck.

Her heart was pounding, but she continued to thrust herself through the icy water, stroke after stroke. Willing herself to survive.

Finally she paused to catch her breath, treading water. Fear was gnawing at her. The glowing beam of the distant lighthouse swept by overhead, continuing its endless rotation, but the lights on shore seemed no closer.

Lys screamed for help and waited for a reply, but none came. Taking a deep breath, she called out again. Nothing.

Fatigue was setting in. She could no longer feel her fingers.

She commanded herself to swim … kicking numb legs through icy waters. Her pattern repeating with endless monotony… two strokes, then dive, then a breath… two strokes…

Her arms were burning. Her muscles quivered with exhaustion.

And then she was sinking. Her arms and legs had stopped moving. Her body demanded rest.

*Get a grip, Lys!*

She struggled clumsily to the surface and gasped for air. Her body was sluggish.

*Got to keep moving, Lys. One more time…*

Focusing on the distant lights Lys forced herself to swim, but she realized now she'd never make it. It was simply too far. A few more strokes left her exhausted and gasping. She knew she didn't have the strength to keep going.

In desperation, Lys shouted for help again, but there was still no answer. She cried out one last time, then the surging waters engulfed her and she sank.

It was cold and dark beneath the surface, yet somehow welcoming. It felt good to stop struggling.

Her body was numb. She no longer felt the pain or the cold. *Is this how it ends?*

There was no way to go further. No way to survive. She was far from shore with no one to help, and her strength was gone.

In utter hopelessness, she relaxed and awaited death's icy embrace.

But as she felt her body slipping silently into the depths of the Firth, Lys remembered something Eliel had said. It was just one brief phrase, but it exploded within her, releasing a faint surge of hope.

*There IS a way to get there.* She told herself. *There has to be!*

Laying hold of Eliel's words; Lys reached into the deepest recesses of her being, searching for some hidden pocket of strength, then steeled herself to make one last desperate drive for the surface.

# Chapter Twenty-two:  Ben

## THE ISLAND OF MULL, ARGYLE, SCOTLAND

At first Holmes didn't know what awakened him.  He lay still for a moment.  Then he heard it.  It was a sound.  A deep throbbing roar like the rumble of distant thunder.  But it did not dissipate.  It increased steadily, like the lumbering growl of an approaching locomotive, building in intensity until it seemed to reverberate in his body.  Even his bones seemed to be shaking.

And then the room around him joined in.  The glasses on the bathroom counter began to clatter.  The pictures on the wall, the lamp beside the bed, all joined in the rising cacophony.

"What the…" Holmes mumbled as he and Piper both sprang from the bed, pulled on robes, and headed out the door.  The sound was louder outside.  The ground beneath their feet was shaking.

It was a clear, crisp morning.  The sun had not yet risen, but the light of the approaching dawn had already spread across the sky, illuminating the distant red peak of Ben More.

In the ancient past Ben More had been the largest volcano in northern Europe, a beautiful, snow-capped peak, ten-thousand feet in elevation.   But before the dawn of human history a massive explosion had blown away most of the mountain, leaving only a three thousand foot remnant. The titanic force of that explosion had collapsed Ben More's subterranean passages, cutting it off from its magma source and rendering it virtually extinct.

But as Holmes and Piper slept, an army of Archon warriors had unsealed the ancient lava tubes and reopened the long-closed channels, releasing once again the massive power of the earth's core. By morning, Ben More, the last active volcano in northern Europe, had ended its long dormancy.

The mountain now thundered angrily as a river of magma, churning with explosive gases, surged from the planet's depths.

"Watch for Ben," Holmes muttered.

"What?" asked Piper.

"Erin's word yesterday... That's what her gift was telling her. 'Watch for Ben.' Ben isn't a person, it's a mountain.

"That's the Archon strategy. They're trying to cut off access to Iona by rekindling the fires of Ben More."

The rumble of the volcano increased in volume.

Suddenly there was an explosion. They saw it before they heard it... a huge ash cloud silently blossomed near Ben More's peak and rose hundreds of feet above the summit. Moments later, the shock wave arrived: a violent, shuddering roar impacted their ears and shook the ground beneath them. A volcanic vent had opened.

By now, Erin and Michael had joined them in front of the inn. Every eye was focused on the mountain.

"That's what the Archons were doing," Michael said to Erin. "They were re-activating the volcano."

"But that's impossible," Erin objected. "A volcano can't form that quickly."

"You'd be surprised how quickly dormant volcanoes can awaken." Michael answered, "In 1975, a 1000-foot-high volcano was born in six weeks on the Kamchatka Peninsula of Russia. Then in 1989 the Redoubt Volcano in Alaska erupted after only 24 hours of activity. And that was without the help of Archons."

As they watched, the smoking peak shuddered from a new round of explosions. More tremors shook the ground and the smoke became darker.

A thick column of ash and smoke belched skyward. Growing rapidly, it rose twelve thousand feet into the air and spread out laterally in the atmosphere. From the base of the cloud, a dark curtain of falling ash trailed earthward. Like thick gray snow, cinders and ash began to rain down on Mull.

Seeing the power of the eruption, Erin's mouth fell open. She quietly spoke one word: *"Pele!"*

"We need to get moving," Holmes said, shouting over the roar of the volcano. "Piper and I will head across to Iona. We need to let Eliel know what's happened. If we leave right now I think we can make it across before conditions deteriorate too badly.

"Michael, I'll leave you in charge here. Have the innkeeper contact the local constable. They need to gather everyone from this end of the island to the ferry terminal. The *Isle of Mull* lands in one hour. Make sure they get everyone on board. This end of Mull must be evacuated."

As Holmes and Piper headed back to their room to make preparations to leave, Michael pounded on the innkeeper's door.

After a minute's hesitation, the old man opened the door a crack and peered out. It was obvious he'd slept through everything.

"Call the constable. Ben More is erupting!" Michael shouted.

"Impossible!" the old man wheezed. "That mountain's been dormant for millions of years."

"Come out here and look for yourself," Michael shouted, pointing to the sky. "Does *that* look dormant?" The old innkeeper took a step out the door, then stopped in disbelief, staring at the mountain above them.

Thick black smoke was continuing to billow into a darkening sky. More vents were opening. Broad sheets of flame lit up many parts of the mountain. One vent hissed out blue flame, like a gigantic Bunsen burner.

"The *Isle of Mull* is due here in less than an hour." Michael continued, "We must get everyone in town ready to board the ferry when it arrives... and don't let anyone get off. You must clear this end of the island immediately."

Even before the constable arrived, people were gathering at the ferry terminal from all over the eastern end of Mull.

Michael and Erin rejoined Holmes and Piper as they loaded their bags into the Mercedes. Large flakes of gray ash were falling around them like snow.

When everything was loaded, Holmes turned to Michael. "Stay with Erin," he said. "Make sure she gets on the ferry to Oban. I don't know what conditions will be like by that time. If you see a way to get across to Iona, join us... otherwise, take the ferry with Erin. It's not going to be safe on this end of the island."

Michael and Erin watched as Holmes and Piper pulled out onto the road to begin the long journey across Mull.

From its newly opened crater, Ben More belched incandescent fragments of rock hundreds of feet into the air, spreading a constellation of sparks, hot ash, and cinders that swirled against the darkened sky. The sound had now dissipated to a low, growling rumble.

"Nothing to do now but wait," Michael said, "and hope Holmes and Piper make it across to Iona. The *Isle of Mull* should be here in forty-five minutes."

"Michael, thank you again for last night," Erin said, leaning close to be heard over the volcano's roar. "I'm feeling much better today, but I know I'm not settled yet. I'm going to go down to the shore for a few minutes and try to clear my head. I'll be back before the ferry leaves."

Michael stood and watched the volcano, transfixed by its fierce beauty. He was amazed at the variety of sounds it produced. His ears were assaulted by a cacophony of bellows and growls, punctuated by a high-pitched whooshing and hissing. From time to time there was even a chugging sound, like a steam locomotive. Behind it all was a continuous background roar like distant cannons.

Michael began to notice a pattern in the mountain's activity. Ben More was breathing. Each breath began with a slight trembling in the ground--then came the rumbling, a deep echoing roar of escaping gasses. The roar increased in pitch, becoming a raucous scream, and finally softening to a subdued moan, only to begin again a few moments later.

The crowd gathering at the ferry terminal continued to build. Many were covering their faces with wet towels to protect against the volcanic ash.

BEN

Although the sun had risen, the sky was totally dark. Ash continued to fall, and earthquakes were coming more frequently.

A cheer went up from the crowd as the ferry finally came into view.

The constable had been in contact with *Calmac* by radio to work out a plan of action. The eruption had not yet begun when the *Isle of Mull* left Oban, and at the height of tourist season, the ship carried a full complement of passengers and vehicles.

Before the ferry pulled up to the dock, the captain got on the ship's speaker system. "Attention all passengers," his voice rasped, "This is your captain speaking. A state of emergency has been declared on the Island of Mull. The eastern end of the island is being evacuated. We will stop to pick up evacuees, and then return to Oban. But we *must* clear the auto deck. If you have a vehicle on board, you must exit the ferry. We'll need every inch of space on the auto deck for the evacuees. I repeat. Every car *must* be unloaded. A local constable will show you where to park. Please leave your keys in the car in case it needs to be moved, and then reboard the ferry immediately. We must be underway in thirty minutes."

The constable had deputized several of the locals to help him direct traffic to the parking area. As each car was parked, the deputies herded the occupants back to the ferry.

The crowd at the ferry terminal was still growing. It was amazing how many people were on the small island. Counting tourists, the crowd now numbered well over eight hundred, and was still increasing. All were dragging suitcases and personal belongings.

One of the last cars off was a gleaming-white Hummer H2. The driver was furious. Standing beside the Hummer's open door, he waved his arms belligerently as he argued with the constable. "Just go off and leave it here? You're out of your freakin' mind! I just bought this last week--paid sixty thousand pounds for it--no bloody way I'm leaving it here!"

Just then, there was another titanic explosion on the mountain. The roar of Ben More increased as another plume of fire and smoke belched into the sky. Red-hot, basketball-size globs of ejected lava began crashing to the ground all around them.

The crowds waiting beside the terminal screamed in terror as they rushed forward, jamming the ramp to the auto deck.

Without another word, the driver of the Hummer grabbed a few personal belongings, slammed the door, and ran to join the crowd pressing their way onto the ferry.

Fresh tremors shook the island. The whole island now seemed to be shaking.

Then, just as the boarding was completed, the mountain fell silent. The rumbling ceased. A heavy cloak of silence fell across the entire island. All eyes turned to the volcano.

Michael looked around. *Was it over?* For a full minute, there was complete silence.

Then the explosion came. Ben More literally blew itself apart. There was no warning. The pressure of the ash-filled steam and gas ripped open the southern flank of the volcano, blasting out horizontally from the mountain at up to 500 miles per hour. A massive surge of superheated ash, magma, and rocks, known to geologists as a pyroclastic flow, plowed across the island, reaching sixty stories high and spreading eight miles wide as it poured down valleys and over ridges.

Fortunately, Craignure was not in the path of the blast, or few of those present would have survived. The blast swept across the southern end of the island, knocking down anything in its path. The superheated gas, hotter than 900 degrees Fahrenheit, instantly carbonized all structures and vegetation.

As Michael watched in horror, the ferry horn gave its final blast.

The *Isle of Mull* was about to leave. *Where was Erin? She should be here.*

He looked around frantically for her. The ash on the ground was already several inches deep and increasing rapidly now. Visibility was decreasing. Michael held a handkerchief across his face and headed toward the shore to find Erin.

\*\*\*

As Holmes and Piper made their way across the southern end of Mull, the ash on the ground was already six inches deep. Progress was slow. The darkened sky, combined with the blizzard of falling ash, made it hard to see the road. Several times the Mercedes lost traction, spinning its wheels in the ash.

They hadn't gone far when the side of the mountain opened up, sending the surge of hot gases and rock pouring down the volcano's flank.

Holmes and Piper heard nothing as the pyroclastic flow approached. The surge was so dense with sand and ash it literally absorbed all sound. Without warning, the storm of churning darkness was upon them.

Fortunately, the Mercedes was in the lee of a steep hill when it hit. The main force of the surge passed hundreds of feet above them, but they didn't escape its destructive power entirely. The flow's trailing edge rushed downslope at close to 200 MPH, catching up the Mercedes in a roiling cloud of superheated ash.

As Holmes gripped the wheel in helpless terror, the Mercedes shuddered violently, skidded sideways, then was picked up and literally blown off the road. Flipping twice, it landed right-side up in a ditch, snapping the left front axle. As a blast of intense heat charred the paint, fine ash clogged the air filter, killing the engine.

And then the surge was gone.

For a long moment Holmes and Piper sat in stunned silence.

"Are you okay?" Holmes asked when he finally caught his breath.

"Yes! Thank God for seat belts," Piper responded, still trembling. "And you?"

"A little sore, but I'm okay," Holmes replied, wincing as he gingerly massaged his right shoulder.

The air around them slowly cleared. The two stared in unbelief at the ruined landscape around them.

In the shuddering air and disorienting noise, the world they knew had vanished, replaced by a barren lunar wasteland. Nothing that had been visible a moment earlier was still there. No road. No streams. No vegetation of any kind. Instead, they now surveyed a cindered plain swirling with sulfur and ash. Holmes felt like the blast had picked them up and deposited them on a different planet.

"What *was* that?" Piper asked.

"I'm not sure," Holmes replied. "But I think Ben More just exploded. I hope Michael and Erin made it safely off the Island."

"What do we do now?" she said, still trying to comprehend the devastation around them.

"We wait here 'till someone finds us. It may take a while. With Ben More erupting, it could be days before a rescue party comes. The Archons did a very effective job cutting Iona off from the rest of the world."

"You don't think we should go for help?"

"I doubt there's another living thing on this end of the island," he sighed hopelessly. "And the ash out there looks almost knee-deep now. We wouldn't get far walking."

Piper leaned close to Holmes. He put his arm around her, and for a long time they sat in silence, thankful to be alive, yet wondering what would come next.

The blast had uncorked Ben More and opened a massive vent where, for the next five hours, a half-mile-wide river of ash and magma spewed skyward. Residents of Oban, many miles to the east, reported ash and pebbles raining down on the city.

Falling ash continued to build up around the Mercedes. From time to time, small cinders clattered on the roof like hailstones. In the darkness around them, lit only by the faint red glow of the volcano, Holmes and Piper lost all sense of time. The air in the car was getting stale, and the sulfur fumes made it difficult to breathe.

"Ginny?" Holmes finally asked.

"What is it?"

"When we get out of this, what do you say we get married?"

Piper laughed. "Holmes, you are *such* a romantic!"

"What do you mean?"

"Some men choose a quiet candlelight dinner to propose. Some pick a moonlit night at the beach. You pick an erupting volcano surrounded by armies of flying demons."

"But will you marry me?"

"Holmes," she smiled broadly, "you know I would marry you, any time, any place."

"Then your answer is *yes?*"

"Absolutely!"

"Good," Holmes replied. "Now we just need to get out of here."

The constant roar of the volcano was deafening, but a new sound now blended in. It sounded like a car horn blasting repeatedly

Peering out the ash-streaked windows, Holmes stared incredulously as headlights appeared through the falling ash behind them.

# Chapter Twenty-three:  Lys's Story

## THE ISLAND OF MULL, ARGYLE, SCOTLAND

Michael trudged through ankle deep ash, heading down toward the water's edge, calling Erin's name.  His heart sank as he saw, in the distance, the *Isle of Mull* pulling away from the dock.  He was too late.  They'd missed the ferry.  They were stranded on Mull.

Then someone was calling *his* name… it was Erin.  She was running toward him through the blizzard of falling ash, and someone was with her.

*Lys!*

Michael stopped, and his mouth fell open at the sight of Lys.  Then he ran forward and embraced them both.

"Lys, how… how did you get here?" he stammered.

"I'll explain that later." Lys shouted, returning Michael's hug and laughing out loud in her joy at seeing him again.  "First we need to figure out how to get out of here."

"We've missed the ferry," he shouted, "There's no way to get back to Oban."

"I don't want to go to Oban," Erin cut in, "I *must* get to Iona."

"We can't get to Iona either." Michael answered, his voice barely audible over the roar of Ben More, "The southern end of Mull was just hit by a pyroclastic flow. Iona is cut off from the world."

"But there's got to be a way," Lys objected. "I have to get to Iona. I have to open the portal."

Michael just shook his head.

They walked back toward the deserted inn. The town of Craignure was dark and empty. The abandoned cars in the parking area were already coated in a thick layer of ash. Behind it all, Ben More continued to rumble, belching forth more clouds of ash.

Lys walked over to one of the abandoned vehicles and opened the door. Seeing a set of keys on the front seat, her face brightened.

"Michael!" she shouted. "I can get us to Iona!"

"You don't understand what a pyroclastic flow can do," he answered. "The whole southern end of the island is a wasteland. The road is gone. There's no way through. It'll take weeks to re-open."

"But this is a *Hummer!*" Lys came back. "It's the H2, the big one. My dad has one just like this. I love these things. It can go *anywhere!*"

The name *Hummer* came from the well-known *Humvee* military vehicle. The idea for the H2 had been to take the basic *Humvee* design, add luxury features, and sell it as a high-end sports utility vehicle.

While the now defunct H2 could be awkward in city traffic, it remains virtually unstoppable off-road. Its fans boast it can plow through 20 inches of water, climb a 16-inch wall, or go up a 60 percent incline.

At Lys's urging, Michael and Erin retrieved their luggage from the inn and quickly found seats in the big SUV. Despite the thick coating of ash, the Hummer's big

6.2 liter V8 responded eagerly, roaring to life. Lys flipped on the lights and put the Hummer into gear. The massive wheels spun in the ash for just a moment, then gripped. They began rolling forward... driving into the depths of hell.

As she drove, Lys told her story, beginning with her sighting of Kareina on Wednesday morning. Michael and Erin hung on every word as she described her capture and the boat ride out to the Firth of Lorne.

She described her plan of escape... allowing herself to be thrown overboard... and her struggle to get free of the anchor line, only to find herself in frigid water far from shore. She told them how she pressed on toward the only lights she could see, moving mechanically, numbly, exhausting the last of her strength, yet choosing to keep moving.

Finally, she was sinking for the last time. Her arms and legs were no longer responding... she knew she could go no further. Through the pain and exhaustion she was ready to accept defeat.

But as she felt herself sinking into the icy depths of the firth, she remembered the portal. She was the only one on earth who could open it! More than *her* life was at stake.

What had Eliel said? It was her *destiny* to open the portal. That simple phrase caused hope to surge within her. If opening the Iona portal was her destiny, there must be a way to get there! She *had* to try again, no matter how impossible it seemed. Summoning her last reserve of strength she determined to make one last desperate push for the surface.

*It's my destiny to open the portal.* She told herself, *I*

*MUST get to Iona!* ... then thrust herself toward the surface with resolute determination.

She didn't make it.

Approaching the heaving surface of the firth, her involuntary breathing reflex finally cut in. Her body, now starved for oxygen, could be denied no longer. Her mouth opened and her body gasped for air, but took in cold saltwater. Her chest heaved convulsively. Her throat and lungs exploded with fire. She was drowning.

Her upward momentum was broken, but then a swell lifted her up, and her mouth at last cleared the surface. Coughing and gagging, she spat out the water, and drank in the crisp night air.

The dark water swirled around her. She tried to swim again, pressing forward with her last remnants of strength toward the distant lights. She'd only gone a few more strokes when a huge wave lifted her up, and smashed her down, slamming her onto a hard surface of solid rock.

Ignoring the pain, Lys looked around in unbelief. She was still far from shore. The jagged rock barely broke the surface. Each new swell that passed crashed down around her, threatening to wash her back into the sea. But in the troughs between the waves she was high and dry. She drew numb legs under her and stood up shakily. Waves continued to crash against her feet, but she stood on solid ground. The rock was not large, but it was *land*.

The beam of the distant lighthouse continued its steady sweep across the sky. Off to the west she could still see the distant lights of shore. If only she could make it till morning, there would be hope of rescue.

As dawn approached, the receding tide left her well above the surging swells. The waves no longer crashed against her. When the first light of dawn broke, Lys sat shivering on the exposed rock.

"Lady's Rock!" exclaimed Michael.

"What's that?"

"I'll explain later. Keep going. How did you get off the rock?"

"Just after dawn, some passing herring fishermen heard me calling and came to my rescue. Ben More was already erupting by that time. They insisted on taking me north, up the coast to Tobermory, but when we saw the ferry coming they agreed to drop me at Craignure.

"Erin was standing on the shore when we landed. We've been talking ever since."

"Michael, I'm sorry we worried you," Erin broke in from the rear seat, resting her hand on Michael's shoulder, "I didn't realize how much time was passing. When Lys told me her story, it completed the process you began last night. When Lys described how she kept pressing forward, even after she lost all hope of survival, I remembered something Piper told me right after the incident at the ranch.

"One evening I was laying in bed, paralyzed by fear, reliving the horrors of the ranch over and over in my mind. Piper came in and sat with me for a long time. She told me something that didn't really penetrate at the time. She said, 'It may be that none of us survive this, but we can't focus on that. We're in a battle, and the stakes are bigger than all of us. All we can do is take things one step at a time and keep moving forward.'

"Michael, that's what Lys was doing. She saw what was at stake and determined that, no matter what, she *had* to find a way through. I've been so focused on my own pain, I forgot the big picture. But now I understand."

Erin looked at him with a strength and resolve Michael had never seen in her. "I may die on Iona, Michael, but I won't hold back in fear. Araton once told me I'd have to face death to fulfill my destiny. I'm ready to do that now. I *must* get Iona, no matter what."

As they talked, the Hummer continued its steady pace across the darkened island. Even for the Hummer it wasn't an easy path.

They traversed a hellish landscape of swirling ash and cinders, glowing red in the light of the distant volcano. No road was visible, though a few shattered and burned-out remnants of houses still stood. But the four-wheel drive Hummer plowed steadily through the knee-deep ash, a twenty-first century lunar rover crossing a surreal moonscape.

To the north, Lys caught a glimpse of something new… a river was slowly winding its way among the steep hills and ash-covered glens of Mull. It was a river of fire, glowing dark orange-red and searing yellow. In places it was crusted over with black slag, but the leading edge glowed white hot as it steadily advanced. The lava was headed south, slowly snaking its way toward the sea.

And then, up ahead, peering at them across the infernal landscape, Lys saw two eyes, glowing red, staring at her.

As they approached, Lys squinted through the blizzard of falling ash. The glowing eyes became clearer. Horizontal slits, shining in hellish red.

She finally knew what they were. They were tail lights! Coming into view was a twisted lump of charred metal and glass that had once been a Mercedes C220.

Could Holmes and Piper have survived? Lys began

mashing her hand on the horn, blasting it repeatedly.

Then she saw the lights of the Mercedes begin to flash on and off.  Piper and Holmes were alive!

# Chapter Twenty-four:
# The Fionnphort Gun Club

## THE ISLAND OF IONA, ARGYLE, SCOTLAND

As they made their way into western Mull, the Hummer emerged from the path of the pyroclastic flow and conditions steadily improved. A light grey coating of ash still covered everything, and the sky overhead remained dark with swirling clouds from horizon to horizon.

Drawing near to Iona, Michael noticed new movement in the sky. The sky ahead seemed to be alive, a churning maelstrom that swung across the sky, completely encircling the island of Iona. Raising his binoculars, he saw that within the storm of smoke and ash, a massive winged army made up of millions of Archon warriors, had surrounded the ancient island.

Directly over Iona, a cloud of Irin circled, standing guard against the overwhelming horde. More than 30,000 Irin had gathered on Iona, but the dark forces now circling the place numbered many times that. And they were steadily drawing closer, slowly hemming in the island's defenders.

From time to time, Michael could see clumps of Irin break away from the cloud and move to confront the

Archons, but they were immediately surrounded by packs of Archon warriors, and in a flash of light, fell from the sky.

Arriving at Fionnphort, the waters of Iona Sound were churning as undersea earthquakes still rocked the area, but the intrepid crew of the Calmac ferry agreed to take them across.

As they emerged from the ferry on the Island of Iona, Patrick and several others were waiting for them on the ramp.

Patrick, Reetha, Marty and Ron excitedly embraced the new arrivals as they walked up the ramp from the ferry. They were particularly thrilled to see that Lys had been found.

"We've been so worried about you!" Patrick began. "All communications here went down yesterday, and then when the volcano erupted this morning we feared the worst. You must tell us the whole story, but first let me introduce some allies from Mull."

Gesturing to three new additions to their party, he said, "I'd like you to meet Angus MacLean, Catherine Campbell, and Malcolm MacKinnon. They call themselves the Fionnphort Gun Club." Holmes shook hands with all three and introduced them to the rest of the group.

Angus and Malcolm were tall and muscular, both in their mid twenties. Rugged outdoorsmen, they wore their hair long and unkempt, with Angus sporting a full and untrimmed beard.

But Catherine was something special. About the same age as her companions, she had the healthy glow of a woman who lived much of her life outdoors. She was dressed casually in jeans and a man's flannel shirt with the sleeves rolled up to her elbows, yet her attire only served to accentuate her natural femininity. Tall and slender with a good figure, her unkempt raven tresses fell softly over her shoulders, framing a face that was gentle, yet strong. Like the men, she carried a Remington 12-gauge pump-action shotgun.

As they walked together toward the local pub, Holmes gestured toward the sky. "Interesting weather you're having today…"

"Living near Iona we're used to strange sights in the sky," Angus answered in a thick Scottish brogue. "But I never seen anything like this. Looks like Armageddon."

"These three know all about the angels," Patrick added.

"You don't live across the water from Iona an' not know about angels," Malcolm explained.

"And Michael…" Marty interjected. "Angus here has read all your books." Turning to Angus, he added, "By the way, Angus, this is Michael Fletcher, the author of those books on angels." His warm greeting revealed that Michael had discovered a fan.

They sat together around the big table in the corner of the pub, and Holmes ordered drinks all around. The first order of business was to bring the group up to date on the adventures of the last twenty-four hours. They sat enthralled as they listened to the accounts of Lys's escape from death, Erin's deliverance from the shades, and the rescue of Holmes and Piper from the ruined Mercedes.

After the quick briefing, Holmes directed the group's

attention to the situation at hand.  Turning to Angus, he said, "Tell me about your gun club."

"It's not what you'd call a real club," Angus answered. "Malcolm, Catherine an' I have been pals since we was wee bairns.  Even as children, we spent our summers hunting and fishing all over the island.  So the club is just us--just pals who go huntin' together."  Noticing their fascination with Catherine, he added,  "Y'know, Catherine here is one of the best shooters in the Highlands."

"What do you hunt?"

"Ducks, hare, an' pheasant mostly, and sometimes vermin."

"Today we've been huntin' vermin!" Malcolm added with a laugh.

"So tell me, what's been happening here since yesterday?"

"Those boggin' cowboys drove in with their fancy guns, and tried to take over Fionnphort."  Catherine said, eyes flashing with anger. "They shot up the town, pulled down the cell tower, and cut off the phones.  Then they tried to shut down the Calmac ferry, not lettin' anyone on or off Iona."

With a look of satisfaction on her face, Catherine added, "So we got our guns, and after a bit of a barnie, we drove the choobs off the island!"

Malcolm continued, "The damn cowboys stole a wee boat and escaped here to Iona where they've barricaded themselves at the fairy mound."

"That's pretty impressive," Holmes observed, "driving Rex and his gang off Mull.  They're pretty tough."

"Most of you Yanks think the Scots are weak 'cause of

the kilts," Malcolm commented, smiling, "But we Celts have always been fearsome fighters."

"We even stopped the Romans," Catherine added with pride. "The Romans conquered everything else in the world, but when they got to our wee isle, Emperor Hadrian said, 'those Scots are too tough for us.' So they built a wall from sea to sea to keep us out."

Angus glanced at Catherine with a twinkle in his eye, "Y'know, among the ancient Celts, the women went into battle right along with the men. And it's said the women were the fiercest fighters of the lot."

"And *none* of 'em wore kilts." Malcolm added, "They all fought stark naked, not a stitch of clothin' on their bodies."

"Even the women?" Patrick questioned, glancing at Catherine.

"Even the women!" answered Angus.

Catherine smiled mischievously, "See, the Celtic women used to paint their bodies all over with hideous war paint. Then, when they went into battle…" Catherine grasped the front of her shirt as though preparing to rip it off… "they'd rip off their clothing an' go chargin' after the enemy. One look at them and the enemy went runnin' for their lives!"

"That certainly gives new meaning to the term 'painted lady,'" laughed Reetha.

"'Course Highland lassies don't need war paint to make the men go runnin' from 'em nowadays." Angus laughed, as Catherine punched him in the arm.

"But Holmes…" Patrick interrupted, trying to get the conversation back on track. "We have a serious problem. Rex Vanderberg and his thugs are heading up a small army of Archon supporters. I counted more than twenty of them. They're camped at the foot of *Cnoc Angel*. Even with our friends from Mull, I don't see a way to get past them. They're armed to the teeth with M-16s, Kalashnikovs, and Uzis.

"Yet over our heads that circling Archon army is getting closer by the hour," he continued. "I don't see a way we can get close enough to the Hill of the Angels to open the portal."

Listening to Patrick's analysis of the problem, Michael burst out laughing. "Well, if that's our problem, we can all relax and have another pint!"

Everyone turned to Michael in surprise. Erin grasped Michael's arm, "Michael, it sounds like you see something we're missing. What is it?"

Michael looked at Erin and then to Patrick. "Don't you see? It's all a game! It's the Archon strategy. Rex is just a diversionary tactic."

"Patrick," Michael said, "what made you think you needed to get to *Cnoc Angel*? It's because Rex and his gang have set up their camp there. They've barricaded themselves at The Hill of the Angels because *that's* where they *want* us to focus our attention."

"But don't we need to get to the hill to reopen the portal?"

"Patrick... I've been pondering this since we left Texas. Your cousin Columba used to pray at the Hill of the Angels, but nobody said that's where the portal was located.

"The ancient legends say that on the night Columba died, a huge pillar of fire was seen on the eastern tip of Iona as the island filled with thousands of angels who had come to honor their friend Columba.

"My theory is that the pillar of fire was formed by thousands of shining angels pouring through the portal.

"But..." Michael continued, "the record specifically said the pillar of fire was on the *easternmost* part of the island. Any map will show you that the Hill of the Angels is not on the eastern part of the island. It's located in the exact center of the island. So the Hill of the Angels is NOT the location of the portal."

"Then where is the portal?" demanded Patrick.

"Remember your map of Iona, Patrick. The easternmost part of the island is found on Iona's northeastern shore. In other words, at the location of Columba's monastery. So the Portal was located at the monastery, not the Hill of the Angels."

"But the monastery covers a big area," Patrick responded, "much of which is now covered by a medieval Catholic church."

"Yes, but we have *another* hint as to the location of the portal," Michael explained.

"The ancient Celts had a practice of erecting cairns--pillars of stones--at places where they sensed the spiritual barrier was thin. So if the monks of Iona knew there was a portal into the heavens, they would have marked it. All we need to do is find the location of the cairns."

"But there are no cairns on that part of the island now," Patrick came back. "I've been all over that area many times."

"Of course," agreed Michael. "Any cairns, along with any other structures from Columba's day, would have been torn down by peasants scavenging for building materials during the medieval period.

"But there's one place within Columba' monastery where we know cairns once stood. In fact, it's a hill that eventually came to be known as the Hill of the Cairns."

"*Cnoc nan Carnan*!" Patrick exclaimed, "The Hill of the Cairns! That's Columba's hill, where his cell once stood between the upright slabs of stone."

"That's right Patrick. I believe the portal was directly over Columba's cell."

"When Columba died and the angels poured through the portal, the monks marked the spot by erecting cairns of stone where his cell had been. So they renamed the place, the Hill of the Cairns.

"And that means we don't have to capture the Hill of the Angels from Rex's army…" Michael continued, "We just need to walk up the road to *your* Hill."

"If that's true," Holmes said with rising excitement, "then we have our direction." Glancing around the table, he added. "I believe it's time to go and open the portal."

"Wait a minute, Holmes," Erin cut in, "I need to say something before we go."

All eyes turned to Erin. "As we walked into the pub and sat down, I felt my gift activate. I got a strong impression I believe could be important."

"What is it?" Holmes inquired.

Brushing a lock of chestnut-brown hair from her eyes, Erin looked around nervously at the group, "It's a word for all of us," she said, "including our friends from Mull. What I heard was this, *'The enemy has formed a strategy to destroy you. Today you will face the powers of evil. But you are now twelve. Your number is complete. Each of you has been called here for a purpose, and if you stand with each other, you will have what you need. Stand together and do not fear.'"*

"I've been hearing something similar," Patrick agreed. "I've sensed we're heading into a major confrontation, and all of us need to be ready."

Looking at Holmes he continued, "I also have a personal word for you. What I heard is this... *'In the confrontation to come, don't hesitate to act. Do what you know is right, and don't fear the consequences. This is your destiny.'"*

When Patrick finished, the group sat in silence for a moment, trying to digest what had been said. Holmes, in particular, focused on their new friends from Mull, seeing them as if for the first time. With their addition, the group had, indeed, increased to twelve. But he wondered what the next few hours would hold for all of them.

Looking at Patrick, he said quietly, "I think we better get to your hill. Show us how to get there."

# Chapter Twenty-five:
# Releasing the Angels

## THE ISLAND OF IONA, ARGYLE, SCOTLAND

Although it was only four in the afternoon, the landscape around them was shrouded in thick darkness. The churning clouds of dust and ash still blanketed the sky while the distant fires of Ben More cast a dull, red glow over everything.

With Patrick leading the way, the members of the synaxis followed the twisting road past the ruins of the medieval nunnery and the Columba Hotel. The Fionnphort Gun Club followed close behind.

They'd almost reached *Cnoc nan Carnan* when three dark figures stepped out of the shadows, blocking their path. In the lead was Rex Vanderberg.

When the lookouts reported to Rex that his wife was on Iona with the synaxis, he'd gone mad with rage. Leaving Grat in charge of the men at the camp, Rex, Reno and Bryce had come hunting for Erin. Reno and Bryce held black Kalashnikov assault rifles slung loosely over their shoulders while Rex carried a Beretta automatic pistol tucked into his belt.

Seeing Rex and his men, Patrick motioned for the

group to stop, and the synaxis spread out across the road with every eye on Rex.

"What do you want?" Patrick demanded.

"I want *many* things," Rex smiled smugly. He glanced from Patrick to the members of the group, "By this time tomorrow I want all of you *dead*. Your *synaxis* ends tonight!"

Shifting his gaze to Erin, Rex pulled the Beretta from his belt and flipped off the safety. "But first," he said, "I want my wife."

Leering at her, he said coolly, "Come here, *Honey!*"

"No, Rex!" Erin answered firmly, her voice quivering with the fierce, pent-up anger of twenty years. "You lost the right to call me *wife* long ago." With rising intensity, she continued, "Until now, I've been too fearful to resist you, but I'm not afraid of you anymore!"

*"Silence... TRAITOR!"* Rex roared, cutting her off. His face went blood dark as he raised the Beretta, his hand trembling with rage, and pointed it directly at Erin's heart. "When I take you back to camp," his voice hardened, "I've decided to leave you with Grat Dalton for the night. While your Irin friends are dying in the skies overhead, Grat and the boys will show you what happens to a woman who betrays me by joining my enemies."

Taking a step closer, he softened his voice and grinned malevolently, "It'll be an educational experience for you, Honey. Grat will *teach you* to be afraid again.

"And when the boys are finished playing their little games with you … and when I've heard your sweet voice whimpering in fear between your anguished screams …" he said as he lowered the gun, "I'll come for you."

Rex glared at her for a long moment, but Erin stood her ground, unwavering and defiant.

Then, in a tone that pierced like a hardened steel knife, he added, "...I *will* come for you, my dear wife, and you can be very certain of this... this time I *will* kill you."

As he was speaking, Rex began moving toward Erin, ready to seize her in his iron grip; but he suddenly found his way blocked. A tall, powerfully built man with piercing green eyes had stepped forward and positioned himself directly in Rex's path.

Holmes had been pondering Patrick's word since they left the pub, and knew this was his time to act. Planting his feet firmly, he looked into Rex's face, now dark and twisted with rage, and said firmly, "Hold it, Rex! You're not taking Erin anywhere. Everyone in this group is under my protection."

Startled by the unexpected intervention, Rex regarded the unarmed man blocking his way through dark, sunken eyes, then smiled thinly. "You must be Derek Holmes, the leader of this tiresome group. I've heard many things about you from my Archon friends.

"You shouldn't have brought these people here, Dr. Holmes. After tonight there will be no more Irin, and you will all be dead.

"But first," he said, glancing at Erin, "I'm taking my *wife*."

"And I said, *no!*" Holmes said firmly, taking a step closer. In a smooth motion, Reno and Bryce unslung their AK-47's, but Holmes continued, "To get to any of these people, you'll have to deal with me first."

Rex's face twisted in a look of honest bafflement, then his eyes darkened, "Your request is granted," he said, icily.

"I *will* deal with you first." Rex raised the Beretta again and calmly pointed it at the center of Holmes' chest, just feet away.

"Hold it right there!" a woman's voice ordered. It was Catherine Campbell, stepping into view from the shadows at the side of the road with her shotgun raised and her long, ebony hair feathering softly in the wind. "I don't know who you think you are, you bloody berk, but you fire one shot at this man and it'll be your last!" She was aiming her shotgun right between his eyes.

"What a big gun for such a little girl," Rex spat contemptuously. "Too bad you can't afford to pull that trigger. You shoot me, young lady, and my boys will kill every last one of you before my body hits the ground."

Fire burned in Catherine's eyes. "Don't test me!" she warned. "I *promise* you, I'll blow your bloody head off!"

Rex gave her a condescending smile, then turned and nodded to Reno and Bryce, who raised their Kalashnikovs into firing position, pointed directly at Catherine.

Shifting his gaze back to Catherine, Rex took several steps in her direction and stood over her menacingly. Glaring at her, he drew his lips back sharply, deliberately baring his teeth. And just for an instant his face was distorted, a beast's face, leering at her in unearthly rage.

Caught off guard by the intensity of his gaze, Catherine wavered for a moment. Her mouth opened slightly and, taking a step back, she lowered the barrel of the Remington just an inch.

That momentary hesitation was all the encouragement Rex needed. Seeing Catherine pull back, his cruel grin broadened to a look of smug satisfaction. Without another word, he turned back to Holmes and raised the Beretta.

Then, before anyone could move, Rex took aim and calmly squeezed the trigger.

Piper heard the shot, and from the corner of her eye saw the bullet impact the center of Holmes' chest. She closed her eyes and screamed.

Rex had cultivated such an aura of intimidation that no one ever dared oppose him. But he didn't know Catherine Campbell. At the moment his shot was fired, the air echoed with the sound of an even louder retort, as Catherine firmly pulled the trigger of her shotgun.

And so, Rex Vanderberg's death was as violent as his life. Firing her Remington 870 twelve-gauge--loaded with double-aught buckshot--at close range, Catherine Campbell fulfilled her promise to Rex by quite literally blowing his head off.

Reno and Bryce had not anticipated Catherine's response, and also had not noticed Angus and Malcolm standing in silent darkness by the edge of the road with their shotguns at the ready. Before Rex's thugs could react, two more shots rang out, and in a moment, Rex, Reno and Bryce all lay dead on the pavement in front of *Cnoc nan Carnan*.

Piper turned back to Holmes, and screamed again. Holmes was gone. In the distraction of the other shots, she never saw that when the bullet impacted his body, he'd simply disappeared.

Then, as quickly as he had disappeared, Holmes was back. He stood before her, hands clutching his chest, but there was no blood. He drew his hands away, and examined his chest, looking perplexed.

"Holmes, what happened?"

"I don't know. I felt it hit… and found myself in the

shadow realm." He felt at his chest again and winced. "I have a nasty bruise and maybe a broken rib. But the bullet didn't penetrate--the force of the impact just knocked me out of this dimension. Eliel said I had that ability. I just didn't expect…"

He winced again as Piper literally threw himself against him, holding him in a tight embrace.

He returned the embrace, ignoring the pain for a moment, then quickly pulled away. "More of that later…" he whispered, "Let's get this thing done."

The swirling storm of Archon warriors had almost reached the island.

The entire synaxis, along with their friends from Mull, were staring at Holmes in disbelief, not comprehending how he was still alive. He turned to them and barked, "Lys, and Patrick--all of you--let's go. We need to get that portal open."

"Not so fast!" …a voice called, this time from the top of *Cnoc nan Carnan*. "I've come for my old friend, Lys." It was Kareina. Botis and Turell walked at her side as she calmly strode down the embankment to the road. "I must say, Lys, you're remarkably resilient, but your luck just ran out. Rex was right about one thing. All of this ends *now!*"

Reaching the bottom of the embankment, Botis and Turell separated and circled around behind the synaxis, while all eyes remained on Kareina.

Smiling malevolently, she approached Lys. "You survived the BMW. You survived the bullet through the hospital window. You survived the shades. You even survived the Firth of Lorne. This time I've decided to do it the old-fashioned way." Coming face-to-face with Lys, Kareina purred, "Let's see if you can survive my *knife.*"

As she spoke, Kareina brought her hand up, revealing a pitch-black, twelve-inch-long obsidian knife with a jagged edge. She raised the knife swiftly until the tip just indented the soft flesh of Lys's neck.

Seeing the raw terror in Lys's eyes, Kareina bared her teeth in a sadistic grin, savoring her long-delayed triumph as she prepared to make the fatal thrust.

But then, from just behind Kareina, came another voice… "Hold it Kareina. Before you use that blade on her, you'll have to get past *my* blade." It was Araton. His shining, white wings were outstretched, and he floated ten feet above the ground. In his right hand he clasped a three-foot-long, glowing scimitar.

Recognizing Araton's voice, Kareina whirled to face him, as the pent-up fury of twenty-thousand years exploded within her.

Forgetting Lys for the moment, Kareina threw aside her knife and slid a shining, three-foot blade from the black scabbard at her side. Then, opening her mouth in a long, rasping cry, she unfurled dark, bat-like wings and rose to meet her ancient adversary.

Botis and Turell joined her in the air. Suddenly, from the shadow realm, twenty more Archon warriors appeared, surrounding Araton with drawn swords.

Araton hovered with wings outstretched and scimitar raised, face-to-face with Kareina. Kareina shifted her sword from side to side, dark eyes glaring at him in searing hatred, searching for her opening.

Turell remained on station, just behind her. But at a gesture from Kareina, Botis retreated, gliding silently away into the darkness.

Spreading dark leathery wings--almost invisible in the

gathering gloom--Botis flew unnoticed in a wide arc around the encircling warriors, then rose into the ash-darkened sky to a position behind and several hundred feet above Araton.

Botis paused for a moment in mid-air, wings outstretched, feeling the cold evening breeze blowing in from the Sound of Iona. Then, seeing Araton's attention still locked on Kareina, he bared his teeth and angled into a sharp dive, plummeting downward toward Araton with sword held high, ready to strike a decisive blow.

But Araton sensed the movement behind him. At the last moment he whirled and struck out at his attacker. Botis saw Araton turning and, for an instant, a look of horror flashed across his face. His mouth opened in a tortured scream but his momentum was too great to turn aside. Araton's glowing blade caught Botis directly across the chest. In an explosion of blinding white light Botis was literally torn apart, the shredded remnants of his mangled body tumbling to the ground in smoke and fire.

"*That* was for Sylvia!" Araton spat, as he whirled on Kareina.

Araton lashed out with his scimitar again, and Kareina jumped back, barely avoiding his blade. The others were on him immediately. The Archon warriors swirled around him, slashing and thrusting, driving in close, then leaping to escape his flashing sword.

Their attack was intense and furious, but Araton was too fast for them. As they pressed in closer, two more Archon fighters were dispatched. But the rest kept coming.

Araton fought valiantly, but was vastly outnumbered. The Archons were pressing him on every side.

Suddenly, falling from the sky like a shooting star,

Eliel was there. She was dancing again, twirling in a blaze of white light, tumbling and twisting among the Archon warriors. And in her hand was a shining sword. In a moment, three more Archons tumbled to the ground in flames.

More Irin arrived--Rand and Khalil and two others. Araton was wounded now, but the others closed ranks around him.

But the Archons increased their numbers also.

Then, in the sky overhead, the two massive armies finally engaged. While the Irin darted and flashed, the massive horde of the Archon army rapidly tightened the circle around them.

The Archons had great numbers, but moved independently. Their attack was ferocious but not well-coordinated. As the Irin held their ground, more Archons died.

But still more Archons were moving into view. Irin began to fall also. The Irin were being overwhelmed by the sheer number of their adversaries.

Holmes turned to the synaxis… "Let's get that portal open."

As the battle overhead intensified, Holmes led the way to the top of the hill. In the gathering darkness, the twelve planted their feet on the soft heather between the upright slabs of stone.

Instinctively, Holmes knew what to do. Eliel had never told him how to open the portal, but he *knew*.

"Patrick, stand in front of that slab on the right. Lys, you stand before the slab on the left, facing him. Everyone else, gather around them. Now, Patrick… you give the word."

Patrick looked at Lys for a long moment and their eyes met. He smiled broadly, then spoke one word, *"Sing!"*

Lys returned his smile, then opened her mouth and began to sing, repeating the simple song she'd made up as a child.

At first the song was forced and halting, a weak and silly song a child would sing--just nonsense syllables in a childish melody. But gradually the song took on a life of its own. It rose from deep within Lys and flowed out, syllable after syllable. The words made no sense, but then they took on a meaning that went beyond human understanding. The song increased in volume. It had rhythm and meter, and the melody grew more complex. It rose and crested in crescendo after crescendo, gaining power.

And as Lys sang, something happened.

The stone slabs around them, and the earth under their feet seemed to vibrate to the sound of her song.

The hill beneath their feet began to glow... and then turned transparent. The ground between Patrick and Lys, the green heather and dark earth beneath, became as clear as glass. Patrick felt a wave of vertigo. Looking down at his feet, he could see into the depths of the earth.

Suddenly, from the heart of the earth, a shaft of light shot skyward, a pillar of white light that pierced the clouds of ash overhead. The dark clouds retreated, as though cringing from the power of the light. And a tunnel formed above them--a glowing tunnel that penetrated into the depths of the sky.

Then, answering the light from the earth, came a light from the heavens. Through the tunnel, a shaft of brilliant light flooded the whole island. The light was more than white. It was a shimmering rainbow of blinding radiance, brighter than the brightest day.

And then the angels came. A shining spark fell through the tunnel, shooting like a falling star, then spreading its wings and extending a flaming sword, it joined the battle. Then another. Then three more... and suddenly there were thousands, and then tens of thousands. And more came. The Irin were flooding into the earth-realm.

In a moment, the battle turned. Archons were falling in flames all around them.

The Archons hesitated... then, seeing the battle was lost, they broke off their attack and fled.

And suddenly it was over.

# Chapter Twenty-six:  A New Beginning

## THE PORT OF OBAN, ARGYLE, SCOTLAND

Four weeks later, the synaxis assembled again, this time on the beautiful, grassy lawn in the center of McCaig's Folly.

Standing on the lookout platform, Holmes and Piper gazed out across the Firth of Lorne to the battered Island of Mull, still recovering from its thick coating of ash.  Crews had been sent in, and the road across the island had already been restored.

By the time the eruption ended, Ben More had actually grown in size.  A picturesque cone more than four thousand feet high now rose in the center of the island.

Following Ben More's eruption, geologists from all over the earth had rushed to Mull.  After careful study, it was declared that the eruption, though unprecedented, was merely an unfortunate geological "burp."  The experts agreed that further damage was unlikely.  Government officials were already studying how to draw geothermal energy from the newly active volcano, greatly enhancing the island's economy.

Holmes and Piper turned and walked across the grassy knoll to where the minister of the local Congregational church was standing, surrounded by a crowd of their friends. Behind the minister, through one of the archways, Piper could see out across Oban Harbor to the distant isles of the Hebrides. But Holmes was looking only at Piper.

When they'd taken their position in front of the minister, Holmes slipped his arm around Piper's slender waist and drew her closer. Piper looked up at him, smiling broadly, and their eyes met.

It was a wedding such as no one had ever seen. The minister, a short, balding man in his mid-sixties, glanced from person to person in this unconventional wedding party with genuine perplexity.

The bride and her attendants were dressed in matching light pale-blue garments, of a style and fabric the minister didn't recognize. The dresses were gifts, the bride had explained, from her maid of honor--a beautiful young brown-haired woman named Eliel.

The groom, though an American, wore a kilt of the MacLean tartan, also a gift from a friend. Holmes was resplendent in full Highland dress; an Argyll jacket with a wool tie to match his kilt, a black leather sporran trimmed in badger fur, and Ghillie Brogues with kilt hose and garter flashes. His kilt pin bore the MacLean clan crest, a tower with battlements surrounded by the proud motto "Virtue is my honor."

The best man, a large black fellow named Araton, was dressed in a kilt of the MacKinnon tartan. In addition to the normal accessories of traditional Highland dress, Araton also sported an imposing two-handed Scottish Claymore dress sword at his side.

There was one more kilted figure in the wedding party, an American named Patrick O'Neill. Michael had informed Patrick that not all of his ancient relatives had

returned to Ireland.  The *Ui Neills* who remained in
Scotland changed their name to the Scottish form,
"MacNeil," and settled on the Island of Barra-- just north of
Iona--where they gained renown as warriors and pirates.
Patrick stood beside Araton, proudly wearing a kilt with the
tartan of the Barra MacNeils, purchased in one of the tourist
shops on George Street.

Music for the ceremony was provided by Angus and
Malcolm, who played with surprising skill on the bagpipe
and highland flute.  They began with a stirring rendition of
"Highland Cathedral," and as the sound of flute and bagpipe
echoed and reechoed around the stone walls of McCaig's
Folly, it sounded like all twenty-four bagpipes of the Royal
Scottish Dragoons had joined in.   Then the music softened
as Catherine began the ceremony by singing a lovely Gaelic
love song.

As the wedding plans had progressed, Michael
revealed that--among his other talents--he was an amateur
photographer.   He requested the honor of recording the
moment for posterity.  Michael stood to the right of the
group, camera in hand, with Erin at his side.

Friends old and new gathered around as Holmes and
Piper took their places in front of the minister.

The minister, speaking in a thick Scottish brogue,
began, "Dearly beloved, we are gathered here today in the
sight of God and this company to join together this man and
this woman in the bonds of holy matrimony..."

Aidan's Pub had never hosted a wedding reception
before and the management had been reticent, but when
Holmes explained that all their regulars would be invited to

attend, and also mentioned free drinks for everyone, an exception was made.

After the toasts were offered, Eliel lifted her *Guinness* and spoke a special blessing over the bride and groom.

When they were seated again, Piper glanced at Eliel, "So what are you and Araton going to do now that the *Archons* are defeated?"

There was a long moment of silence as Eliel and Araton looked at each other, then back to Piper. Eliel spoke first, "Piper, we thought you understood. The Archons are not yet defeated. In fact, the battle has just begun. What you did on Iona gave us a chance for victory, but the outcome is far from assured. The greatest part of the conflict is still ahead."

"There's much you don't understand yet," Araton cut in. "And much you still need to learn. Right now you have one synaxis, not yet fully trained. To drive back the Archons, this group must come to maturity, then multiply into thousands of groups all over the earth. The Archons will do everything in their power to prevent that."

Holmes looked around at the group. "Eliel told me yesterday that if the portal on Iona is to remain open, a synaxis must be formed on Iona immediately."

Erin spoke up. "Holmes, if you and the Irin would approve, I'd like a part in that. I have nothing in Dallas to return to. I'd like to build a home on Iona and help to establish a synaxis here."

Holmes studied her for a long moment. "That's truly interesting," he said with a subtle smile, glancing briefly at Araton. "You don't know this, Erin, but Araton has already recommended you to head up the synaxis on Iona. He said to tell you it *is* your destiny.

"Of course," he continued, "you must realize it won't be easy. Iona is a major historical site, owned and supervised by the National Trust for Scotland. It won't be easy for an outsider to obtain property there."

"You forget, Holmes," Erin grinned, brushing back a soft lock of chestnut-brown hair, "I'm now Rex Vanderberg's *widow*. I checked with my lawyers yesterday. Rex was so confident of my imminent demise, he never even bothered to file for divorce. So, since my husband's tragic 'hunting accident' a few weeks ago, his grieving widow is now a *billionaire*."

*...And as they say in Dallas,* she thought to herself, smiling, *Erin Vanderberg can do anything!*

Taking a sip of her Velvet, she looked up at Holmes and continued, "I'll call my lawyers in the morning and get them working on it. I'm sure we'll get exactly what we need on Iona."

"I wouldn't doubt it for a moment," Holmes laughed. "The Iona synaxis appears to be in very capable hands.

"And..." he added. "I think our friends from Mull could well form the beginnings of that new synaxis." The members of the Fionnphort Gun Club, hardly recognizable in their recently trimmed locks and newly acquired finery, raised their glasses in hearty agreement.

Erin hesitated and, glancing at Michael, continued, "If Michael would agree, I'd like to ask him to stay on Iona and help us build the synaxis here."

"I'd love to!" Michael said. Leaning close to Piper, he confided, "Since that night in Craignure, I believe Erin has come to view me as something of a father figure."

Piper gave Michael a curious smile and, leaning near, whispered in his ear, "Michael, I've noticed how Erin has looked at you the last few weeks. Believe me, a father-daughter relationship is *not* what she has in mind!"

For the second time since meeting the Irin, Michael Fletcher was speechless.

After more conversation, Eliel and Araton excused themselves and left the pub. The remaining wedding guests continued in conversation, but Piper got the distinct impression that they were all waiting for a big surprise to break, though she had no idea what it was.

Holmes had kept the honeymoon plans top secret, saying only that things were "in the works." As the evening drew to a close, Holmes was deep in conversation with Michael and Erin, seemingly in no hurry to leave.

Finally, Piper could take the suspense no longer. She leaned over to Holmes and whispered, "Okay, Holmes, you proposed to me in a volcanic eruption surrounded by flying bat-winged demons. We married in a Roman Coliseum on a cliff overlooking the islands of the Hebrides--with angels for our best man and maid of honor, no less. And now we've had our wedding reception in a Scottish pub. I can't wait to find out where you're taking me on our honeymoon!"

Holmes smiled at her, "Are you ready to find out?" His smile broadened to a mischievous grin.

"It's about time, Holmes! I've never seen you so secretive about anything. I've hardly seen you the last two weeks. So tell me, where are we going?"

"It's a place Eliel found for us, and I guarantee you'll love it."

Then Holmes stood up in the middle of the pub and held out his hand to Piper. He asked again... "Are you ready to see it?"

"Holmes, I don't understand."

"You don't need to understand, Ginny, just come."

"But… we need to go back to the hotel and pick up our luggage," Piper objected.

"Eliel already took care of that for us. It's all been arranged."

Piper stood up and looked around in confusion. From the looks on the faces of everyone in the wedding party, it was obvious that the big secret was about to be revealed. She turned back to Holmes, looked up into his eyes, and gently slipped her hand into his.

Holmes enfolded her softly in his arms, and they enjoyed a long, lingering, passionate kiss, to the delight of everyone in the pub. And then, in the middle of the cheering crowd… in a move that is sure to be pondered over many a pint at Aidan's for years to come… Piper and Holmes simply disappeared.

# EPILOGUE

Erin gazed out the plate glass window at the barren expanse of the Kilauea caldera. It was one year to the day since she'd last been here.

The massive clouds of steam and sulphurous gas had finally stopped pouring from the *Halema'uma'u* crater. The floor of the pit had hardened and cooled.

The longest-running volcanic eruption in recorded history was finally over. Pele, the goddess of the volcano, had been among the Archons summoned to Mull to reopen the fires of Ben More. In the melee that took place when the Iona Portal opened, Pele was one of the many Archons destroyed.

Erin took a deep breath and let it out slowly. Like the crater before her, she was at peace--for the first time in many years. Ghosts of the past still occasionally haunted her dreams, but in waking hours the unbearable burden of stress was gone.

Gazing across the Caldera to the darkened pit of *Halema'uma'u*, she fought back tears. *One year ago today I sat at this same table after almost ending my life.*

She remembered standing before *Halema'uma'u's* hellish pit, carefully measuring out the steps that would lead to her destruction. She'd come so close… if Araton had not been there… a shudder went through her body.

Sensing her distress, Michael reached out and gently took her hand. She looked into his eyes and the distress faded.

Their whirlwind romance had surprised them both. Wanting to avoid a Dallas society media circus, they'd kept the wedding small, secret, and informal, exchanging vows on the broad deck of Piper and Holmes' lake house, overlooking the peaceful waters of Cedar Hills Lake. They'd invited only the members of the synaxis and a few close friends.

The first three nights of the honeymoon had been spent at their beach house on Hawaii's big Island. The place had been thoroughly renovated in the past six months, erasing every memory of Rex.

But Erin knew they needed to be at Volcano House this morning. They'd checked into the hotel the evening before, then driven out at 5 AM to watch the sun rise over the darkened pit of *Halema'uma'u*. Returning to the hotel, they'd warmed themselves with steaming mugs of coffee before the old stone fireplace. It somehow brought a sense of closure.

Erin's mind thought back over the last eight months. So much had happened.

The Iona synaxis was coming together quickly. In addition to their friends from Fionphort, the Irin had been in contact with a woman on Iona and a married couple from Mull. As an added bonus, Lys and Patrick both recently announced plans to relocate to Iona. Their arrival would bring the Iona synaxis up to the minimum number of ten. A *minyan*, as Marty Shapiro fondly called it.

Erin had leased a small cottage on the island until her new home, already christened *Iona House*, could be built, though Michael had steadfastly insisted on staying at the hotel until the wedding.

Erin looked up at Michael… "I can hardly believe this is real, Michael."

"I can't either," Michael smiled warmly, giving her hand a squeeze. "I mean… how a beautiful woman like you could *ever* fall for an old fart like me." It was a phrase he'd repeated several times a day for the past week, and he meant it every time.

"Michael! You've *got* to stop saying that!" Erin scolded gently. "You're eleven years older than I am... Rex was nine years older, and I was married to him for 20 years. I guess I just have this thing for older men."

Then, looking tenderly into his eyes, she continued. "And Michael… I've been around a lot of men… rich men, famous men, powerful men and cruel men. But you're the first *kind* man I've ever known. I wasn't about to let you get away. Besides, Araton assures me that you *are* my destiny."

They ate in silence for a few moments, then Michael looked up. "I got an email from Holmes last night. He and Piper just returned from Alaska. They've officially begun synaxis number 28… Believe it or not, it's a group of Eskimos in a little Inuit village called Kotzebue… above the Arctic Circle in Northwest Alaska."

"That's amazing," Erin said. "I can't believe how quickly these new groups are springing up. It's like the Irin have been in contact with people all over the world, just waiting for the right time to begin."

"By the way," Michael continued. "Have you noticed the pattern developing in these new groups?"

Erin tilted her head to the left... her body language for *I don't understand what you're talking about.*

"Think about it," Michael said. "Before the Alaskans there was the group of native Hawaiians at Kailua-Kona... There were Mongolians living in primitive *gers* on the steppes outside Ulaanbaatar. Last month Holmes and Piper established synaxis groups among the Ashanti tribesmen in Ghana, the Ethiopian Jews in Jeruselem's old city, and a group of Maoris in southern New Zealand..."

Erin's face lit up in recognition... "I hadn't noticed that before. Most of the new groups are forming among *native* peoples. How interesting."

"I'm developing a theory about it. Our western culture has a rationalistic mentality--we think it's necessary to *understand* something before we accept its reality. That makes us tend to discount anything supranormal. We don't want to admit the possibility of angels... and we find it hard to accept and operate in our special abilities.

"But native peoples don't have that problem. They're much more open to accept what they don't yet understand."

At that moment, Erin was distracted by a sudden motion in her peripheral vision. Someone was approaching their table. Looking up, Erin saw a powerfully built man with shaved head and rich dark skin.

"I'm sorry to disturb the honeymooners..." A deep resonant voice spoke.

"Araton!" Erin smiled broadly, jumping up to gave him a quick hug. "I'd hoped you'd be here this morning. Come and sit with us."

Araton pulled up a chair at the end of the table and eased himself into it. "I can only stay for a moment," he said, a tone of urgency in his voice. "There's something I need to tell you."

"The Archons are on the move again. They're using their mental powers to cloud our view of the future, but we sense they're very close to their goal.

"I've come to bring you a warning. The Archons know the threat you pose, Erin. For your protection, we believe it's time to activate the next level of your gifting. It will provide you both a way of escape when the enemy tries to destroy you."

"You believe the Archons will still try to kill me?"

"Erin, the Archons know your potential… as do I. In the end, you're the only one who can thwart their plans to annihilate the human race."

He grew more serious. "In fact… we believe they've a plan to kill you both *today*."

Araton glanced around, eyes darting nervously, then seemed to focus on something beyond their range of vision. "I'm afraid I must ask you to cut your honeymoon short," he said, standing to his feet. "There are Archon sympathizers approaching this mountain, even as we speak. I need both of you to come with me… *now*."

Responding to the urgency in his voice, both Michael and Erin immediately rose to their feet.

Araton led them from the restaurant, walking purposefully, though trying to appear calm and unhurried. As they headed down a narrow hallway and out a door at the back of the hotel, his speed steadily increased. Michael and Erin both soon found themselves running to keep up.

They followed the path beside the edge of the caldera, walking north along the rear of the hotel. Passing through a cluster of Ohia trees, they entered a secluded area behind a thicket of giant Hapu'u ferns, where Araton stopped and glanced around again.

Trying to catch his breath, Michael gasped, "*Araton…* where are we going?"

Araton reached out quickly and took them both by the hands. He looked at Erin, and then to Michael, and said simply…

"To *Basilea!*"

\* \* \* \* \*

Watch for Part Two of the *Synaxis Chronicles*:
IONA STRONGHOLD

# ABOUT THE AUTHOR

Robert David MacNeil is an author, wine-lover, and investigator of things supernatural. Over the last twenty years he's traveled to 31 nations researching, writing, and teaching on angels, demons, and supernatural encounters. His travels have taken him from the steppes of Mongolia to the jungles of Thailand, and from the Eskimo villages of Northwest Alaska to *le fin del mundo*, the "end of the world," at the tip of South America.

Long addicted to sci-fi and suspense thrillers, Robert also has a love for history–especially ancient Greece, Rome and medieval Europe. He's particularly fascinated with Patrick, Columba, and the ancient Celts of Ireland and Scotland. The Celtic monks had a special relationship with the angels. They also loved beer and invented whiskey. The Irish really did save civilization.

Robert and his wife, Linda, live near Dallas, Texas. He has authored five non-fiction books under a different pen-name. Iona Portal is his first novel.

You can visit Robert on the web at **ionaportal.com**

Follow him on Twitter at **@RDavidMacNeil**

Or email him at **Robertdavidmacneil@gmail.com**

If you've enjoyed IONA PORTAL, please tell please your friends!

Made in the USA
Columbia, SC
19 September 2022

67583770R00163